P9-AGV-155

BEYOND THE GREAT SNOW MOUNTAINS

BEYOND THE GREAT SNOW MOUNTAINS

LOUIS L'AMOUR

DOUBLEDAY DIRECT LARGE PRINT EDITION

Bantam Books
New York   Toronto   London   Sydney   Auckland

This Large Print Edition, prepared especially for Doubleday Direct, Inc., contains the complete, unabridged text of the original Publisher's Edition.

BEYOND THE GREAT SNOW MOUNTAINS

A Bantam Book/May 1999

All rights reserved.
Copyright © 1999 by Louis and Katherine L'Amour Trust.

No part of this book may be reproduced or transmitted in any form or by any means, electronic or mechanical, including photocopying, recording, or by any information storage and retrieval system, without permission in writing from the publisher.
For information address: Bantam Books.

ISBN 0-7394-0339-7

Published simultaneously in the United States and Canada

Bantam Books are published by Bantam Books, a division of Random House, Inc. Its trademark, consisting of the words "Bantam Books" and the portrayal of a rooster, is Registered in U.S. Patent and Trademark Office and in other countries. Marca Registrada. Bantam Books, 1540 Broadway, New York, New York 10036.

PRINTED IN THE UNITED STATES OF AMERICA

**This Large Print Book carries the
Seal of Approval of N.A.V.H.**

CONTENTS

To John Veitch and Louis L'Amour . . .
together again

BY THE WATERS OF SAN TADEO

The dozen shacks that made up the village of San Esteban huddled, dwarfed and miserable, below the craggy ramparts that walled them away from the world. The lofty circle of mountains, with their ice-choked ravines and thick tangles of beech forest, formed an enclosing wall as impassable as the mountains of the moon. Only in one direction was escape from the village possible . . . through the narrow mouth of the inlet, eight miles from the village.

Julie Marrat had thought of all that many times in the last few weeks, and each time she had come to the same conclusion, and each time that conclusion was just as hopeless. There was but one way of escape . . . by boat.

There were three boats at the inlet, and all of these belonged to Pete Kubelik. One was the schooner that he used for infrequent trips up the coast and to bring in supplies. There were also two fishing boats, not much more than dinghies, far too small in which to brave the sea that lay outside. Yet escape she must, and immediately.

Returning to the bedside, she looked down at the dying man who was her father. Lovable, impractical, and a dreamer with an always restless heart, George Marrat had never been able to remain still. Now, this lonely inlet far south on the coast of Chile had trapped him, and once there he could not leave.

Two things insured that. One was his own health, which failed rapidly in the cold, dreary world of San Esteban, where the sun rarely shone and the sky was overcast nearly three hundred days of the year. Yet had it been his health alone, Julie could have managed. The other element was Pete Kubelik.

From the moment they drew their ketch up to the jetty and Julie turned to look into the piglike eyes of the big trader, she had been frightened. Right then she asked her father to leave, knowing that this was not a place they should stay.

He was amazed. "Why, Julie? We've only just come! We can at least look around, can't we?"

"No, Father, please! Let's go find somewhere else."

Her father had turned to face Kubelik, and the big man's brown face wrinkled in a smile. "I'm afraid my daughter doesn't like it here," he confessed.

"Well," Kubelik had replied, "it ain't much of a place for women, that's true, but there's gold here, plenty of it!"

"Gold?" Her heart sank at the eagerness in her father's voice. What would he do if he found it? she wondered. No man ever cared less for money, but in her father's mind the concept of gold was so much more than money. It was the reward that he was searching for, the last reward that would somehow repair the life that luck had deserted. But, ironically, that life without luck was not his . . . it was hers. "There's gold here?"

"Yes, sir!" Kubelik had turned and waved a hand at the long spit of black sand that pointed into the inlet from a nearby island. "We've washed many a good stake out of that beach! Best beach placer I ever saw! Was that why you came here?"

Had there been anxiety in the big man's voice? Julie had looked at him again, and felt such revulsion that she could scarcely stand to be near him.

Plodding along beside her father, Kubelik had dwarfed him with his huge body. His face was round and moonlike under the thick black beard. Wrinkles ran out in a network of tiny lines from the corners of both eyes, eyes that were small and cruel. His hands were dirty, the fingernails black and broken. And then, for the first time, she'd seen the gun. It was in a holster under his sheepskin coat.

Not until later did Julie wonder that none of the others came near them. An Indian woman standing in the door of a driftwood cabin hurriedly stepped back and closed the door when Julie started toward her. Despite the inhospitable gesture, Julie had not been alarmed, taking it for granted that the woman was naturally shy.

By midnight, when they moved into the inner room at Kubelik's station and to bed, they had met only one other man. He was a pasty Austrian named Rudy, and seemed to be Kubelik's shadow. He rarely spoke, but whenever Kubelik and Rudy shared a look,

Julie realized there was some silent communication. She saw other people moving among the shacks, but they did not come near the store.

That inner room had been Pete Kubelik's suggestion. She had wanted to return to the boat, hoping that her father could be talked into leaving, but Kubelik laughed at her and waved her objections away with an impatient hand. He would take it as an insult, he said. By all means, they should stay. Entranced by his stories of the coast, her father listened, and they remained. And in the morning, their boat was gone.

She had just gotten out of bed when she saw through the small window the empty pier where the ketch had been left. Fear gripping her heart, she awakened her father. George Marrat's face went pale, and for the first time, he was afraid.

They rushed down to the beach, but the ketch was nowhere to be seen.

Kubelik had come from the house, rubbing his eyes. "What's the matter. Something wrong?"

"Our boat's gone!" Marrat exclaimed. "Lord, man! What will we do? What could have happened to it?"

"Wind, maybe," Kubelik suggested, "or some thief. No use standing here. Come in an' let's fix breakfast. Then we can take one of my boats an' look around."

Yet when her eyes happened to meet those of Kubelik, his had been triumphant.

Her father, despite his interest in the gold, was genuinely worried. He knew the mountains were impassable, that the forests were undergrown with thick moss, laden with moisture, and a man could sink to his waist in trying to struggle through. And by the end of the day, they realized that the boat was gone and they knew they would not find it.

"How about taking us to Puerto Montt?" Marrat had suggested. "You have the schooner, and we can't stay here. I have money in the bank back in Santiago. Take us out, and I'll pay your price."

"All right," Kubelik had said thoughtfully. "But you'll have to wait until I'm ready to go for supplies. A week or so, maybe."

Yet when the week had passed, he said nothing about leaving. Her father had been placer mining on the beach and caught a severe cold. By that time, they had moved to a small shack, refusing to accept more of Kubelik's hospitality.

"I'm sorry, Julie," George said. "When I get well, we'll get out of here and I'll make it up to you." He coughed, the breath rattling deep in his lungs.

"Get some rest," she said. He nodded and relaxed, breathing more easily. She sat there in the dark, a twenty-six-year-old woman who had failed in life, failed in marriage, who had fled back to her father, a ne'er-do-well adventurer, and ended up here, in a narrow fjord at the end of the earth.

Her grandfather had been a Chilean who migrated north with his son to fish the waters of British Columbia and Alaska. Her father had spent much of his life in Canada, and she was born there, schooled there, and had been wed there.

Like many young girls, Julie had thought that marriage would change her life, and indeed it had. But she discovered that the qualities in a man that had appealed to her when she was being courted were not the qualities that made a good partner for life.

Her husband had been a dashing young bohemian who could quote enough Spencer, Marx, or Freud to prove any point. Unfortunately, for all his obsession with the working man, he could not seem to hold a job. What she had mistaken for intensity turned out to be self-obsession, and the wild ways that she once thought were delightfully liberated proved to be simple self-indulgence.

After six months he had disappeared to prowl the bars and jazz clubs of San Francisco by himself, and she fled back to her father in shame. Julie hid herself away from the world on her father's boat, ashamed because she had not been wise enough to choose the right man and hadn't been strong enough to confront that man about their problems.

George Marrat had never questioned her. Although he had made many a poor choice himself, and life had dealt him many a blow, he still met the morning with a smile and fixed his eyes on the horizon. He planned a trip south to show his daughter his homeland, to take her mind off her problems. They would prospect on the southern coast. If they could find a cannery and take on a crew, they would fish the southern waters as he had in Ketchikan and Port Albion.

But now they were here in this dismal settlement. And George Marrat was very sick.

Julie put her father to bed and hurried to the store for medicine.

Pete Kubelik shook his head. "Medicine?" he said. "Ain't got much. Aspirin, an' some cold tablets. Anything more I can do, let me know."

He came around the counter and leaned against it. Despite her fear, she forced herself to stand still, but couldn't look him in the eye.

"You know," he said, "we could get along, you an' me. Gets mighty lonesome here, of a winter." In the corner, Rudy stifled a whispering laugh.

"I'm sorry, Mr. Kubelik. I couldn't do that. When Father gets well, we will leave."

"Suppose he doesn't get well?"

Cold fear welled up within her. "Oh, he will," she said firmly. "He often has touches of cold like this. He'll get well, and then we'll leave."

Kubelik grinned at her, his teeth yellow and broken. "Well, maybe," he said. "*If* I decide to take you up the coast. Then again, I may just keep you here, sort of company for me."

"That's ridiculous!" She looked up at him for the first time. "You couldn't get away with anything like that! What about the authorities?"

"The Chileans? The army? The police?" He laughed with genuine amusement. "They don't come here. Know why these folks don't come near you? Because I told 'em to stay away, that's why. Know why they stay here? Because they can't get away, either! They are pilin' up gold for me. Me an' Rudy, here!"

He chuckled. "Why, the government thinks this place is abandoned. Nobody ever comes here, at least," his voice dropped to a whisper, "nobody that goes out again."

Two days later her father died.

He died suddenly, in the night. Only for a moment was he rational, and seemed to realize there was little time left. He called her to him. "Julie . . ." His voice was hoarse. "I . . ." He fumbled for words. "I know what happened to the boat. He . . . Kubelik . . . he towed it away. He hid it over at Rio de San Tadeo. One of the others told me, that last day, workin' on the spit."

"It's all right, Dad," she said gently, "we'll manage!"

The long gray miles of cold sea and the

towering cliffs that flanked it filled her with horror. In all the world, there could be no more desolate place than this coast north of Magellan. "We'll manage," she whispered, but she knew he was dying.

They buried her father at the foot of a huge rock three hundred yards up the canyon from San Esteban. Several of the villagers were out for the funeral, but had she ever hoped for help from them, she gave up now. They were a thin, woebegone group, obviously afraid of Kubelik, who towered above them.

There were six men in the village, she discovered, four of them Chileans and two Yahgans, natives from the Beagle Channel area. The four women were all Yahgans but one, an Ona woman from Tierra del Fuego.

After the funeral, she talked with them while Pete Kubelik and Rudy ignored her. They had the only weapons among the group, and aside from the pistol which he always carried, Kubelik possessed two shotguns and a rifle. He had killed a man only a few days before their ketch arrived.

Recalling Kubelik's anxiety over their discovery of the place, she realized that was his greatest fear. Here in his little kingdom, he ruled supreme while they slaved for him and lived in abject fear of his rages. As he controlled the only means of escape as well as the only source of food, tobacco, and liquor, he was firmly in the saddle.

"But what about the boats?" she said to Aleman, one of the villagers. "Couldn't you steal one and get away?"

"Not a chance!" he told her. "His schooner has an auxiliary engine, and he'd have us before we made a dozen miles. Besides, where could we go on the supplies we'd have? We are a long way from the nearest port."

During the afternoon preceding her father's burial, she tried to recall exactly what the chart had pictured. The inlet was in the southeast corner of the Gulf of San Esteban, and the Rio San Tadeo was to the north. Although the chart indicated little of the nature of the country back of the coast, she knew it was rugged mountain and glacier. Of the beech forests, she knew only by hearsay, but they were pictured as dark, fearsome places, well nigh impenetrable.

It was raining when they finished the funeral service. She started away when the grave had been filled, but Pete Kubelik overtook her. "Get your stuff, whatever you got," he ordered, "an' move over to my place."

It didn't take much to bring her to tears, but she intentionally pushed her sorrow and terror to the forefront. "Oh, not now! Please!" She sobbed hysterically, fell to her knees moaning, "My father . . . my father . . ."

She made the most unappealing spectacle of herself possible. Finally, in disgust, he shrugged it off. "All right, tomorrow, then," Kubelik said, and trudged away.

She was rolling up her father's jacket when she found the knife. Evidently, he had planned to use it himself, yet it was no knife she had ever seen aboard the boat. That meant he had acquired it since coming ashore, either finding it or getting it from one of the others.

The thought filled her with excitement. Perhaps . . . if one of the men had given the knife to her father, she might have a friend out there. How could she know who he was?

Holding the coat so anyone peeking through the window could not see the knife, she examined the blade. It was bright and gleaming, and obviously had not been lying out in the weather.

The knife gave her courage. At least she could kill herself. The thought of killing Kubelik came first, but she dismissed the idea at once. He was too big, too strong, and he wore too many thicknesses of clothing. She would never have strength enough to drive the knife home.

Then she remembered the tobacco. Her father had come ashore prepared to trade, carrying a small sack filled with plugs of tobacco, some large packages of smoking tobacco, and a few cartons of cigarettes. In this place, it was a veritable fortune.

She had seen how avidly the men clutched the tiny packets of tobacco that Kubelik passed out. Maybe that was how her father got the knife.

For a long time she thought, wondering about the mountains and the inlet itself. If she could manage to steal a boat, she might get to the San Tadeo at least, and from there perhaps she could find her father's ketch. She would need neither food nor water to go that far. The thought of the eight miles against the engine of the schooner changed her mind. The river was out of the question.

Julie got up and put out her light, yet scarcely had the cabin become dark when there was a scratching at the window. Going to it, she stood to one side and peered out. In the vague light she could see a figure crouching in the darkness. Gently, she lifted the window.

"Missy? This Cuyu . . . you got tobac' . . . si?"

Cuyu was one of the Yahgans. She remembered him at the funeral. He had been one of those who carried her father's body to the grave and helped fill it in. She remembered his eyes as she'd turned away, how they had seemed strangely gentle and compassionate.

"Yes! Yes, I have tobacco! Come to the door!"

"No door! He watch. He watch alla time! You speak me here!"

"Cuyu, can you get me away from here? Can you? Please!"

The Yahgan was silent. What sort of man was he? Would he be even worse than Kubelik? She dismissed that idea at once. Nobody could be worse.

"Can you get me to our ketch? My father was told it was anchored over on the San Tadeo!"

"San Tadeo? Si. The boat, it there." There was sudden eagerness in Cuyu's voice.

She was almost frantic with excitement. "Oh, Cuyu! Take me to it and I'll give you all this tobacco! Yes, and more, too. Can we steal a dinghy?"

"No." The finality of his voice ended that possibility. "Maybe mountain." His voice was doubtful. "You strong? Walk fast? Climb?"

"Yes, oh yes!" Suddenly he hissed, and then like a shadow, he was gone.

Outside, in front of the cabin, she heard a crunch of boots on gravel. Had Kubelik changed his mind? Was he coming *now*? Or was he suspicious?

Instantly, she slipped off her shoes and got into bed, hunching the blankets around her. He came to the door, and she heard her latch lift, but the bar was in place. He hesitated, and there was no sound. Fear welled up within her. Suppose he broke down the door? Certainly, it would be little effort for a man of his brute strength. Praying she could make it sound right, she turned in the bed, as though in sleep.

Footsteps crunched around the house, and she felt rather than saw his head at the window. She had been unable to close it in time, and hoped he would believe she'd left it open for the air. He stood listening, and she kept her breathing deep and regular, hoping he would not look beneath the window for tracks. Suddenly, a light flashed on her face. After a minute of examination, he turned and walked away. Julie lay rigid, listening to the retreat of his footsteps on the coarse gravel.

It could have been no more than a minute before she heard the Yahgan again. Instantly, she was at the window. "I take," he whispered, "you bring tobac', si?"

Swiftly, she dressed. She pulled on her boots and thrust the knife into the capacious pocket of her coat. It took her only a moment to climb through the window. She passed the tobacco to the Yahgan, but he returned it to her. "You keep—for now," he whispered.

Tugging at her sleeve, he moved off and away. Almost before she realized it, they were working their way through the gray trunks of ancient, long dead trees, and then into the timber itself. Her feet tangled in a soft, sinking bed of moss and she almost fell.

Cuyu caught her sleeve again and guided her in the darkness to a deadfall. She perceived his purpose; by walking on the fallen tree, they could keep out of the moss. Yet it was only a short distance, and then they were struggling in the knee-deep moss again. It was heavy with moisture, and before they had gone fifty yards she was soaked from the knees down. Yet Cuyu seemed to have eyes like a cat, for he found one deadfall after another.

How long they struggled and fought against the clinging, wet fingers of the forest she had no idea. Time and again she fell. She scratched her hands and face, but she kept going, fighting with the strength of desperation for every inch of distance. Suddenly, they emerged from the forest.

She was amazed. Before them, white and wide in the night, lay a glacier! Overhead, the clouds had momentarily parted and a few friendly stars shone through, but the Yahgan was looking at neither the stars nor the glacier. He was moving swiftly out over the icy surface, and the measure of his fear was the measure of her own. From time to time he glanced back. Was he expecting pursuit so soon?

Yet they made better progress now. Nor did Cuyu waste time. He led off swiftly and she almost had to run to keep up. That the Yahgan was frightened was obvious.

Leaving the glacier, they went up a steep, rocky trail along an icy black cliff, then down through a ravine. It was growing gray in the east, and despite all their travel, she had the feeling they had gained little ground. From time to time now, Cuyu stopped. He kept staring ahead, then listening.

Something worried him. She was fighting exhaustion now, for they had not only encountered the roughest possible travel, but had kept up a pace far beyond her strength. Yet the Yahgan showed no evidence of tiring and no intention of slowing down. It was plain that he knew that if they were caught, while she might be taken back to the inlet, he would be killed on the spot.

Cuyu turned now, changing his course to proceed more directly north, but his eyes continued to watch toward his left. Once, through a break in the curtain of trees shrouding the cliff on her left, she thought she saw water.

Was the fact that they must go down to

the water what Cuyu feared? Kubelik, guessing their route or seeing their tracks, might use the boat to come around the point and head them off. It would be pitifully easy, and in a matter of an hour he could render useless their night of struggle.

The dim game trail they had been following dipped sharply down into a fantastically rugged gorge. Here the moss was scarce, but the trees were laden with snow, and there was an occasional patch of ice. They went down the steep side, passing themselves from tree trunk to tree trunk to keep from sliding or falling all the way to the bottom.

A brawling stream roared along over stones, and Cuyu dropped on his stomach and drank. Julie followed suit, then got to her feet and looked around.

The gorge curved sharply right before them, and the course of the stream led down toward the north. While the direction was perfect for them and would make travel easier, it must also lead to the inlet she thought she had seen. Now she comprehended the reason for Cuyu's hurry. He hoped to get to the mouth of the river before they could be headed off.

He started again, with only a glance at her, nearly running wherever the path was smooth enough to permit it. At times they had to climb down over great tumbled masses of white boulders, or walk gingerly across slippery rocks, some of them covered with encroaching peat moss from the forest.

They came out of the trees and into the open delta of rocks and sand where the inlet met the mouth of the San Tadeo River. There was no boat in sight, but they ran now, trying to cover the exposed area as quickly as possible. They reached the woods where the river poured forth, a wide course of dark water rushing down from the mountains, and Cuyu paused to let her catch her breath. For a brief moment he grinned at her.

"Almos' to boat . . . you'll see."

Slowly, they started upstream along the watercourse, and soon, through the branches of the trees ahead, she could see the white of the ketch's hull. It was only a matter of minutes to reach the vessel. The trim craft was tied up in a deep backwater out of the main flow of the river. A good anchorage, Julie realized, but a difficult one for her to maneuver out of even with Cuyu's help. The ketch would have to be carefully backed and turned into the river, with most of the backing being into the current.

Without bothering to pull the boat in to shore, she climbed out on a low hanging branch and dropped to the deck. Cuyu followed as she made her way to the pilot house.

"You take us away?" he asked.

She could see that he was more terrified than ever, now that they had reached their destination. Terrified because, unlike the stretches of forest and glacier, this was a place where Kubelik would have to come on any search for them that he might make. She thought of the difficult job of fighting the river's current with a reversed engine, of how the ketch would slip sideways even as it moved back, and feared what roots or rocks lurked beneath the black waters of the San Tadeo. Sometime toward morning there would be a tide, and that would make her job much easier, but high tide was hours away and she was sure they didn't have an hour, let alone hours.

"I can try," she mumbled. The thought of the miles of gray, whitecapped water frightened her. She had spent many months at sea, but never without her father. She took a deep breath and reached out for the switch that activated the pumps. Nothing happened. She tried again.

But the moment she touched the console, she heard it. Off in the distance, but not distant enough, was the low *thot-thot* of an auxiliary engine. It could only belong to Kubelik's schooner. She turned, and through the open hatchway could see a movement through the trees that blocked her view of the river.

"Quick!" she said to Cuyu. "We must get off the boat and hide." But the native was already headed across the deck. He jumped for a branch and pulled himself up. Julie, desperate to know the full extent of her troubles, flipped up the cover and glanced into the electrical console. The battery cable had been removed, and the deck boards were scarred where Kubelik had yanked it up through the narrow channel. He had made sure that no one was going to be taking the ketch out of the river, at least not without winching it out of the backwater and upriver against the current. She dropped the cover and ran.

Back on deck, she saw Cuyu motioning frantically from the bank. She'd started for the branch when a shot rang out.

The Yahgan fled. The schooner was drawing into the backwater, and standing in the bow, a rifle in his hands, was Pete Kubelik!

"Cuyu!" Her cry seemed lost in the space between the trees. *"Look out!"*

She saw the Yahgan glance back, and then he left his feet and dove into the brush and in that instant the rifle barked. Did he stumble? Or was he already falling of his own volition?

The rifle barked again, but she heard no whine of bullet nor was she hit. Cuyu must have still been alive then, and another shot had been sent to finish the job. She heard Kubelik shout, and turned back to the companionway. Dropping down the ladder, she ran for her father's cabin. Just as she unlatched the door she both heard and felt Kubelik's schooner bump up alongside the ketch.

Hanging from leather loops attached to the side of the bunk was George Marrat's old Mannlicher carbine. Julie jerked it free and grabbed up the leather cartridge wallet that hung with it. Footsteps pounded overhead. She had no time to load and barely time to think. Kubelik was coming down the ladder. As she ducked into the companion-way she could see the back of his legs as he descended. She slid through the galley door and threw the lock, although that would hold him only an instant.

Scrambling onto the mess table and pushing open the skylight, she tossed the rifle through and started to crawl out herself. Behind and beneath her, the door splintered open. She rolled through the hinged skylight as Kubelik roared, charging across the cabin.

Julie grabbed the carbine and plunged overboard. The icy water hit her like a fist, a cold, solid hammer in her stomach. Down she went, striking out toward the shore but still sinking. Her clothes, heavy shoes, and seven pounds of rifle carried her to the muddy bottom. Her ears popped and she pushed off, hitting the surface and gulping air. She saw a vague shape to her left and grabbed out, her hand scraping along the side of Kubelik's schooner. Her eyes cleared, and looking past the bow, she saw Kubelik stalking along the rail of the ketch, rifle in hand.

Julie Marrat took a deep breath and sank away from the boat. A couple of strokes and she felt the bottom again, and then the dirt and roots making up the side of the back-water. A submerged branch hit her in the face, and she grabbed at it, pulling herself up and along a fallen log to the shore. She stumbled up and water poured from her clothes in a rush.

There was a whip of air by her body and then the slam of a rifle shot. Pete Kubelik jacked another round into the chamber of his rifle, the spent case bouncing off the deck of the ketch. On the schooner, Rudy came running forward, shotgun in hand. She fell, rather than ran, into a dark space between the trees.

"You come back here!" Kubelik roared. "You come back or I'll kill you!"

Now it was the air that was a freezing fist closing on her lungs. Her sopping clothes clung to her as she slogged, almost knee deep in moss, deeper into the forest. Even as she ran she was sobbing with fear. Soon she slowed, realizing that she was leaving a trail even a blind man could follow, and found a deadfall like Cuyu had used. She worked her way deeper and deeper into the immense stand of beeches, and finally, shivering, collapsed from exhaustion.

Her breath came in shuddering gasps, but as she slowly caught her wind she became aware of the silence. There was no noise of pursuit . . . there was almost no noise at all. For the moment she was safe.

Except the cold would kill her. It was still in the mid-forties, but her wet clothes would rapidly give her hypothermia, and in the night the temperature would drop another ten or fifteen degrees. She tried to hold herself still and quiet her chattering teeth. There were still no sounds of pursuit. She crawled around behind a fallen log and pulled off some chunks of bark, but they seemed too damp to burn. A long crack in the fallen tree, however, gave her access to the inside of the trunk, hollowed out by heart-rot, and from there she used the knife to scrape out some light, dry, strips of wood.

Using a box of safety matches that she had taken from the shack in San Esteban, she struck match after match with no answering flame; they had become too wet. Finally, she tried holding the match head against the striking area with the ball of her thumb as she rasped it along. The match flared but the pain in her hand made her drop it in the moss, where it went out. Blowing on her burned thumb, she was not surprised to find herself cursing in a manner befitting a sailor or dockhand. Gritting her teeth, she struck another match. There was the smell of burning sulfur, and even as she pulled her thumb away she knew she'd blistered it again; however, she lit her tiny fire and slowly fed the flames. Then she stripped the achingly cold clothes off, wrung them out, and laid them out across the log near the fire.

Shuddering, half frozen, and naked, she huddled by the log and prayed for her clothes to dry. In the dark and silent wood, exposed in every way, Julie was sure that this was when Kubelik would find her. He would follow her tracks, even where she had tried to make it hard for him. He would smell her fire. He would find her and . . .

She turned and, fumbling with the cartridges, loaded the gun. She put a round in the chamber and set the safety. "Damn you," she whispered. "Damn you, if you come here, I'll kill you!"

Then she laughed.

She laughed at the picture of herself, stark

naked and freezing in a primitive forest, clutching a rifle and daring a man like Pete Kubelik to come and get her. What made it funny was the thought of her husband, champion of the working class, seeing her now. That her often drunk, ineffective coffeehouse bolshevik could never even imagine this, which made her cough out a hard, mean laugh from lips that were set in a snarl.

"Come on, damn you."

From somewhere inside her there came a deep swell of emotion. Some of it was the loss of her father. Some of it was fear of this terrible man. Some of it was anger, finally not with herself, but with her no-good husband. But most of it was an emotion that had no name, something ancient and primal, the feeling that a tiny animal might have when, after being pursued to the end of its endurance, it turns and bares its teeth. Not only does it have to fight, but something inside it has changed . . . now it *wants* to fight.

Morning found Pete Kubelik painfully awake in his room at the San Esteban trade store. He'd clumsily fallen off one of the deadfalls that Julie Marrat had skillfully negotiated in her escape the previous day. Kubelik had sprained his ankle, and now the swelling had become serious and excruciating. He took a swallow from a bottle of vodka he had half finished the night before and limped to the front door of the store. Throwing off the heavy bar, he stepped out into the gray and drizzling dawn.

Today he and Rudy would have to finish up what that damn girl had started. Regardless of the pain that shot through him every time he took a step, regardless of the hangover pounding in his temples, he'd find Julie Marrat, and if he couldn't make her come back with him, he'd kill her. He'd kill her anyway, but there'd be more pleasure for him if he brought her back alive.

He surveyed the long beach and the high cliffs. Time to get moving. He shook his head, trying to clear it, but that movement made his vision blur with pain.

Maybe he'd just kill her.

An invisible club knocked Pete Kubelik's bad leg out from under him. He went face first into the sand, gasping in shock. He lurched around, trying to sit up even as the crack of the gunshot echoed back from the cliffs. Looking down, he saw blood welling from a hole dead center in his knee. He clawed for the pistol behind his hip.

Down on the beach, less than one hundred yards from the door of his store, the dark sand moved and shook. Julie Marrat stood up from the place where she had lain, half buried, through the night, the sights of her father's old carbine trained on Kubelik's front door. She worked the bolt on the rifle, and when Rudy came charging out of the building, shotgun in hand, she shot him in the stomach. Then she started forward.

Kubelik half raised the .45, but she spoke before he could bring it to bear.

"Don't! I won't kill you if you throw it away."

He was tempted to try, but the barrel felt heavy, too heavy, and down in his leg the pain was starting to rise like a giant comber. He dropped the gun and began to curse, a long quiet stream of the foulest language Julie had ever heard.

She picked the gun up. "I came back for my battery cable," she said. "You shouldn't have taken it . . . or stolen our boat." She went up to the store and took the bolt from Kubelik's rifle. Then, using a rock, she beat the hammers from the trader's shotguns. The cable she eventually found lying on the deck of the schooner.

She fired up the schooner's auxiliary and threw off the lines. Several of the other inhabitants of the station had come down to the water and were watching her curiously. She called out to them.

"I'll leave this boat in the mouth of the San Tadeo River if you want it." They looked at her as she turned and headed down the inlet and toward the gulf. The last time she looked back, they had walked over to where Pete Kubelik lay in the sand. They had all taken up sticks or rocks, but were not striking him. They were just standing there. Finally, they slipped out of sight as she rounded the headland and started down to the sea.

MEETING AT FALMOUTH

Night, and the storm . . . howling engines of wind roared over the Lizard and above the slate roofs of Falmouth. Volleys of rain rattled along the cobblestones like a scattering of broken teeth.

Shoulders hunched against the wind and rain, the rider stared through the darkness toward a bend in the road ahead. It was January of 1794, and the worst storm of the winter was raging over the Atlantic, screaming above Land's End and lashing Mount's Bay with its fury.

Suddenly, a woman darted from the rocks beside the road and lifted her hand. Startled, the man drew up sharply, one hand dropping to his greatcoat pocket.

"Oh, sir! Sir!"

He looked down into the white, rain-wet face of a girl. She was shabbily dressed, with an old piece of sailcloth serving as a shield from the rain.

"What are you doing out here, girl?" he demanded. "You'll get a nasty bit of cold!"

"Sir, beggin' your pardon, but are you Mr. Talleyrand?"

"Talleyrand?" He was puzzled. "No, I'm not Talleyrand, and what would a serving wench like you be wanting with him?"

"It's up ahead, sir. I'm maid at the Bos'n's Locker, sir. The inn, it is. There's a bad lot there, a-plottin' they are, a-plottin' against Mr. Talleyrand."

"And you came out here to warn him?"

"I did, sir. I'd want no man murdered by them, not even a Frenchman, sir."

"And what makes you think Talleyrand will be here tonight? Only yesterday he sailed from England for America."

"I know that, sir. They talked of it. But they think he will be coming, sir."

"Thank you, girl. Now you'd best get inside before they find you're gone—" His voice broke off sharply as two men came running through the rain.

Both were roughly dressed, and in a momentary lull in the storm, he saw one of them wore a black patch over his eye. A tall, lean man he was, with the face of evil on him.

"So here you are!" His voice sounded shrill in the storm. "What are you doin' out here on the road, wench?" He grabbed at her shoulder and the girl stepped back.

Instantly, the rider pushed his horse between them. In his hand was a drawn saber. "Get back there, man! Leave the girl alone! She came to bring me a message, and it will be none of your affair!"

"Who're you?" The man with the patch peered up at him from the rain, careful to keep free of the saber point. He blinked his eyes, then drew back, smiling suddenly, almost leering. "Ahhhh, Tom! It's the Yank! It's that American who's been about the tavern. He's no bit of trouble for us, let's be back inside."

Without another word, they turned and hurried back through the rain.

When they had gone, the rider glanced down at the girl. "Put your foot in my stirrup, girl, and we'll have you back to the inn in no time."

When she had her foot in his stirrup, he put an arm about her waist to steady her.

"Say nothing of this now, not to anyone. You understand?"

"Oh, yes sir! I'll not speak, sir!"

Dropping her to the ground, he then rode around to the stable. A hard-faced man with a wooden leg limped toward him, peering through the rain. "Oh, it's you?" He accepted the bridle. "Don't you worry, sir. I'll be carin' for the mare."

The American stamped his feet to shake off some of the water, then walked swiftly across the worn cobbles to the side door of the inn. There he repeated his stamping, and opened the portal.

Wind almost tore the door from his hand, and the candles gasped and went out. He stood stock-still, listening carefully until the lights were glowing again. The inn shutters rattled and, on the hearth, the flames guttered and spat.

The man with the black patch over his eye was hunched over a table with two other men. "I tell you, Tom, they will never pass the Lizard this night!"

"What then?" Tom was a burly man in a shabby cloak.

"Then it's here they will come! Only this morning, Brynie sighted their ship, and fighting a head wind she was! They'll put in here or be blown miles off their course."

"And if they come, we can still earn our guineas."

The American gave them no second glance, walking to a table near the fire and stripping off his rain-wet cloak. He removed his saber and placed it beside the cloak, but within easy grasp.

A compact, well-built man he was, but not large. Obviously a gentleman, but more than that. His was a strong, handsome face, his hair silvering at the temples. With it he wore the air of one born to command, yet it was a face that showed suffering, and was marked by some deep tragedy.

Drawing a book from his pocket, he opened it. He glanced up at the innkeeper. "Sherry," he said, "and if you have it, a bit of bread and cheese."

He glanced at the pages of the book, then at the three men. Slovenly rogues they were, if he had ever seen them. Scum, but a bloody, dangerous sort of scum, and plotting no good to anyone.

"Simple," Tom said then, waving a dirty hand, "they will come ashore, and if they come ashore, it's here they must come. So then, we have them."

"You speak of *them* . . . it is *him* we want."

"Garnet will know him."

"A tall man, he is, a tall man with a limp, a fair bit of nobleman and church."

The American turned a page of his book. The plotters had spoken in low tones, but their voices carried to him. Still, they had said nothing to be noted . . . had he not been warned by the maid.

Talleyrand . . . he knew the name well. A refugee from the French revolution now living in England, but about to leave for America. His was the reputation of a shrewd diplomat, cool but charming. He had a narrow escape from the guillotine, but evidently had not left all his enemies when he fled from France. These rogues were British if he had ever seen them, the sort of scum that can be had to kill for hire. But Garnet—that name had a French sound.

Obviously, the plotters were correct. No ship could beat past the Lizard on such a night, and if by some chance she did pass, then she could never hope to get beyond Land's End in the face of such a wind.

Tom jerked his head toward the American.

His voice lowered, but could still be heard. "Who's that one? What . . . ?"

One of the others whispered a name, and all their faces turned toward him. The American felt shame mingled with anger send hot blood creeping up his neck and face. He turned a page of the book and the print blurred before his eyes. Dimly he heard the words, "Not him. He'll not interfere, not the likes of him."

So they thought him a coward as well, did they? Many things, but never that. He had been no coward at Saratoga, he——

On the hearth, the flames hissed as a drop of water fell down the chimney. The host, seeing his empty glass, crossed the flags to him. "Yes, Salem, if you please," the American said. "It's a foul night and the wine warms a man. They bottle with this, I think, some of the sunshine of Spain."

"That they did, sir. Would you have me leave the bottle?"

"If you will . . ."

Battalions of wind threw their weight against the shutters, then withdrew, rattling them with angry fingers.

So they would never forget? A man made

one mistake . . . but it was the worst mistake. The worst of all.

The maid moved about the room, frightened and pale. From time to time she darted a glance at him, but the American continued to read.

Finally, the three arose, drew their cloaks about them and left the tavern. The innkeeper moved to stoke the fire, then placed a heavy chunk on the coals. He threw a glance at the American, then jerked his head after the departing trio. "A bad lot that, sir. Gallows bait for sure."

"They are staying here?"

"The night only, sir. I'd not have them longer if I had to call the watch from Falmouth."

"A good idea." The American turned a page of his book, then picked up his glass and drained it. "Salem?"

"Sir?"

"There will be some Frenchmen coming alone. One will be named Talleyrand. Would you tell him, from a friend, to have a care? To be on his guard?"

"From *them*, sir? There's that in the wind?"

"More than we know, I'm thinking. You'll tell him?"

"Of course, sir. But—"

"As a precaution only. I'll be back."

The maid started to speak, then stopped. Yet she hurried to the door and looked up at him, her eyes frightened. He chucked her gently under the chin. "You worry too much," he said.

He opened the door then, stepped out and drew it to behind him. Falmouth was a cluster of roofs several hundred yards away. The Bos'n's Locker stood on the harbor road away from the town. Overhead the sign creaked dismally in the wind.

Drawing his collar tighter, the American bent his head into the wind and turned down the road in the direction of the docks. There was no trusting the men he had seen. It would be like them not to wait for Talleyrand to come to the inn, but to murder him along the coast and throw his body in the sea.

It was not in him to sit idly by while a man was attacked without warning. Or was it in part because he was irritated with inaction?

Rain whipped his face and pounded at him with tiny, angry fingers. He could see the men ahead of him along the road, and when they stopped near some dark buildings along the wharf, he drew back into the shadows himself.

From the darkness nearby a man stepped. "Followin' 'em, are ye? Now Dick'll be proud to know that. He—"

The American stepped quickly from the shadows and one hand grasped the newcomer by the throat, the other by the shoulder. Fiercely, he slammed the man back against the building, took a twist of the man's collar and let up only when he became afraid unconsciousness would keep the other from understanding his words. "Open your mouth," the very calmness of the American's voice was more frightening than rage would have been, "and I'll have the heart out of you. Get away from here now, and be glad that I haven't opened you up with my saber."

Gagging and pawing at his bruised throat, the man staggered back, then turned and hurried away into the storm. The American watched him for a few minutes, then glanced back to where the others waited in the darkness. Far away down the channel he thought he saw a light, and he moved along the building, well back in the darkness, his saber in his hand.

"Bloody awful night!" It was the man the others had called Dick.

"It is that."

"Any sign of her?"

"I be'ant lookin'. Soon enough when they put down a boat. If she comes, she'll come soon, you can mark that."

"Where then, Dick? Where'll we do't?"

"We've got to see him, first. Garnet will show us the man."

An hour passed on heavy feet. The wind did not abate, but the ship came. Her sails rolled up slowly, and the sailors at the canvas were unseen in the howling dark. They heard the rumble of her anchor going down, and later the chunk of oars, a sound caught only at intervals when the wind hesitated to gather force.

The American shifted his saber and dried his palm on his trousers beneath his greatcoat. Then he clutched the sword again.

He did not hear the boat come alongside, only suddenly there were men walking and he heard the sound of them speaking French. It was a language he knew, and he listened. He learned much of what he knew in Quebec, and this was but little different. But no names were called, and the three men went by, two tall men and one short, stout, and slipping as he walked. At times he ran a few steps to keep up, and puffed when he slowed down.

Dick and his companions fell in behind, and the American followed them. And so they came again to the inn.

By then he was before them. He had run, and gotten around them and into the back door as from the stable. When they entered, he was again at his table, a glass of sherry poured, and engrossed in his book. They entered, and he glanced up.

"You are from the port?" the American asked.

"From the sea." The man who replied was tall, cold of eyes, and walked with a slight limp. The American knew him from description to be Talleyrand. "We are for America," the man said.

"It is my country."

Talleyrand glanced at him with quick interest. "Then you can tell us of your country. We go there as strangers. What can you tell of America? Is it a fair land?"

The American closed his book carefully. "A fair land? Yes, it is. If I were to tell you of it as I think of it, you would think me a poet rather than a soldier. And I do think of it, I think of it always.

The newcomers warmed themselves at the fire and the American went on, speaking to them but to himself also. "You will find it colder there than here, but the houses are strong and tight and warm. There will be less talk of art and more of the frontier, less of books and more of land, but there will be good food, and good drink. You will find it a land of strong men, of full-breasted women, fit to mother a race of kings."

"And this man Washington? Have you met him? We in France have heard much of him."

The American hesitated, glancing at his wineglass. "Washington? Yes, I knew him. He is a great man, a greater man than most of us believed. Though he does not, you might say, have a flair. He is a shrewd, thoughtful, considering man, but he has a temper."

"So I have heard." Talleyrand clasped his hands behind his back. "It needs a great man to retreat when all around him are demanding a victory. He knew the important thing was not to risk his army, to keep his fighting force intact."

The American gestured to the table. "Will you join me, gentlemen? With the wind as it is, you must plan to stay for hours, perhaps for days. You are Monsieur de Talleyrand?"

"I am. And this is Monsieur de Fougier. And our companion, Paul Garnet."

The American looked around at the name. Garnet had a hard face with cold eyes and a tight-lipped mouth. So this was the traitor? He hesitated over that thought.

"You will like my country," he said gently. "It is a fine, strong land. The earth will be frozen now, beneath the snow. The rooftops will be white, and a thousand chimneys will lift their fingers of smoke toward the sky, but soon after you are there, the spring will come. The trees will bud and the fields grow green, and the men will plow the earth and you will hear the heavy wagons along the dirt roads. It is a young land, monsieur, a growing, raw, wonderful land, and . . . and . . ."

Talleyrand smiled slightly. "And it is your country."

"Yes," the American said quietly, "it is my country. It will always be my country, the only one for me. I have only learned that now . . . and now it is too late."

Suddenly, he looked up and saw that Dick was in the doorway. Tom was moving nearer, and Garnet suddenly arose and stepped back.

The American's hand was beneath his coat. "Talleyrand, watch yourself, sir. I have been waiting to warn you. Your life is in danger."

Talleyrand did not move from the table. His eyes flickered over the faces, came to rest on that of Garnet. If he was surprised, he gave no evidence of it. This man, who was for many years to be Europe's master of intrigue, who was to think always of his country and not of its ruler, was never to be surprised.

"You are clumsy, Paul. Had it not been for the storm, we would have gotten away from you."

"It does not matter. There was the storm!"

"But we are warned."

"And unarmed," Garnet replied coolly, triumphant now.

"I am not."

Their eyes turned to the American. He had drawn a pistol from beneath his dress coat. In his right hand he held the hilt of the still-sheathed saber.

There was something in that still, cold, handsome face that sent a shiver of apprehension through Garnet. This man . . . this man would not be afraid to die. He would die hard, and not alone.

De Fougier lurched backward, his face white. The three men faced the assassins. One pale and cowering, one tall and straight and cool, one the mysterious soldier, with a pistol in his hand.

"Well, gentlemen," Talleyrand said coolly, "what is it to be? Are you ready to die, or will you retire quietly?"

Garnet was furious. He glared at the American. "He has but one shot, and there are four of us!"

The American smiled. "One shot, for *you*. And then the saber. I fancy the saber, my man. I was of the cavalry before this."

Dick spoke up angrily. "Belay the gab! It's him you want, ain't it?" He pointed an outstretched finger at Talleyrand. "Then by the . . . !" He lunged, a dagger suddenly gripped in his fist.

The American's pistol exploded and Dick halted in mid-stride, his mouth falling open. At the same instant there was a second explosion and Garnet turned half around, then fell across the corner of the table. The table tipped, crashed on its side, and the wine bottle rolled off, struck the fallen man on the back, then rolled off onto the floor. The American stood with drawn saber. But the two others fled into the storm, the wind slamming closed the door behind them.

The second shot had been fired by Talleyrand, who held a small pistol. There was a flicker of irony in the Frenchman's eyes. "Yes, my American friend, even a diplomat knows that words must occasionally be backed with force." He glanced at the fallen man. "Very likely you've saved my life."

The American bent and retrieved the bottle from the floor. "And we did not break the wine."

Talleyrand glanced at the bodies of the two men. "It would be just as well if we went to some other place. There'll be trouble here soon."

"Monsieur?"

Talleyrand turned to face the American. "Yes?"

"If you will take the advice of one who is gone from his own country—go back to France. If that is not politically possible now, then go back when you can, as soon as you can. Believe me, monsieur, far better than any other, I know there is no country like one's own, and you will not be happy serving another."

"It is good advice, but now we go to America. Could you give me letters of introduction to someone there? It would be a great favor."

The American shook his head regretfully. "I am sorry, that I cannot do. I am perhaps the only American who cannot."

Their eyes held. Talleyrand hesitated. "Then, your name, sir? You can tell me that."

The American stiffened. His face was resigned and cold with pride and tragedy. "My name is Benedict Arnold."

ROUNDUP IN TEXAS

I

The instant Ward McQueen saw the horsemen in the basin below, his heart leaped with quick apprehension. That would be Kim Sartain astride the sorrel, and the other riders, three of them, had him neatly boxed.

Touching spurs to the strawberry roan, McQueen went down the hill at a dead run, then slowed up as he neared the group. He saw Yost's face flash with anger and disappointment as the man recognized him. Ward drew up.

"All right, boys," he said. "Break it up!"

In a moment the situation had changed appreciably. The three riders had Sartain in such a position that he would be covered from three sides if he started to fire.

There would be no chance for escape.

Ernie Yost's expression showed his uncertainty. The odds favored them three to two, but now one of the three, Ike Taylor, had his back to McQueen. Ward had stopped his horse to the left rear of Sartain, and could fire at all three men without endangering Sartain. Taylor was now in the middle, between Ward and the guns of his two friends.

"If any shootin' starts, boss," Kim suggested quietly, "I'll take Yost!"

Ernie's face flamed with dark blood, but he hesitated. He was no fool. Kim Sartain had once flashed a gun in his presence at Sotol, against a half-crazed Mexican killer who had Kim covered, but the Mexican never got off a shot.

As for Ward McQueen, the foreman of the Tumbling K had held a reputation in Texas long before he went off to Wyoming and Nevada. He was known to be a deadly gunfighter. Taylor was as good as dead if shooting started, and without Taylor, Ernie Yost wanted no part of it.

Yost spoke calmly. "This rider of yours is on the prod, McQueen. He ordered us off the range."

"What business have you here?" McQueen demanded.

Ike Taylor was sweating blood in his present position. He started to shift around.

McQueen's voice was sharp. "Ike, you sit still or I'll drill you!"

Taylor swallowed and sat still, his eyes haunted. He was filled with regrets, wishing he were in Sotol, or any other place but here.

Yost's face had darkened again. "A man has a right to ride anywhere he wants!"

"No, he doesn't!" McQueen wasn't hedging. Had he arrived thirty seconds later, Sartain might have been dead. "You don't run any cattle, Yost. You have no business on this range at any time. We're working cattle here, and we don't like rustlers. Now you get off and stay off!"

Yost was bursting with hatred. His hands trembled as he strove to compose himself. "Some day you'll go too far, Ward!"

"Call it when you're ready!" Ward answered sharply. He stepped his horse nearer at a walk. He was angry and ready. "Why not now?"

No one had ever accused Ernie Yost of cowardice, yet, in this situation, he could see no hope. He had never faced deadlier gunmen than Ward McQueen and his dark-faced *segundo*, Kim Sartain.

"All right," he flared suddenly. "I'll stay off!" He turned his horse with a jerk and started to walk away. Villani and Taylor wasted no time in following.

The two riders sat on their horses and watched until they were over the rise. "Reckon we ought to follow?" Sartain wondered.

"No. Let's get back. There's work to do."

Sartain glanced up at him. "You showed up at the right time, boss," he said dryly. "Another minute and they would have had me."

"They were set for a killing, all right," Ward agreed. "I don't savvy it. Ever had any trouble with them?"

"Not until I ordered them off." Sartain was puzzled. "But there's more to this than meets the eye."

They rode away. But as they topped the rise, Ward removed his hat and anxiously mopped his brow as he stared down at the dusty herd below them. When Ward had bought that stock from Old Dick Gerber, it had looked like a godsend. Long ago, he had worked for Gerber, and knew the tight-fisted old rancher well. That was before Ward had gone to Nevada and become foreman of the Tumbling K, Ruth Kermitt's ranch.

In all his dealings, the old man had seemed to be strictly honest and reliable, so when he showed McQueen a tally book, and the records amounted to over four thousand head, Ward decided to buy. The price seemed reasonable enough. Ward had, however, insisted upon a guarantee. At first Gerber had balked, but finally agreed to guarantee three thousand head.

The guarantee was something on which Ward would never have insisted had he been buying the herd for himself. He just wanted to be sure that Ruth got her money's worth. The price he paid had been for four thousand head, the whole procedure handled in the somewhat loose and careless manner typical of the West of that era.

Now, however, the number of cattle was running far below four thousand, and McQueen could not understand it. He still firmly believed that Dick Gerber's count was honest, and knowing the old man, he knew that Gerber's methods were not slipshod.

"The tally's fallin' short, ain't it?" Sartain

asked. He knew McQueen was worried. "Do you suppose Yost would know anything about that?"

"How could he? Our own boys are handlin' this roundup. Yost hasn't been around—just my riders and the few of Gerber's I kept on to handle the branding."

Buying as he had, without waiting for the completed tally, he had saved money, for Gerber had insisted that the deal be made before the roundup. The difference was considerable. Now it could take all their profit away.

The ranch in Nevada had been making money steadily, and it had been Ruth Kermitt's idea to stock it with more cattle. They could, she suggested, pick up a herd in Texas and drift it north, letting it feed as it moved.

McQueen liked the plan. With luck they could sell enough cattle at the railheads in Kansas or Nebraska to pay expenses, and possibly, with luck, even pay for the herd.

Buying cattle on the range could often prove very profitable, for in many cases the completed tally would run higher than the estimate. McQueen, knowing Gerber, had little hope of exceeding the tally.

"Bud" Fox and "Baldy" Jackson, the two hands that had come south with them, were drifting their way. "Brought in about thirty head," Bud volunteered as they drew near.

"Any unbranded stock?"

"Nope. Gerber must have figured wrong on that because most of the stuff we're findin' has to be vented."

"Where is that KT rep?" Ward asked. He started to build a smoke, studying the cattle thoughtfully.

"Buff Colker?" Jackson rubbed a hand over his bald pate. "He's off to Sotol, as always. Said he had to mail a letter."

Sartain chuckled. "Shucks, Baldy! You're just jealous because you can't go in, too."

"Jealous?" Baldy snorted. "Of that Kansas City cowhand?"

"Buff sure ain't around much," Bud Fox agreed. "He takes his reppin' job easy."

"If those outfits he's workin' for can stand it, we can," McQueen said. "How's it look back in the breaks, Bud?"

"Cleaned out, almost. There's a few steers around that we might pick up, but most of them are wild as deer."

"Forget them," Ward advised, "they aren't

worth it. We could waste a month combing that chaparral an' never get them out."

Kim Sartain spoke thoughtfully. "You know that Colker hombre sure puzzles me. He says he goes to Sotol, but remember that time you sent me in after some smokin' for the boys? Well, Buff was supposed to be there, too, but I didn't see him."

"Maybe you just didn't run into him," Bud said.

"In Sotol?" Sartain stared at Fox with utmost disgust. "You couldn't hide a pack rat in that place! You could cover the whole durned town under a Mexican's saddle blanket!"

Ward McQueen reined in and lounged loosely in the saddle, staring unhappily at the herd. Tonight he would ride in and have a talk with Ruth. He would have to tell her that his deal had been a poor one. Scowling, he tried to think if there was any spot they had somehow missed. Still, with Perkins, Gallatin, Jensen, and Lopez working for them, all men who knew this range, there was small chance of overlooking anything.

When the hands finished bunching the herd, Kim drifted his way again. "Riding into Sotol, boss?"

McQueen slanted his eyes at the casual young rider. "Yeah, what about it?"

"Nothin'." Kim shrugged carelessly. "Figured you might let me ride along. Sort of wash some of the dust out of my throat!"

Ward grinned. Few men cared so little for drinking as Kim Sartain. The rider was a top hand, but he liked a good fight, and Ward knew he was thinking of Yost.

"I don't want any trouble, Kim. You know how Miss Kermitt is."

Sartain turned his horse, riding toward the ranch house beside McQueen. "Boss, when are you and Miss Kermitt tyin' the knot?"

Ward looked around. "We don't plan on gettin' married until we get back to Nevada." He shrugged. "Maybe after she hears what a bad deal I made for her, she won't want to."

"Boss," Kim said hesitantly, "did you ever figure that maybe this Gerber lied? He wouldn't swear there was over three thousand."

Ward spat and swung the horse up to the corral. "Did you ever see the time you could swear to how many head you had on a ranch? I never could."

Sartain got down and began stripping the

saddle from his sorrel. "I could guess within a thousand head," he replied.

Ward McQueen stopped a moment and frowned uneasily. Maybe he had been wrong in trusting Gerber. After all, the old man was notoriously tight-fisted, and he might not be above dishonesty with a man who came from so far away, and was on his way back. The thought rankled McQueen.

II

Ruth Kermitt was waiting for him on the steps of the hotel when he cantered up the street and swung down. She was smiling as he joined her.

"After you talk to me," he said, "you may not look so happy. Have you eaten?"

"Yes, but I want some more coffee with you."

She was a tall girl, her dark hair gathered in a loose knot at the nape of her neck. Her wide, blue eyes examined his face as he lifted his cup. She could see the lines of weariness etched there, the worry in his eyes.

"What's wrong, Ward?" she asked.

He sighed. "We bought four thousand head accordin' to Gerber's tally book. We won't get more than three thousand."

Her lips tightened. "Oh! I was afraid of something like that."

"Me, I'd have sworn by Gerber."

The door to the room smashed back suddenly, and Ward looked around. Five men had come into the cafe. In the lead, his blue eyes flashing from his brown, wind-burned face, his untrimmed white hair falling to his shoulders, was Old Dick Gerber. Behind him were four hard-faced riders.

Gerber sighted Ward and crossed the room swiftly.

"McQueen!" Gerber's voice rang in the narrow room. "It's come to my ears that you say I lied about my tally on that herd! Did you call me a liar?"

As Ward McQueen carefully got to his feet, the door opened quietly behind him.

"I'm with you, boss." It was Kim Sartain's voice.

"No, Dick, I didn't say you lied."

"The great McQueen, takin' water!" sneered one of the riders. A big man known as Black.

Ward's eyes shifted to Black. "I'm not

takin' water. It's just I've known Dick Gerber a lot longer than I expect to know you."

His eyes turned to Gerber's. "Dick, you sold me four thousand head of cattle according to your tally. I took your word and the word of your book. I worked for you, an' that tally book of yours was somethin' to swear by. I had no doubts."

Gerber stared at him, still resentful. "What's the fuss about then?" he demanded.

"Because we've had our roundup, an' we've only netted three thousand head."

"Three thousand?" Gerber stared. "Ward, you're crookin' me! If you only found three thousand head, you've snuck some off somewheres." His mouth tightened. "Ah? Maybe that's it? Maybe you figure to get me on that guarantee! Well, I won't stand for it, Ward!"

Ward's face flushed. "All I want is a square deal."

"He's askin' for trouble, Gerber," Black said. "Let me have him."

"Listen, big ears," Sartain took a step into the room, "if you're so anxious to throw iron, suppose you come out in the street an' throw it with me?"

"*Kim!*" Ward barked. "Stop it!" Ward

wheeled on Black. "And you shut up! Gerber, get that man out of here, and get him out fast! If we start shootin' in this room, nobody will get out alive. And we've a woman here, remember that!"

Dick Gerber's anger left him. Realization broke over him that what Ward said was true. Ruth Kermitt was there. To throw a gun when a woman was present was out of reason.

"Quiet down!" Gerber snapped. "You, Black, mind what I say." He turned back to McQueen. "I'm sorry, Ward. Maybe I went off half-cocked, but I sure ain't the man to bunco anybody. I figure you of all people knew that."

"Mr. Gerber," Ruth said quietly, "just before you came in Ward was saying that even though there was a problem he would swear by you."

The old man looked around. "I guess I'm a fool," he said, and dropped into a chair. "I never figured on makin' a shootin' match of it, Ward. I was just too mad to think."

"Forget it and let's have a talk." Ward glanced at Sartain. "Kim, we don't want any trouble."

"That goes for you boys, too," Gerber told

his men. "Ward an' me'll find some peaceful way to handle this."

As the hands trooped out, the door pushed open and into the room swaggered a big man, broad shouldered and blond. He was nattily dressed in black and he smiled when he saw Ruth.

"Oh, Miss Kermitt! I was looking for you. They told me in the office that you had come in here with one of the hands. Are you ready now?"

Ward McQueen looked around, astonished. The man was Buff Colker, the rep for the KT outfit, but he had never looked like this on the range. Then, as Colker's meaning swept over him, his face flushed and he glanced around at Ruth.

"Why, yes, Mr. Colker, just one minute." She turned quickly to Ward and put her hand on his. "I wasn't sure that you'd be in tonight," she said, "and Mr. Colker asked if he might call. Do you mind?"

For a moment Ward McQueen sat still, resentment burning within him. He had a half notion to say that he certainly did mind. Then he shrugged it off.

"No," he said, "I've got to talk with Gerber, anyway."

Yet as she arose and walked with Buff Colker into the other room, he glared after them. "Make a nice-lookin' couple," Gerber suggested thoughtfully. "She ain't married, is she?"

"We came here to talk about cattle." McQueen's voice had a faint rasp.

"Sure," Gerber agreed. He pulled his tally book from his pocket. "Got money, that young Colker has. I often wonder why he works for the KT, but maybe he figures to go into the cattle business."

He put on his glasses and peered at the book. "Now let's see: there were a couple of hundred head in Seminole Canyon. Did you get those out?"

Two hours later Ward McQueen stalked into the saloon, irritated and unhappy. Despite their discussion and the careful checking of the record Gerber had kept, there was no accounting for the missing cattle. Yet a thousand head of cattle cannot just vanish, nor can they be hidden with ease.

Sartain was sitting alone at a card table idly riffling a deck of cards. He had his flat-brimmed gray hat shoved back on his head and was watching Black like a cat. The big gunman looked around when Ward came in, and watched as he walked over and dropped into a chair with Kim.

Sartain riffled the cards through his fingers and, without looking up, commented, "That Black has money. He buys drinks pretty free for a forty-dollar cowhand."

He has money. The words flitted through McQueen's mind, and then were lost as the door shoved open and Ernie Yost came in, accompanied by Villani and Taylor.

Taylor averted his eyes hastily. One of the three, McQueen reflected, was content to let well enough alone. Watching them, Ward was struck by the fact that Yost, staring straight across the bar, was speaking out of the corner of his mouth. The man beside him was Black.

Black's eagerness for trouble and a few words exchanged with Yost lingered in Ward's brain. What was between those two? Was Black tied in with Yost? What was going on around here?

"Let's leave, Kim. We've got a hard day tomorrow."

Mounting, they turned down the trail toward the ranch, but as he glanced back,

Ward saw Ruth saying good night to Colker on the steps of the hotel. "He's got money." That was what Gerber had said of Colker. It was also what Sartain had said of Black. Could there be a tie-up there? Did their money come from the same source? Or was jealousy leading him down a blind alley?

What was the source of Black's money? The man had the earmarks of an owlhoot.

"Glad you got me out of there," Kim said, "I reckon I'm sleepier'n I thought."

Sleepier was right. *Sleep—er*. Ward's dark mood was gone in a flash. He jerked around in the saddle. "Kim, have you been over to that herd of cattle we've cut for the other brands?"

Kim looked up, half awake. "No, why should I? We're through with them."

There must be at least two or three thousand head of KT, Broken Arrow, and Running M cattle in that herd, McQueen thought. That was a big herd, a very big herd.

It was almost noon the next day when he rode down to the roundup crew. McQueen had been thinking and checking. Sartain was sitting on a small gray horse, and Jackson was nearby. They had just knocked off for a brief rest.

Perkins and Lopez were sitting on the ground while Gallatin and Jensen were just riding up. Ward dropped from his horse and walked up to Lopez.

"Lopez, what horse did you ride yesterday?"

Lopez hesitated. "Bay pony, *señor*."

"A bay?" Baldy looked around. "You must be forgetful. You rode that blaze-faced black with the broken hind hoof." The Mexican looked at him, then got to his feet, and he suddenly looked sick.

"That's right, Lopez." McQueen's thumbs were tucked in his belt, and around him the other riders were silent. "Now tell me what you were doing moving cattle at midnight."

"I, *señor*?" Lopez's eyes shifted right and left. "I was moving no cattle. I was in my bunk, asleep."

"A lie!" Ward's tone was brutal and he moved a step nearer. "You took that black horse out again, and you an' somebody else cut some cattle from the unbranded herd and moved them over into those mixed brands!"

"Sleeperin', by golly!" Baldy slapped his leg. "Sleeperin'! Why didn't I figure that? An' nobody ever checks that herd of mixed brands. After we're finished here, they'll just be left to drift back on the range from that long valley where you're holdin' 'em."

"And then these rannies could move in an' brand the unbranded stock for themselves. Nice business." Bud Fox dropped a hand to his six-shooter. "Do we down him, boss?"

"Not if he talks." Ward walked up to the Mexican, whose face was a sickly yellow now. "Lopez, who's bossin' this show? Tell me an' you can go free."

"Let me have a hand at him!" Gallatin shoved forward, his face grim and his eyes narrow. "I'll fix him for you!"

"Keep out of this!" Ward snapped. "I'll talk to you, later! I've a good notion you're the other one in this mess!"

Gallatin sprang back, his face suddenly wolfish. "Oh, you think so, do you? Well, by—" His hand swept down for his gun.

"Stop!" Ward yelled. "Drop it or I'll kill you!"

Gallatin was crouching and his gun kept lifting. "Drop, nothin'!"

Ward palmed his six-gun in a flashing

movement and flame stabbed from the black muzzle. His own gun coming up too slow, Gallatin caught the lead slugs in the stomach. He gulped, then staggered slowly back, his eyes glazing, the gun slipping from nerveless fingers.

III

Hooves clattered and a shout went up. McQueen whirled in time to see Lopez streaking away on the horse the Mexican had just freshly saddled. Ward's gun came up, but the rustler was in a direct line with two men on the far side of the herd, and he dared not fire.

"Gone!" He swore. "He got plumb away."

Baldy Jackson reached for his bridle reins. "Boss, we'd better get at that mixed herd. Now they'll probably move in an' try to rustle the works. We'd better start cuttin' her."

"We're not in on any deal with Gally or the Mex," Jensen said. "You can ask Dick Gerber. I rode for him four years."

Ward glanced around at them. "Either of you know their friends? Who did they see in Sotol?"

Jensen hesitated. "Well, I reckon that Black who still rides for Gerber was the only one. They were pretty thick when they both rode for this spread. And then Villani. He worked for Gerber for a while, then left him after some trouble over a bridle, and he went to hangin' out with Ernie Yost."

"That fits." Sartain nodded. "They all run together. The same brand wears well on them. Let's go coyote huntin', boss."

Ward McQueen hesitated. That was one thing, but the cattle came first. He must at all costs protect Ruth's cattle. "No, we'd better start workin' that mixed herd an' cuttin' our unbranded stock out of it."

"Boss, that Mex didn't head for Sotol," Bud suggested. "He took out for the mountains an' I've a good idea he's more set on gettin' safe away than tellin' Yost what happened here. Why don't we lay low an' check that herd today?"

"All right." Jensen was facing Ward, and he motioned to the body of Gallatin. "Plant him over by those trees, will you? Before anybody sees him. And I don't want it mentioned all day, you hear? Not in front of anybody!"

Sartain crooked a leg around his saddle

horn. "Boss, I reckon Buff Colker will be out here soon."

"I said *anybody*." Ward turned to Bud. "I like your idea. We'll start cutting the mixed herd again tomorrow. Today we'll keep on with the branding, and tonight," he glanced at Baldy, then at Kim, "tonight we'll stand guard by that unbranded herd. If anybody starts to move those cattle we'll be ready for them."

The day drew on, hot and dusty. There was no breeze, and Ward nervously glanced at the sky from time to time. It felt like a storm was building up.

A cloud of dust hung over the corral where the branding was done, and the hands kept working up new bunches of cattle from the herd of the unbranded. Sartain was handling a rope, and Baldy was working with a branding iron. Buff Colker had arrived and sat his paint horse near the corral.

"KT, one calf!" Baldy yelled, slapping the iron on the animal, which bawled plaintively. "Tumblin' K! One calf!"

Colker checked the KT in his tally book and wiped the dust and perspiration from his brow. Ward McQueen was studiously avoiding the KT rep. He put his rope on a white-face steer and spilled the beast close to the fire. Baldy slapped the iron and yelled, "Tumblin' K! One steer!"

Colker slapped his book shut and turned his horse. "Guess I'll ride along, McQueen," he said, "I've got business in town!"

Ward glanced around, his lips tight. "Go ahead," he said. "We don't need you here."

Buff laughed sardonically. "Maybe there's somebody else that needs me."

McQueen's face flamed. "I don't know what you mean by that, Buff," he said evenly, "but you'd better be ridin'."

"That lady boss of yours seems to like what I say. Pretty little thing, I'll say that for her."

McQueen turned his roan. "If you're goin'," he warned, "you better hightail it while the goin's good."

Colker laughed, his eyes hard and the sneer evident. "Ward," he said, "you're a fool! After I've had my way with her, I'll come back here an' teach you a couple of things!"

He wheeled his horse and started at a gallop toward the Sotol trail. Ward McQueen's face went hard and white, and he wheeled his horse and went after Buff like a streak.

"Lord help that Colker now!" Baldy said. "The boss is sure boilin'. I wondered how much he'd take from that four-flusher!"

"Look!" Kim yelled excitedly. "This is goin' to be good!"

Too late, Buff Colker turned to see what was happening. Ward's roan had covered the ground in a short dash that brought him alongside Colker's galloping horse. Quickly, Ward reached down and grabbed the paint horse's tail and whipped it to one side, shoving the horse hard with his knee.

It was a process used often on the range to throw a steer, and when the animal, whether horse or cow, was traveling at all rapidly, it would invariably be spilled on the head and shoulder. It was known as "tail-ing," but was rarely used on a horse unless the animal was of little or no value.

Colker and the animal went flying. He sprang to his feet and clawed for his gun, then stopped. Ward was on the ground facing him, and had him covered. Colker had never even seen Ward draw.

A dozen cowhands had crowded around. "Bud," Ward said, "take his gun. I'm goin' to teach this cowboy a lesson!"

"What do you mean?" Colker snarled. His

face was white, but his eyes blazed. "You aimin' to shoot me down like a dog?"

"No, *amigo*," Ward said harshly, "I'm goin' to beat your thick skull in with my fists."

Abruptly, Buff grinned. "You're goin' to fight me with your hands? I'll kill you!"

Fox slid the gun from Buff Colker's holster, and Ward stepped over to Kim Sartain and hung his own gun belts around his saddle horn. Then he turned.

Across the wide ring of horsemen, he faced Buff Colker. Buff was the bigger man, young, wide-shouldered, and tough. He was smiling and confident. Buff paused long enough to strip off his shirt. Ward did likewise. Then the two men moved together.

Colker came fast and lashed out with a left that caught Ward coming in, but failed to stop him. McQueen crowded Colker and threw a short left, palm up, into Buff's midsection as they came together, Ward turning his body with the punch. It jolted Buff, but he jerked away and smashed both hands to Ward's face. Ward tried to duck a left, and caught another right. Then he closed in and threw Colker hard with a rolling hip-lock. Buff came up fast and dived at Ward's knees and they both went down, and then they were up and fighting, toe to toe, slugging. The two men came together, throwing their punches with everything they had in them.

Eyes blazing with fury, Buff sprang close, swinging with both hands. The dust rose from around their feet in a thick cloud, so at times the fighting could scarcely be seen. Neither man would give an inch and they fought bitterly, brutally, at close quarters. This was old stuff to Ward, for he had battled in many a cow camp brawl, and he kept moving in, his head spinning and dizzy with rocking blows, his hands always set to punch.

Blood trickled from a cut lip, and he had the taste of it in his mouth. Overhead the sky was like a sheet of iron, molten with heat. Ward set himself and slammed a right to the body. Again Buff was jolted, and he stepped back, and McQueen moved in, advancing his left foot then his right. He worked in, then threw his right again. Buff's hands came down and Ward lunged, swinging high and hard with both fists, and Colker went down in the dust and rolled over.

"Put the boots to him!" Baldy said. "He'd give them to you!"

"Let him get up!" Ward panted. "I want more of him!"

Colker staggered to his feet and stood there weaving, the hatred in his eyes a living thing. He lunged, suddenly. But Ward met him with a stiff left hand that stopped him flat-footed and left him wide open for a clubbing right. It caught Colker flush on the ear, and Buff went down to his knees, the ear beginning to puff almost as he hit the ground.

Ward moved in, staggering with exhaustion. He jerked Colker to his feet and, holding him with his left, struck him twice in the wind and then three blows with his right in the face. Then he shoved the man from him, and Buff staggered and tumbled into the dust.

McQueen walked back to his horse and leaned against it for an instant, then picked up his shirt and began to wipe his face and body with it.

"Better get started on those cows," he commented. "We've a lot to do."

Baldy stared at him grimly. "You better go up to the cook shack and get that face fixed up," he suggested. "You look like chopped beef. But not," he added with satisfaction, "near so bad as he does!"

Colker was still stretched on his face, and Bud Fox glanced at him. "Shall we pick him up?" he asked.

"Let him lay!" Baldy told him. "He needs the rest!"

When he had bathed his face and repaired the cuts as best he could, Ward McQueen studied the situation. He was wrong to have let Buff Colker goad him into a fight. Nobody ever gained anything permanent by violence despite the satisfaction derived from a solid smash of a fist.

Colker was not his problem. He knew that Gallatin and Lopez had been sleepering cattle, and there seemed to be a connection between them and the Yost crowd, and possibly with Black.

He must find something more concrete in the way of evidence. Without returning to the corral, he dropped to a seat on a wooden bench in the shade near the back door of the cook shack. From where he sat he could see the dust rising from the branding corral, and the hills beyond.

The cook stuck his head out of the door and grinned at him. "Coffee, *señor*?"

"You bet, Pedro! An' thanks."

Sleepering cattle by day was a risky job, but it had been done. Baldy and Bud had the right idea, to check the herd by night and watch for the rustlers. Gerber himself might even be in it, but McQueen could not bring himself to admit that, nor could he quite believe that Ernie Yost, crooked as he was, would be the ringleader in any such scheme. Yost might run off forty or fifty head and sell them over the border, but dangerous as he might be at times, he was not a man who planned big.

Sartain had suggested that Colker did not always go to town when he left the roundup. If not to Sotol, where did he go? To a hideout in the hills? Or was he, himself, drifting unbranded stock away from the main herd?

Ward McQueen mounted the roan and headed back for the branding corral. Baldy rode up to him as he approached.

"The boys workin' back in the hills say the stock is mostly down out of the brush," he commented. "Also, Bud seen Old Man Gerber back there in the woods."

"Gerber? Out here?" Ward scowled. "What was he doing? Did Bud talk to him?"

"No, he didn't. Bud found a few more Slash Seven cows for us and was starting them back. They showed no liking for open country, so he had his work cut out for him."

"How long ago?"

"Right after the fight. He must be still back there because we heard a shot 'way back in the canyon, maybe a half hour ago."

"A shot? What would he be shootin' at?"

Baldy Jackson shrugged. "Want me to ride back an' see? Maybe the old feller is skinnin' you, Ward."

"No, he's honest enough. I think I'll ride back there, though. You come along."

"Kim was tellin' about your run-in with Yost, an' then with Black. You reckon they are in on this steal?"

Ward shrugged. "Could be. Lopez and Gallatin weren't in it alone."

The grass was parched and brown in the valley, and they were leaving the scattered growth of oak, Spanish dagger, and mesquite for higher ground and the cedar. The air felt thick and heavy. Across the shoulder of the mountain they pushed down into the thick brush, and here they ran into

Jensen with four head of Slash 7's, two YT's, and a 21.

"You see Gerber here?" Ward demanded.

"No, I sure haven't. Heard a shot a while back, then two more. I had these critters, though, an' couldn't chase over to investigate. Somebody shootin' at a wolf, maybe, or a panther."

"Start those cattle over the ridge and then come with us. We may need an outside witness."

IV

Ward McQueen's gray eyes swept the tangle before him. It would be like hunting for a needle in a haystack to search for anything down there. Still, if Gerber was out here, he was here for a reason.

The sun was blazing hot, and in the chaparral the heat was oppressive. It felt even more like a storm than before. If it rained, it would at least make travel better, and Ward's plan was to start the herd within forty-eight hours if possible. It wouldn't give the men much rest, but he wanted to be driving north to where the grass was better.

Along the trail north they could take their time. He wanted the cattle to feed all the way to Kansas, anyway.

Sweat trickled down his face, cutting a furrow through the dust. It was hot. He wiped his palms dry on his pant legs and let the roan find its way through the brush that now was higher than his head.

"More to the left, I reckon," Jensen said. "You can't always swear to the direction."

"I smell smoke," Baldy said. "Hold up! I smell smoke close to hand."

"Who would want a fire on a day like this?" Jensen asked, of nobody in particular. "This place is like an oven."

"Wait a minute!" Ward lifted a hand. "There's something over here." He turned his horse and pushed through the shin oak, then drew up sharply, and the roan snorted and backed up. "Dead man," he said.

He trailed the bridle reins and dropped to the ground. He needed to go only a step nearer to recognize Dick Gerber. The white-haired old man was lying on his back, one arm thrown across his eyes to shield them from the sun.

Jensen dropped from his horse and bent

over the old man. He placed a hand on his heart.

"Dead, all right. That's too bad, he was a pretty good old boy, at that."

"What was he doin' with a fire?" Baldy demanded. "Hey, there's a runnin' iron!"

Ward scowled. "Gerber? With a runnin' iron? What would he be brandin'?" He stared at the man, and then at the fire. "Hunt up his horse, Baldy, while Jensen an' I have a look around."

"He always carried a runnin' iron, Mr. McQueen," Jensen said. "The old man claimed it saved a sight of time to brand stock where he found it. Never went out but what he carried it."

Ward looked around thoughtfully. Obviously, Gerber had used the iron. He bent over it and touched it. It was lying in the shade and it was still warm.

Gerber had been shot twice through the chest, never able to get his gun out. It was a plain case of murder.

"He had a critter down, Mr. McQueen," Jensen said. "Here's the tracks. He throwed it, an' from the look hog-tied it."

"Yeah." Ward squatted on his heels. "Here's a piggin' string. But what would he want to brand back in here on a day like this?"

"It wasn't dishonest," Jensen said stubbornly. "I knew the old man well, as I guess you did. He was on the level."

"Sure! But what was he doin' here? An' who shot him?"

Jensen scratched his jaw. "You know what they'll say. They'll say you done it. They'll say after that trouble in town that you had more trouble and that you killed him in an argument over cattle."

McQueen stared at the old man's body. So far as he could see, nothing had been touched. He got up, studying the angle of the shots, but apparently the old man had not died at once, but had moved around some, and it was hard to figure. Yet, when he looked again, there did seem to be one possibility.

On the brow of a hill, not over fifty yards away, was a cluster of boulders. It was worth looking at.

"Baldy, go back to the ranch and get a buckboard," he said. "Come as far as you can, an' we'll pack the body out to it."

"You ought to be havin' a look around, Mr. McQueen," Jensen said seriously. "This here was murder, an' you better find who done it. Folks sure liked this old man."

Who had the opportunity? Jensen, of course. Bud Fox, too. Both of them had been working the brush, and there were probably two or three other hands who had been in the vicinity. But it wouldn't make sense for any of them to kill him. It had to be someone else, and somehow it was sure to tie in with the sleepering of Slash 7 cattle.

Ward turned and fought his way through the brush to the nest of boulders on the hill. From atop a boulder, he studied the earth behind them. From here he could see Jensen standing over Gerber's body, and the unknown murderer could have done the same. Behind the rocks were boot tracks, a number of them. He could find no cartridge anywhere around.

Jensen was waiting for him. "Find anything?"

"Tracks. That's all. Probably whoever shot him did it from there, but that doesn't tell us anything."

Jensen scratched his unshaven jaw. "It does tell you a little, Mr. McQueen. It tells you the chances are that whoever killed him was following him. Nobody gets in this here brush by accident, an' nobody's goin' to convince me that two men are in the brush by accident an' one seen the other down here, then killed him."

"It could be that way, though." Ward pushed his hat back, then removed it and mopped the sweat band. "The thing is, the killer had a reason, an' that's where we've got to think this out. The killer must have seen Gerber down here with that critter thrown, an' he didn't want him to do what he was doin'."

"Well, anybody could say he was rustlin'," Jensen suggested. "I'll never believe it of the old man, but it sure does look funny, him down here with a runnin' iron an' a critter throwed in this heat."

"Or maybe there was something else. Maybe he was inspectin' a brand somebody didn't want him to look at too close. Could that be it?"

Jensen agreed dubiously. "Could be. But what brand?"

Baldy Jackson came up leading a horse. "Got the buckboard. There's a passel of folks at the ranch. Sheriff, too."

"The sheriff? Already?" Ward shrugged. "The law always gets there fast when you don't want him. All right, we'll have a talk."

Ward McQueen rode back to the ranch followed by Baldy with the buckboard, and Gerber's horse and the horse that packed him out of the brush trailing behind. Jensen brought up the rear, his face doubtful.

Buff Colker was there, and not far from him was Ruth Kermitt. Ward glanced quickly at her, but her eyes were averted and he could not catch her glance.

Other men walked up from the corrals and he saw Ernie Yost, Villani, and Black. Taylor was nowhere in evidence. Apparently, he, like Lopez, had decided he had enough.

Kim Sartain loafed nearby, leaning against an old Conestoga wagon. He nodded toward the tall man with the drooping mustache.

"Sheriff Jeff Davis, this is Ward McQueen."

"Howdy." Ward swung around. "What's the trouble, Sheriff?"

"I hear there's been some shootin' around here. Who killed Dick Gerber?"

"That's something I'd like to know," McQueen told him. "We heard the shots, or some of the boys did, and later went to look around. We found Gerber, already dead."

Davis stocked his pipe. "You had trouble with him in town?"

"Nothing serious. We were friends, only somebody told him I said he lied about the number of cattle we had here and he went off half-cocked. I bought four thousand head, but when we finished our gather the tally showed only a few over three thousand."

"Then what happened?" Davis eyed him thoughtfully. Ward met his eyes and shrugged.

"We had our words in town, then sat down together and straightened things out. I didn't see Dick again until we found him in the brush, dead."

"He had a brandin' iron alongside of him, an' a fire goin'. He'd branded something." Baldy made his offering and then shut up.

Davis glanced at him, one bleak, all-seeing glance. "The killer could have planted that. You could have planted it, McQueen."

"I could have, but I didn't. Dick Gerber never misbranded a cow in his entire life, and I'd bet on it. He drove a hard bargain often enough, but he was honest as they come."

"You ask us to believe," Colker interrupted, "that you parted from Gerber last night on a friendly basis when you had a thousand head missing from the tally? That sounds pretty broad-minded to me."

For a moment Ward looked around at him. "What's his part in this, Sheriff? As you can tell by the expression I pounded into his face, I don't like him!"

"I'm a witness." Colker smiled grimly. "I'll have my say, too."

"Want me to start him travelin', boss?" Sartain asked. "I'd like that."

"I'm in charge here." Davis looked around at Kim. "I'll start who movin' when I want."

Kim Sartain straightened away from the wheel. "Ward McQueen is my boss, and I'll take his orders."

"Are you takin' that, Davis?" Yost thrust forward. "There have been two killin's committed on this place today. Gallatin was shot down by McQueen, and then Gerber was bumped off. That Sartain is a killer; McQueen as much as admitted it the other day."

"Was Gallatin killed?" Davis inquired gently. Ward found himself liking the man. Obviously, Sheriff Jeff Davis was no fool, and he was a man who knew his own mind.

"Yes, there was a gunfight. I accused Lopez of handling cattle at night. Gallatin interfered, and when I called him on it, he went for a gun. I tried to stop him, but couldn't, so I drew."

"I seen it, Jeff," Jensen said flatly. "Gally asked for it. He was rustlin' cows."

"What about that thousand head?" Davis asked. "Found hide or hair of them?"

"I reckon we did," Ward said, and his eyes swung to Buff Colker. "I think we've found 'em all!"

By the light that leaped suddenly in Colker's eyes, McQueen knew he had guessed right. Buff Colker was the brains of the rustling on the Slash 7.

"They were sleeperin' 'em, Sheriff. Driving unbranded stock around the pens at night an' mixing them in with the mixed brands we were going to release. Lopez was in on it, an' so was Gallatin. I think that Gerber smelled a rat, an' when the killer trailed him an' saw what he was doin', he killed him."

"Sheriff." Ruth Kermitt spoke gently. "Have you had trouble with rustlers around here before?"

"Sure. Matter of fact, that was the reason

Gerber was sellin' his stock. Too much rustlin'."

"And Gerber's brand is a Slash Seven," Ruth continued. "Can you think of a brand that a Slash Seven could be made into, Sheriff?"

"Ma'am, we've been over that here for months," Davis said. "There ain't a brand in this part of the country like that. Not one it could be done with, not anywhere easy."

"There's one brand," she insisted gently. "I refer to the brand that Buff Colker has registered."

Ward happened to have his eyes on Colker, and he saw the man start as if struck with a whip. His head jerked around, and hatred blazed in his eyes, hatred and fear. But then the fear was gone.

"Colker ain't got no brand!" Davis said, frowning. "Nor no cattle I know of."

"He has, though, Sheriff." Ruth glanced at Ward, then away. "I checked with Austin. He has a Box Triangle registered there. Any child could make a Slash Seven into a Box Triangle.

"Mr. Colker spent the whole evening telling me how he didn't have to be a cowhand, that he had a ranch of his own, well stocked with cattle, and that he intended to branch out. When Ward told me of the cattle we were missing, I became curious, and I checked with Austin as to Buff Colker's brand."

"Are you accusin' me of being a rustler?" Colker turned on her, his dark eyes ugly. Then he looked back at the sheriff. "You can see for yourself, Sheriff. This is a cheap plot. They are conniving to hang this on me. McQueen is a known gunman, so is Sartain, and they both work for Miss Kermitt."

Davis chewed his mustache. "Do you have a brand?"

Colker's eyes shifted. "Yes," he said finally.

"Is it a Box Triangle?"

"Well, yes, but that doesn't mean that I'm a rustler."

Davis dropped to his haunches and with a stick, drew a Slash 7 in the sand, and then opposite it, a Box Triangle.

He glanced up at Colker. "You've got to admit it's awful easily done." He straightened to his feet. "Now, folks, I ain't much on a man havin' an alibi. Them as needs 'em can get 'em, an' them as don't need 'em never has 'em.

"If McQueen has found the Tumblin' K

cows, like he says, I don't see no reason for any shootin' on his part. Far's I know, the two of them are friends. There has been some rustlin' here, I can see that. I reckon afore we can do much else we'll have to send a deputy to your ranch an' have a few head of your cows killed so we can check the brands. If we can find any Slash Sevens made over, I reckon we'll have Gerber's rustler, an' maybe a powerful suspect for his murder. Until then we'll hold you."

"That don't figure, Jeff," Yost protested. "Just because this girl figured it that way is no sign that Gerber did."

"He knew." Ruth spoke positively. "I was very careless last night. I was drawing Slash Sevens into Box Triangles at the table, and forgot and left my paper there. When I returned for it, the cook told me that Dick Gerber had picked it up, swore, and went out."

Buff Colker was sweating now, and his face was pale. "That doesn't prove a thing!" he declared. "I demand to be allowed to leave. All you have is a lot of suspicion. I can find fifty brands in Texas that could be made from Slash Sevens."

Ernie Yost had fallen back close to Colker,

and Villani had moved toward his horse. A slight movement by Black drew Ward's attention, and he saw that the big gunman was sidling toward his horse and his rifle. And then he saw something else.

Bud Fox had his rope on a steer and he was half leading, half dragging him toward the house. Behind him, Perkins was using his rope as a whip to urge the stubborn steer along.

Ward McQueen shifted his position so he could keep Yost and Colker completely covered if necessary. Out of the corner of his eye he noticed that Kim Sartain and Baldy Jackson were both alert to the shifting of forces. Only the sheriff and Jensen seemed unaware of what was happening.

"Ruth, you'd better get inside," Ward said quietly. "There's going to be trouble." He spoke softly, but he noticed the sheriff's sudden movement and knew he had heard.

Ward shifted his eyes from Buff toward the steer, and for a moment he stared at the weird brand without comprehension, and then it hit him.

"Davis!" he said sharply. "There's your proof of murder!"

Burned with a running iron on the steer's hide was the date, and under it:

```
SHOT BY BUF CLKR RUSTLER, DYIN
            /7 TO BX TRI
            HOT AS HELL
            D. GRBR.
```

"There it is! Burned with a runnin' iron as the old man lay dyin' in the brush! Then he cut loose the steer—had him thrown and ready to check his brand when Buff came up on him!"

Buff Colker stepped back quickly and clawed for his gun, but Ward was faster. Even as Colker's gun started to lift, Ward's first bullet ripped the thumb from his hand and knocked him off balance.

Colker stared at the stub where his thumb had been, now gushing with blood, and with a cry like an animal, rushed for his horse. Ward had swung his gun toward Yost even as a bullet knocked him into the side of the house. He fired, holding his gun low. Sartain had opened up on Black, and the wiry young gunfighter was walking in on him, firing with every step. Villani was out of it. Baldy had fired his rifle right across the saddle bows, and Villani toppled over, clawed at the side of the water trough, and got himself half erect, getting his gun out even as he cursed. Baldy fired again, and the gun slid from Villani's fingers.

Yost screamed as Ward's bullet hit him, and then suddenly, his eyes wild, he ran straight for McQueen, his gun blazing. Ward stepped back and tripped on the stoop. Catching himself on one hand, he looked up into the wild, fear-crazed eyes of Yost as the man threw down on him with a six-shooter at point-blank range! McQueen shot fast, three times, as swiftly as he could thumb the gun.

Ernie Yost went up on his toes, his face twisting in a frightful grimace; then he pitched over on his face, his gun blasting the hard-packed earth within inches of Ward's hand.

McQueen kicked the dying man off his legs and got to his feet, feeding shells into his gun, but the battle was over. In a few seconds four men had died.

Sheriff Davis had fired but one shot, killing Buff Colker as he scrambled to get away.

Ward McQueen holstered his gun and grabbed for support at the well coping. He knew he had been shot; his side felt strangely numb and his mind seemed sluggish, but his eyes were alive and knowing.

Jensen was down, but struggling to get up, with a red stain on his pant leg. Sheriff Davis, in the most exposed position of all, was unharmed.

Ruth rushed to Ward's side. "Darling! You're hurt!"

He put his hand on her shoulder and tried to grin. "Not much," he said. "How's Kim?"

"Never touched me!" Sartain said. "They plowed a furrow over Baldy's ear. Cut off a piece of the last fringe of hair he's got left!"

Neither Fox nor Perkins had managed to get off a shot. Both men came crowding up now, and they helped Ward inside. On examination they found he had only a flesh wound in the side, and while there had been some loss of blood, he was not badly hurt.

Ward looked at Ruth. "I reckon when I get on my feet, we'd better haul out of here. This place looks like trouble."

She laughed, then blushed. "I'm in a hurry to get back, too, Ward. Or shall we wait?"

"No," he smiled, "I've heard that Cheyenne is a good town for weddings!"

SIDESHOW CHAMPION

When Mark Lanning looked at me and asked if I would take the Ludlow fight, I knew what he was thinking, and just what he had in mind. He also knew that there was only one answer I could give.

"Sure, I'll take it," I said. "I'll fight Van Ludlow any place, for money, marbles, or chalk."

But it was going to be for money. Lanning knew that, for that's what the game is about. Also, it had to be money because I was right behind the eight ball for lack of it.

Telling the truth: if I hadn't needed the cash as bad as I did, I would never have taken the fight. Not me, Danny McClure.

I'd been ducking Ludlow for two years. Not because I didn't want a shot at the title, but because of Lanning and some of the crowd behind him.

Mark Lanning had moved in on the fight game in Zenith by way of the slot machine racket. He was a short, fat man who wore a gold-plated coin on his watch chain. That coin fascinated me. It was so much like the guy himself, all front and polish, and underneath about as cheap as they come.

However, Mark Lanning was *the* promoter in Zenith. And Duck Miller, who was manager for Van Ludlow, was merely an errand boy for Mark. About the only thing Lanning didn't control in the fight game by that time was me. I was the uncrowned middleweight champ and everybody said I was the best boy in the division. Without taking any bows, I can say yes to that one.

The champ, Gordie Carrasco, was strictly from cheese. He won the title on a foul, skipped a couple of tough ones, and beat three boys on decisions. Not that he couldn't go. Nobody ever gets within shouting distance of any kind of title unless he's good. But Gordie wasn't as good as Ludlow by a long ways. He wasn't as good as Tommy Spalla, either. And he wasn't as good as me.

Ludlow was a different kinda deal. I give the guy that. He had everything and maybe a little more. Now no real boxer ever believes anybody is really better than he is. Naturally, I considered myself to be the better fighter. But he was good, just plenty good, and anybody who beat him would have to go the distance and give it all he had. Van Ludlow was fast. He was smart, and he could punch. Added to it, he was one of the dirtiest fighters in the business.

That wasn't so bad. A lot of good fighters have been rough. It isn't always malicious. It's just they want to win. It's just the high degree of competitive instinct, and because among top grade fighting men the fight's the thing, and a rule here or there doesn't matter so much. Jack Dempsey never failed to use every advantage in the book, so did Harry Greb, and for my money they were two of the best who ever lived.

If it had just been Ludlow, I'd have fought him long ago. It was Lanning I was ducking. Odd as it may seem, I'm an honest guy. Now I've carried a losing fighter or two when it really didn't matter much, but I never gypped a bettor, and my fights weren't for sale. Nor did I ever buy any myself. I won them in the ring and liked it that way.

The crowd around Lanning was getting a stranglehold on the fight game. I didn't like to see that bunch of crooks, gunmen, and chiselers edging in everywhere. I had ducked the fights with Ludlow because I knew that when I went in there with him, I was the last chance honest fighting had in Zenith or anywhere nearby. I was going to be fighting every dirty trick Lanning and his crowd could figure out. The referee and the judges would be against me. The time-keeper would be for Ludlow. If there was any way Lanning could get me into the ring without a chance, he'd try it.

Yet, I was taking the fight.

The reason was simple enough. My ranch, the only thing in the world I cared about, was mortgaged to the hilt. I'd blown my savings on that ranch, then put a mortgage on it to stock it and build a house and some barns. If it hadn't been for Korea, it would have been paid off. But I was in the army, and Mark Lanning located that note and bought it.

The mortgage was due, and I didn't have even part of a payment. Without that ranch, I was through. My days in the ring weren't numbered, but from where I stood I could see the numbers. I'd been fighting fourteen years, and Lanning had the game sewed up around there, so nobody fought unless they would do business. I cared more about that ranch than I did the title, so I could take a pass on Gordie Carrasco. But Van Ludlow couldn't. Lanning had him aimed at Gordie but he wouldn't look so good wearing the belt if the man all the sportswriters called "the uncrowned champ" wasn't taken down, too. Lanning now had it all lined up. I had to fight or give up on my future.

And then, there was Marge Hamlin.

Marge was my girl. We met right after I mustered out, when I first returned to Zenith. She was singing at the Rococo, and a honey if there ever was one. We started going together, became engaged, and were going to marry in the summer.

I *had* to take the fight. That was more the truth of it.

I went over to Lanning's. Duck Miller was there. We talked.

"Then," Lanning said, smiling his greasy smile, "there's the matter of an appearance forfeit."

"What d'you mean?" I asked. "Ever know of me running out on a fight?"

He moved one pudgy hand over to the ashtray and knocked off the gray ashes from his expensive cigar. "It ain't that, Danny," he said smoothly, "it's just business. Van's already got his up to five thousand dollars."

"Five thousand?" I couldn't believe what I heard. "Where would I get five thousand dollars? If I had five thousand you would never get me within a city block of any of your fights."

"That's what it has to be," he replied, and his eyes got small and ugly. He liked putting the squeeze on. "You can put up your car an' your stock from the ranch."

For a minute I stared at him. He knew what that meant as well as I did. It would mean that come snakes or high water, I would have to be in that ring to fight Ludlow. If I wasn't, I'd be flat broke, not a thing in the world but the clothes on my back.

Not that I'd duck a fight. But there are such things as cut eyes and sickness.

"Okay," I said, "I'll put 'em up. But I'm warnin' you. Better rig this one good. Because I'm going to get you!"

I wasn't the bragging kind, and I saw Duck

Miller looked a little worried. Duck was smart enough, just weak. He liked the easy dough, and the easy money in Zenith all came through Mark Lanning. Lanning was shrewd and confident. He had been winning a long time. Duck Miller had never won, so Miller could worry.

The thing was, Miller knew me. There had been a time when Duck and I had been broke together. We ran into some trouble out West when a tough mob tried to arrange one of my fights to make a cleanup. I refused to go along, and they said it was take the money or else.

Me, I'm a funny guy. I don't like getting pushed around, and I don't like threats. In that one, everybody had figured the fight would go the distance. This guy was plenty tough. Everybody figured me for the nod, but nobody figured he would stop me or I'd stop him. The wise boys had it figured for me to go in the tank in the sixth round.

I came to that fight all rodded up. They figure a fighter does it with his hands or no way. But these hombres forgot I'm a western man myself, and didn't figure on me packing some iron.

Coming out of the Arizona Strip, the way I

do, I grew up with a gun. So I came down to that fight, and when this Rock Spenter walked out of his corner I feinted a left and Rock threw a right. My right fist caught him coming in, and my left hook caught him falling. And at the ten count, he hadn't even wiggled a toe.

I went down the aisle to the dressing room on the run, and when the door busted open, I was sitting on the rubbing table with a six-shooter in my mitt. Those three would-be hard guys turned greener than a new field of alfalfa, and then I tied two of them up, put the gun down, and went to work on the boss.

When I got through with him, I turned the others loose one at a time. Two of them were hospital cases. By that time the sheriff was busting down the door.

That old man had been betting on me, and when I explained, he saw the light very quickly. The sure-thing boys got stuck for packing concealed weapons, and one of them turned out to be wanted for armed robbery and wound up with ten years.

I'm not really bragging. I'm not proud of some of the circles I've traveled in or some of the things I've done. But I just wanted you to know what Duck Miller knew. And Duck may have been a loser, but he never lost anything but money. So far, he was still a stand-up guy.

When I had closed the door I heard Duck speak. "You shouldn't have done it, Mark," he said. "He won't take a pushing around."

"Him?" Contempt was thick in Lanning's voice. "He'll take it, and he'll like it!"

Would I? I walked out of there and I was sore. But that day, for the first time in months, I was in the gym.

The trouble was, I'd been in the service, spent my time staring through a barbed-wire fence in a part of Korea that was like Nevada with the heat turned off, and during that time I'd done no boxing. Actually, it was over three years since I'd had a legitimate scrap.

Van Ludlow had a busted eardrum or something and he had been fighting all the time. It takes fights to sharpen a man up, and they knew that. Don't think they didn't. They wanted me in the tank or out of the picture, but bad. Not that Van cared. Ludlow, like I said, was a fighter. He didn't care where his opponent came from or what he looked like.

Marge was waiting for me, sitting in her car in front of the Primrose Cafe. We locked the car and went inside and when we were sitting in the booth, she smiled at me.

Marge was a blonde, and a pretty one. She was shaped to please and had a pair of eyes you could lose yourself in. Except for one small thing, she was perfect. There was just a tiny bit of hardness around her mouth. It vanished when she smiled, and that was often.

"How was it?" she asked me.

"Rough," I said. "I'm fighting Van in ninety days. Also," I added, "he made me post an appearance forfeit. I had to put it up, and it meant mortgaging my car and my stock on the ranch."

"He's got you, hasn't he?" Marge asked.

I smiled then. It's always easy to fight when you're backed in a corner and there's only one way out.

"No," I said, "he hasn't got me. The trouble with these smart guys, they get too sure of themselves. Duck Miller is a smarter guy than Lanning."

"Duck?" Marge was amazed. "Why, he's just a stooge!"

"Yeah, I know. But I'll lay you five to one

he's got a little dough in the bank, and well, he'll never wind up in stir. Lanning will."

"Why do you say that?" Marge asked quickly. "Have you got something on him?"

"Uh-uh. But I've seen his kind before."

Like I say, I went to the gym that day. The next, too. I did about eight rounds of light work each of those two days. When I wanted to box, on the third day, there wasn't anybody to work with. There were a dozen guys of the right size around, but they were through working, didn't want to box that day, or weren't feeling good. It was a runaround.

If I'd had money, I could have imported some boys and worked at the ranch, but I didn't. However, there were a couple of big boys out there who had fooled with the mitts some, and I began to work with them. Several times Duck Miller dropped by, and I knew he was keeping an eye on me for Lanning. This work wasn't doing me any good. I knew it, and he knew it.

Marge drove out on the tenth day in a new canary-colored coupe. One of those sleek convertible jobs. She had never looked more lovely. She watched me work, and when I went over to lean on the door, she looked at me.

"This won't get it, Danny," she said. "These hicks aren't good enough for you."

"I know," I said honestly, "but I got a plan."

"What is it?" she asked curiously.

"Maybe a secret," I told her.

"From me?" she pouted. "I like to know everything about you, Danny."

She did all right. Maybe it was that hardness around her mouth. Or put it down that I'm a cautious guy. I brushed it off, and although she came back to the subject twice, I slipped every question like they were left-hand leads. And that night, I had Joe, my hand from the ranch, drive me down to Cartersville, and there I caught a freight.

The Greater American Shows were playing county fairs through the Rocky Mountain and prairie states. I caught up with them three days after leaving the ranch. Old Man Farley was standing in front of the cook tent when I walked up. He took one look and let out a yelp.

"No names, Pop," I warned. "I'm Bill Banner, a ham an' egg pug, looking for work. I want a job in your athletic show, taking on all comers."

"Are you crazy?" he demanded, low voiced. "Danny McClure, you're the greatest middleweight since Ketchell, an' you want to work with a carnival sideshow?"

Briefly, I explained the pitch. "Well," he said, "you won't find much competition, but like you say, you'll be fightin' every night, tryin' all the time. Buck's on the show, too. He'd like to work with you."

Almost fifteen years before, a husky kid, just off a cow ranch in the Strip, I'd joined the Greater American in Las Vegas. Buck Farley, the old man's kid, soon became my best pal.

An ex-prizefighter on the show taught us to box, and in a few weeks they started me taking on all comers. I stayed with the show two years and nine months, and in that time must have been in the ring with eight or nine hundred men.

Two, three, sometimes four a night wanted to try to pick up twenty-five bucks by staying four rounds. When I got better, the show raised it to a hundred. Once in a while we let them stay, but that was rare, and only when the crowd was hot and we could pack them in for the rest of the week by doing it.

When I moved on, I went pro and had gone to the top. After three years, I was ranking with the first ten. A couple of years later I was called the uncrowned champ.

"Hi, Bill!" Buck Farley had been tipped off before he saw me. "How's it going?"

Buck was big. I could get down to one sixty, but Buck would be lucky to make one ninety, and he was rawboned and tough. Buck Farley had always been a hand with the gloves, so I knew I had one good, tough sparring partner.

That night was my first sideshow fight in a long time. Old Man Farley was out front for the ballyhoo and he made it good. Then, I don't have any tin ears. My nose has been broken, but was fixed up and it doesn't show too much. A fighter would always pick me for a scrapper, but the average guy rarely does, so there wasn't any trouble getting someone to come up.

The first guy was a copper miner. A regular hard-rock boy who was about my age and weighed about two hundred and twenty. The guy's name was Mantry.

When we got in the ring, the place was full.

"Maybe you better let me take it," Buck suggested, "you might bust a hand on this guy."

"This is what I came for," I said. "I've got to take them as they come."

They sounded the bell and this gorilla came out with a rush. He was rawboned and rugged as the shoulder of a mountain. He swung a wicked left, and I slid inside and clipped him with two good ones in the wind. I might as well have slugged the side of a battleship.

He bulled on in, letting them go with both hands. I caught one on the ear that shook me to my heels and the crowd roared. Mantry piled on in, dug a left into my body and slammed another right to the head. I couldn't seem to get working and circled away from him. Then I stabbed a left to his mouth three times and he stopped in his tracks and looked surprised.

He dropped into a half crouch, this guy had boxed some, and he bored in, bulling me into the ropes. He clipped me there and my knees sagged and then I came up, mad as a hornet with a busted nest. I stabbed a left to his mouth that made those others seem like brushing him with a feather duster and hooked a right to his ear that jarred him for three generations. I walked in, slamming them with both hands, and the crowd began to whoop it up.

His knees wilted and he started to sag. This was too good to end, so I grabbed him and shoved him into the ropes, holding him up and fighting with an appearance of hard punching until the bell rang.

Mantry looked surprised, but walked to his corner, only a little shaky. He knew I'd held him up, and he was wondering why. He figured me for a good guy who was taking him along for the ride.

When we came out he took it easy, whether from caution or because I'd gone easy on him, I couldn't tell. I stabbed a left to his mouth that left him undecided about that, then stepped in close. I wanted a workout, and had to get this guy back in line.

"What's a matter, chump?" I whispered. "You yella?"

He went hog wild and threw one from his heels that missed my chin by the flicker of an eyelash. Then he clipped me with a roundhouse right and I went back into the ropes and rebounded with both hands going. He was big and half smart and he bored in, slugging like crazy.

Mister, you should have heard the tent! You could hear their yells for a half mile, and people began crowding around the outside to see what was going on. Naturally, that didn't hurt the old man's feelings.

Me, I like a fight, and so did this Mantry. We walked out there and slugged it toe-to-toe. What I had on him in experience and savvy, he had in weight, strength, and height. Of course, I'd never let old Mary Ann down the groove yet.

The crowd was screaming like a bunch of madmen. I whipped a right uppercut to Mantry's chin and he slumped, and then I drove a couple of stiff ones into his wind. The bell rang again and I trotted back to my corner.

The third was a regular brannigan. I dropped about half my science into the dis- card because this was the most fun I'd had in months. We walked out there and went into it and it would have taken a smarter guy than any in that crowd to have seen that I was slipping and riding most of Mantry's hardest punches. He teed off my chin with a good one that sent up a shower of sparks, and when the round ended, I caught him with two in the wind.

Coming up for the fourth, I figured here is where I let him have it. After all, Farley was paying one hundred bucks if this guy went the distance. I sharpened up in this one. I didn't want to cut the guy. He was a right sort, and I liked him. So I walked out and busted him a couple in the wind that brought a worried expression to his face. Then I went under his left and whammed a right to the heart that made him back up a couple of steps. He shot two fast lefts to the head and one to the chin, then tried a right.

I stepped around, feinted with a left, and he stepped in and I let Mary Ann down the groove. Now you can box or you can slug but there's none out there that can do both at once. A fighter's style is usually one or the other. Boxing will win you points and it'll keep you from getting hit too much, but slugging puts them on the canvas. The only problem is you have to stop boxing for an instant and plant your feet to do it. It's in that instant that you can get hit badly, if your opponent is on the ball. Mantry took the feint, however, and that was the end of him.

It clipped him right on the button and he stood there for a split second and then dropped like he'd been shot through the heart.

I walked back to my corner and Buck looked at me. "Man," his eyes were wide, "what did you hit him with?"

When the count was over, I went over and picked the guy up.

"Lucky punch!" one of the townies was saying. "The big guy had it made until he clipped him!"

When Mantry came around, I slapped him on the shoulder. "Nice fight, guy! Let's go back an' dress.

"Pop," I said when we were dressing, "slip the guy ten bucks a round. He made a fight."

Pop Farley knew a good thing when he saw it. "Sure enough." He paid the big guy forty dollars, who looked from me to Pop like we were Santa Claus on Christmas Eve. "Why don't you come back an' try it again?" Pop suggested.

"I might," Mantry said, "I might at that!"

That was the beginning. In the following

sixty days, I boxed from four to twelve rounds a night, fighting miners, lumber- jacks, cowpunchers, former Golden Glove boys, Army fighters, anything that came along. Mantry came back twice, and I cooled him twice more, each one a brawl.

Those sixty days had put me in wonderful condition. I was taking care of myself, not catching many, and tackling the varied styles was sharpening me up. Above all, every contest was a real fight, not practice. Even an easy fight keeps a man on his toes, and a fighter of strength can often be awk- wardly dangerous if he knows a little. And every one of these men was trying.

Buck knew all about my troubles. He was working with me every day, and we had uncovered a good fast welter on the show who had quit fighting because of a bad hand. The light, fast work was good for me.

"It won't go this easy," Buck told me. "I heard about Mark Lanning. He's dangerous. If he intends to clear the way to the title, he'll not rest until he knows where you are, and just what you're doin'."

Later, I heard about it. I didn't know then. Buck Farley had voiced my own thoughts, and in a different way, they were the thoughts of Mark Lanning and Duck Miller.

"Well," Lanning had said, "if he's taken a powder he's through. Might be the best way at that, but I hate to think of him gettin' away without a beatin', and I hate to think of blowin' the money we'd win on the fight."

"He ain't run out," Duck said positively. "I know that guy. He's smart. He's got something up his sleeve. What happened to him?"

"We traced him to Cartersville," Gasparo said. Gasparo was Lanning's pet muscle man. "He bought a ticket there for Butte. Then he vanished into thin air."

It was Marge Hamlin who tipped them off. I found that out later, too. I hadn't written her, but she was no dumb Dora, not that babe. She was in a dentist's office, waiting to get a tooth filled, when she saw the paper. It was a daily from a jerkwater town in Wyoming.

CARNIVAL FIGHTER TO MEET PAT DALY

Bill Banner, middleweight sharpie who has been a sensation in the Greater American Shows these past two months, has signed to meet Pat Daly, a local light-heavyweight, in the ten-round main event on Friday's card.

Banner, a welcome relief from the typical carnie stumblebum, has been creating a lot of talk throughout the Far West with his series of thrilling knockouts over local fighters. Pop Farley, manager and owner of Greater American, admits the opposition has been inexperienced, but points to seventy-six knockouts as some evidence. One of these was over Tom Bronson, former AAU champ, another over Ace Donaldson, heavyweight champion of Montana.

She grabbed up that paper and legged it down to Mark Lanning. "Get a load of this," she tells him. He studies it and shrugs. "You don't get it?" she inquired, lifting an eyebrow. "Ask Duck. He knows that Danny used to fight with a carnival."

"Yeah," Duck looked up, "got his start that way. Greater American Shows, it was."

Lanning's eyes lit up triumphantly. "You get a bonus for that, Chick," he tells Marge. Then he turned his head. "Gasparo, take three men. Get Tony Innes. I'll contact him by phone. Then get a plane west. I want Tony Innes to fight in this Daly's place."

"Innes?" Miller sat bolt upright. "Man! He's the second best light-heavy in the business!"

Lanning leered. "Sure! An' he belongs to me. He'll go out there, substitute for Daly. He'll give McClure a pasting. One thing, I want him to cut Danny McClure's eye! Win or lose, I want McClure's eye cut! Then when he goes in there with Ludlow, we'll see what happens!"

Outside in the street, Duck Miller lit a cigarette and looked at Marge Hamlin.

"So he's got you on the payroll, too," he said. "What a sweet four-flusher you turned out to be!"

Marge's face flushed and her lips thinned. "What about *you*?" she sneered.

Duck shrugged. "I'm not takin' any bows, kid," he said grimly, "but at least he knows which side I'm on. He's a square guy. You like blood? Be there at the ringside when he gets that eye opened. You'll see it. I hope it gets on you so bad it'll never wash off!"

"He chose this game," Marge said angrily. "If he doesn't know how it's played, that's his problem."

"And you chose him." Duck snapped his match into the street. "I guess the blood's there and won't wash off already."

All that I heard later. The Greater American was playing over in Laramie, but Pop and Buck Farley were with me, ready to go in there with Pat Daly. All three of us were in the dressing room, waiting for the call, when the door busted open.

Pat Daly was standing there in his street clothes. He had blood all over and he could hardly stand.

"Who in blazes are you?" he snarled. "Y' yella bum! Scared of me an' have your sluggers beat me up so's you can put in a setup!"

Buck took him by the arm and jerked him inside. "Give," he said, "what happened?"

"What happened?" Daly was swaying and punch-drunk, but anger blazed in his eyes. "Your sluggers jumped me. Ran my car off the road, then before I was on my feet, they started slugging me with blackjacks. When I was out cold they rolled me into the ditch and poured whiskey on me!"

"What about this substitute business?" Pop demanded.

Suddenly, I knew what happened. Mark

Lanning had got me located. From here on in, it would be every man for himself.

"You knew all about it!" Daly swore. "When I got in, Sam tells me he heard I was drunk and hurt in an accident, and that they have a substitute. You tell me how you knew that!"

The door opens then, and Sam Slake is standing there. He looks at Daly, then he looks at me. His face is hard.

"Daly can't fight," he says, "which is your fault. Your handpicked substitute is out there, so you can go in with him. But I'm tellin' you, don't bring your crooked game around here again. I'm callin' the D.A., so if you want to play games you can play them with him."

I got to my feet then, and I was sore. "Listen!" I snapped. "I'll tell you what this is all about! Get the newspaper boys in!"

It was time for the main go, and the crowd was buzzing. They had had a look at Pat Daly, some of them, and the arena was filled with crazy stories. The newspaper boys, three of them, came down into my dressing room.

"All right," I said, "this is the story. My name isn't Bill Banner. It's Danny McClure."

"What?" one of these reporters yelped. "The uncrowned middleweight champ? But you're signed to meet Van Ludlow!"

"Right!"

Briefly, quickly as I could, I told them about how I was pushed into the fight with Ludlow, all about the methods Lanning used. How I couldn't get sparring partners, and how I came west and joined the show I'd been with as a kid. And how Lanning had sent his sluggers to the show. That I didn't know who the substitute was, but before the fight was over, they'd know it was no frame. Some of it was guesswork, but they were good guesses.

"Maybe I'll know him. I'll bet money," I told them, "he's good. I'll bet plenty of dough he was sent out here to see that I go into the ring with Ludlow hurt. I got to go, or the commission in Zenith belongs to Lanning and I lose my ranch."

"Wow! What a story! The best middleweight in the game fights his way into shape with a carnival!" The reporters scrambled to beat me to the ring.

By that time the arena was wild. So I grabbed my robe and got out of the dressing room with Buck Farley and Pop alongside of me. I could see both of them were packing heaters.

When I crawled through the ropes, I looked across the ring and saw Tony Innes.

"Who is he?" Buck asked.

I told him and his face went white. Tony Innes was tough. A wicked puncher who had fought his way to the top of the game with a string of knockouts.

The announcer walked into the center of the ring and took the microphone, but I pushed him aside. Gasparo, in Innes's corner, started up. Before he could get over the edge of the ring, Buck Farley tugged him back. The crowd was wild with excitement, but when I spoke, they quieted down.

"Listen, folks! I can't explain now! It will all be in the papers tomorrow, but some guys that want me out of the fight racket had Pat Daly slugged and brought out a tough boy to stick in here with me. So you're goin' to get your money's worth tonight!

"In that corner, weight one hundred and seventy-five pounds, is Tony Innes, second-ranking light-heavyweight in the world! And my name isn't Bill Banner! It's Danny McClure, and tonight you're going to see

the top-ranking light-heavyweight con-
tender take a beating he'll never forget."

The crowd just blew the roof off the audi-
torium, and Tony Innes came on his feet and
waved a wildly angry glove at the mike. "Get
it out of here!" he snarled. "Let's fight!"

Somebody rang the bell, and Buck Farley
just barely got out of the way as Innes
crossed the ring. He stabbed a left that
jerked my head back like it was on a hinge,
and he could have ended the fight there, but
he was crazy mad and threw his right too
soon. It missed and I went in close. Never in
all my life was I so sore as then.

I ripped a right to his muscle-corded middle and then smashed a left hook to the
head that would have loosened the rivets on
the biggest battleship ever built, but it never
even staggered this guy. He clipped me on
the chin with an elbow that made my head
ring like an alarm clock. If that was the kind
of fight it was going to be, I was ready! We
slugged it across the ring and then he
stepped out of the corner and caught me
with a right that made my knees buckle.

I moved into Tony, lancing his cut mouth
with a straight left, then hooking that same
left to the same mouth. He sneered at me

and bored in, rattling my teeth with a wicked uppercut and clipping me with a short left chop that made my knees bend. I slammed both hands to the body and jerked my shoulder up under his chin. When the bell for the first sounded, we were swapping it out in the middle of the ring.

The minute skipped by and I was off my stool and halfway across the ring before he moved. The guy had weight and height on me and a beautiful left. It caught me in the mouth and I tasted blood and then a right smashed me on the chin and my brain went smoky and I was on the canvas and this guy was standing over me, never intending to let me get up. But I got up, and brought one from the floor with me that caught him on the temple and rolled him into the ropes.

I was on top of him but still a little foggy, and he went inside of my right and clinched, stamping at my arches. I shoved him away with my left, clipped him with a right, and then we started to slug again.

You had to give it to Innes. He was a fighter. There wasn't a man there that night who wouldn't agree. He was dirty. He had sold out. He was a crook by seventeen counts, but the guy could dish it out, and, brother, he could take it.

And those people in that tank town? They were seeing the battle of the century, and don't think they didn't know it! The leading world contenders for two titles with no holds barred. Yeah, they let it go on that way. The sheriff was there, a red-hot sport and fight fan.

"Let the voters get me!" I heard him say between rounds. "I'm a fightin' man, an' by the Lord Harry I wouldn't miss this no matter what happens. Nobody interrupts this fight but the fighters. Understand!"

If a guy was to judge by that crowd, the sheriff could hold that office for the rest of his life. Me, I was too busy to think about that then. Van Ludlow, Marge Hamlin, Duck Miller, and Lanning were a thousand miles away. In there with me was a great fighting man, and a killer.

Maybe I'd never fight Ludlow, but I was going to get Innes.

Don't ask me what happened to the rounds. Don't ask me how we fought. Don't ask me how many times I was down, or how many he was down. We were two jungle beasts fighting on the edge of a cliff, only besides brawn, we had all the deadly skill, trained punching power, and toughness of seasoned fighters. A thousand generations had collected the skill in fighting we used that night.

He cut my eye . . . he cut both my eyes. But his were, too, and his mouth was dribbling with blood and he was wheezing through a broken nose. The crowd had gone crazy, then hoarse, and now it sat staring in a kind of shocked horror at what two men could do in a ring.

Referee? He got out of the way and stood beside the sheriff. We broke, but rarely clean. We hit on the breaks, we used thumbs, elbows, and heads, we swapped blows until neither of us could throw another punch. The fight had been scheduled for ten rounds. I think it was the fourteenth when I began to get him.

I caught him coming in and sank my right into his solar plexus. He was tired, I could feel it. He staggered and his mouth fell open and I walked in throwing punches to head and body. He staggered, went down, rolled over.

Stand over him? Not on your life! I stepped back and let the guy take his own time getting up! It wasn't because I was fighting fair. I wanted him to see I didn't need that kind of stuff. I could do it without that.

He got up and came in and got me with a right to the wind, and I took it going away and then I slipped on some blood and I hit the canvas and rolled over. Innes backed off like I had done, and waved at me with a bloody glove to get up and come on!

The crowd broke into a cheer then, the first he'd had, and I could see he liked it.

I got up and we walked in and I touched his gloves. That got them. Until then it had been a dirty, ugly fight. But when I got up, I held out both gloves and with only a split second of hesitation, he touched my gloves with his, a boxer's handshake!

The crowd broke into another cheer. From then on there wasn't a low blow or a heeled glove. We fought it clean. Two big, confident fighting men who understood each other.

But it couldn't last. No human could do what we were doing and last. He came for me and I rolled my head and let the glove go by and then smashed a right for his body. He took it, and then I set myself. He was weaving and I took aim at his body and let go.

The ropes caught him and he rolled along them. He knew he was going to get it then, but he was asking no favors, and he wasn't going to make it easy for me.

Again I feinted, and when he tried to laugh, a thin trickle of blood started from a split lip. He wouldn't bite on that.

"Quit it!" I heard him growl. "Come an' get me!"

I went. Then I uncorked the payoff. I let Mary Ann go down the groove!

The sound was like the butt end of an axe hitting a frozen log, and Tony Innes stood like a dummy in a doze, and then he went over on his feet, so cold an iceberg would have felt like a heat wave. And then I started backing up and fell into the ropes and stood there, weaving a little, my hands working, so full of battle I couldn't realize it was over.

The news report of the fight hit the sport pages like an atomic bomb. Overnight everybody in the country was talking about it and promoters from all over the country were offering prices on a return battle. Above all, it had started a fire I didn't think Mark Lanning could put out. But he could still pull plenty behind the smoke.

Most people will stand for a lot, but once a sore spot gets in front of their eyes, they want to get rid of it. The rotten setup at Zenith, which permeated the fight game, was an example. The trouble was, it was a long time to election and Lanning still had the situation sewed up in Zenith, and most of the officials.

More than ever, he'd be out to get me. The season was near closing for Greater American so Pop turned the show over to his assistant and came east with me. Buck came, too, and he brought that .45 Colt along with him.

Maybe I had spoiled Lanning's game. Time would tell about that, but on the eve of the Ludlow fight, I had two poorly healed eyes, and the ring setup back home was no better than it had been. Despite all the smoke, I was still behind the eight ball.

The publicity would crab the chance of Lanning pulling any really fast stuff. But with my eyes the way they were, there was a good chance he wouldn't have to. I was going into a fight with a cold, utterly merciless competitor with two strikes against me. And with every possible outside phase of the fight in question.

You think the timekeeper can do nothing? Suppose I got a guy on the ropes, ready to cool him, or suppose I get Ludlow on the deck and the referee says nine and there are ten seconds or twenty seconds to go, and then the bell rings early and Ludlow is saved?

Or suppose I'm taking a sweet socking and they let the round go a few seconds. Many a fight has been lost or won in a matter of seconds, and many a fighter has been saved by the bell to come on to win in later rounds.

Duck Miller was lounging on the station platform when I got off of the train. He glanced at my eyes and there was no grin on his lips.

"Well, Duck," I said, "looks like your boss got me fixed up."

"Uh-huh. He's the kind of guy usually gets what he wants."

"Someday he's going to get more than he asks for," I said quietly.

Duck nodded. "Uh-huh. You got some bad eyes there."

"It was a rough fight."

Duck's eyes sparked. "I'd of give a mint," he said sincerely, "to have seen it! You and Tony Innes, and no holds barred! Yeah, that would be one for the book." He looked at me again. "You're a great fighter, kid."

"So's Ludlow." I looked at Duck. "Miller, at heart you're a right guy. Why do you stick with a louse like Lanning?"

Duck rubbed his cigarette out against his heel. "I like money. I been hungry too much. I eat now, I got my own car, I got a warm apartment, I have a drink when I want. I even got a little dough in the bank."

I looked at him. Duck was down in the mouth. His wide face and hard eyes didn't look right.

"Is it worth it, Duck?"

He looked at me. "No," he said flatly. "But I'm in."

"Seen Marge?" I asked.

That time he didn't look at me. "Uh-huh. I have. Often."

Often? That made me wonder. I looked at him again. "How's she been getting along?"

Duck looked up, shaking out a smoke.

"Marge gets along, don't ever forget that. Marge gets along. Like me," he hesitated, "she's been hungry too much."

He turned on his heel and walked away. He was there to look at me, to report to Lanning how I looked so they could figure on Ludlow's fight. Well, I knew how I looked. I'd been through the mill. And what he'd said about Marge I didn't like.

She was waiting for me at the ranch, sitting in the canary-yellow convertible. She looked like a million, and her smile was wide and beautiful. Yet somehow, the change made her look different. I mean, my own change. I'd been away. I'd been through a rough deal, I was back, and seeing her now I saw her with new eyes. Yes, she was hard around the eyes and mouth.

When I kissed her something inside me said, "Kid, this is it. This babe is wrong for you."

"How's it, honey?" I said. "Everything all right?"

"Yes, Danny, but your eyes!" she exclaimed. "Your poor eyes are cut!"

"Yeah. Me an' Tony Innes had a little brawl out West. Maybe," I said, "you read about it?"

"Everybody did," she said frankly. "Do you think it was wise, Dan? Telling that stuff about Mark Lanning?"

"Sure, baby. I fight in the open, cards on the table. Guys like Lanning don't like that." I looked down at her. "Honey, he's through."

"Through? Mark Lanning?" She shook her head. "You're whistling in the dark, Dan. He's big, he's too strong. He's got this town sewed up."

"It's only one town," I said.

Right then I didn't know she was working with Lanning. I didn't know she was selling me out. Maybe, down inside, I had a hunch, but I didn't know. That was why I didn't see that I'd slipped the first seed of doubt into her thoughts.

That evening two plain sedans pulled up the drive and stopped in front of the porch where I was sitting, feet up, reading the newspaper. Something about the men that got out, maybe it was their identical haircuts or the drab suits that they wore, said "government" in square, block lettering.

"Evening," the first one said. "I'm special agent Crowley, FBI." He flipped open his wallet to show me his ID. "This," he indicated a taller man from the second car, "is Bill Karp, with the State Attorney General's office. We'd like to talk to you about a story we read in the newspaper . . ."

Before they were done we'd talked for four hours, and a court reporter took it all down.

Three days I rested, just working about six rounds a day with the skipping rope and shadowboxing. Then I started in training again, and in earnest. We had a ring under the trees, and I liked it there. Joe Moran was with me, and Buck Farley.

It went along like that until two days before the fight. Then Pop came in, he had a long look at me, and he pushed his wide hat back on his head and took the cigar from his lips.

"Kid," he said, "I got a tip today. Your dame's bettin' on Ludlow."

If anybody had sprung that on me, even Pop Farley, before I went west, I'd have said he was a liar. Now I just looked at him. Pop was my friend. Maybe the best one I had. I was like a son to him, and Pop wouldn't lie to me.

"Give it to me, Pop," I said. "What do you know?"

"Saw her coming from Mark Lanning's office. I got curious and I had her followed. I found out she's hocked her jewelry to bet on Ludlow. I traced the sale of that yellow car. Lanning paid for it."

Well, I got out of the ring and walked back to the house. I pulled on my pants and a sweater, I changed into some heavy shoes. Then I went for a walk.

There was work to be done. Fences needed mending, one barn would soon need a new roof, over the winter I would have to repair my tractor, which hadn't worked right in years . . . I always dreamed I was doing it for someone, someone besides me, that is. Suddenly I realized that person wasn't Marge and never would be.

Marge Hamlin meant a lot to me, but hurt as it did, it wasn't as bad as it would have been before I went west. That trip had made me see things a lot clearer.

I walked in the hills, breathing a lot of fresh, cool air, and before long I began to feel better. Well, maybe Duck was right. She had been hungry too much. Somehow, I didn't find any resentment in me.

. . .

We were sitting on the porch the day of the fight when Marge drove up. She'd been out twice before, but I was gone. She looked at my eyes when I walked down to the car. I heard Pop and Buck get up and go inside.

Marge looked beautiful as a picture, and just as warm.

"Marge," I said, "you shouldn't have bet that money." Her eyes went sharp, and she started to speak. "It's okay," I said, "we all have to live. You play it your way, it's just that you'll lose, and that'll be too bad. You're going to need the money."

"What do you mean? Who told you how I bet?"

"It doesn't matter. Copper those bets if you can, because I'm going to win."

"With those eyes?" She was hard as ice now.

"Sure, even with these eyes. Tony Innes was a good boy. I beat him. Outweighed fifteen pounds, I beat him. I'll beat Ludlow, too."

"Like fun you can!" Her voice was bitter. "You haven't a chance!"

"Take my tip, Marge. And then," I added, "cut loose from Mark. He won't do right by you, baby. He won't be able to, even if he wanted to."

"What do you mean? What can you do to Mark?" Contempt was an inch thick in her voice.

"It isn't me. That story from out West started it. Mark's through. He's shooting everything on this fight. He still thinks he's riding high. He isn't. Neither are you."

She looked at me. "You don't seem much cut up about this," she said then.

"I'm not. You're no bargain, honey. In fact you've been a waste of my time."

That got her. She had sold me out for Mark Lanning and his money, but she didn't like to think I was taking it so easy. She had set herself up to be the prize, but now she wasn't the prize I wanted. She started the car, spun the wheel and left the ranch with the car throwing gravel as I walked back inside.

That night you couldn't have forced your way into the fight club with a jimmy. The Zenith Arena was jammed to the doors, and when Ludlow started for the ring, a friend told me and I slid off the table and looked at Pop.

"Well, Skipper," I said, "here goes everything."

"You'll take him," Buck said, but he wasn't sure. It's hard to fight with blood running into your eyes.

When we were in the center of the ring, Buck Farley was with me. I turned to him. "You got that heater, Buck?"

"Sure thing." He showed me the butt of his .45 under his shirt.

The referee's eyes widened. Ludlow's narrowed and he touched his thin lips with his tongue.

"Just a tip." I was talking to the referee. "Nobody stops this fight. No matter how bloody I get, or no matter how bloody Ludlow gets, this fight goes on to the end. When you count one of us out, that will be soon enough.

"Buck," I said, "if this referee tries to give this to Ludlow any way but on a knockout or decision at the end of fifteen rounds, kill him."

Of course, I didn't really mean it. Maybe I didn't. Buck was another guess. Anyway, the referee was sure to the bottom of his filthy little soul that I did mean it. He was scared, scared silly.

Then I went back to my corner and rubbed my feet in the resin. This was going to be murder. It was going to be plain, unadulterated murder.

The gong sounded.

Van Ludlow was a tough, hard-faced blond who looked like he was made from granite. He came out, snapped a fast left for my eyes, and I went under it, came in short with a right to the ribs as he faded away. He jabbed twice and missed. I walked around him, feinted, and he stepped away, watching me. The guy had a left like a cobra. He stabbed the left and I was slow to slip it. He caught me, but too high.

Ludlow stepped it up a little, missed a left and caught me with a sweet right hand coming in. He threw that right again and I let it curl around my neck and smashed both hands to the body, in close. We broke clean and then he moved in fast, clipped me with a right uppercut and then slashed a left to my mouth that hurt my bad lip. I slipped two lefts to the head and went in close, ripping both hands to the body before he tied me up. He landed a stiff right to the head as the bell rang.

Three rounds went by just like that. Sharp, fast boxing, and Ludlow winning each of them by a steadily increasing margin. My punches were mostly to the body in close. In the fourth the change came.

He caught me coming in with a stiff left to the right eye and a trickle of blood started. You could hear a low moan from the crowd. They had known it was coming.

Blood started trickling into my eye. Ludlow stabbed a left and got in close. "How d'you like it, boy?"

"Fine!" I said, and whipped a left hook into his ribs that jolted him to his socks.

He took two steps back and I hit him with both hands. Then the fight turned into a first-rate blood-and-thunder scrap.

Van Ludlow could go. I give him that. He came in fast, stabbed a left to my mouth, and I went under another one and smashed a right into his ribs that sounded like somebody had dropped a plank. Then I ripped up a right uppercut that missed and brought a whoop from the crowd.

Five and six were a brawl with blood all over everything. Both my eyes were cut and there was blood in my mouth. I'd known this would happen and so was prepared for it. Ludlow threw a wicked right for my head in the seventh round and I rolled inside and slammed my right to his ribs again. He backed away from that one.

"Come on, dish face!" I told him politely. "You like it, don't you?"

He swung viciously, and I went under it and let him have both of them, right in the lunch basket. He backed up, looking unhappy, and I walked into him blazing away with both fists. He took two, slipped a left, and rocked me to my number nines with a rattling right hook.

He was bloody now, partly mine and partly his own. I shot a stiff left for his eye and just as it reached his face, turned my left glove outside and ripped a gash under his eye with the laces that started a stream of blood.

"Not bleeding?" I protested in close. "That wasn't in the lesson for today. I'm the one supposed to bleed!"

The bell cut him off short, and he glared at me. I took a deep breath and walked back to my corner. I couldn't see myself. But I could guess. My face felt like it had been run through a meat grinder, but I felt better than I had in months. Then I got the shock of my life.

Tony Innes was standing in my corner.

"Hi, champ!" He looked at me, got red around the gills, and grinned. "Shucks, man! You're a fighter. Don't tell me the guy who licked me can't take Van Ludlow."

"You ever fight Ludlow?" I was still standing up. I didn't care. I felt good.

"No," he said.

"Well," I told him, "it ain't easy!"

When the bell sounded, I went out fast, feeling good. I started a left hook for his head and the next thing I knew the referee was saying "Seven!"

I rolled over, startled, wondering where the devil I'd been, and got my feet under me. I came up fast as Van moved in, but not fast enough. A wicked right hand knocked me into the ropes and he followed it up, but fast. He jabbed me twice, and blind with blood, I never saw the right.

That time it was the count of three I

heard, but I stayed where I was to eight, then came up. I went down again, then again. I was down the sixth time in the round when the bell rang. Every time I'd get up, he'd floor me. I never got so tired of a man in my life.

Between rounds they had my eyes fixed up. Tony Innes was working on them now, and he should have been a second. He was as good a man on cut eyes as any you ever saw.

The ninth round opened with Ludlow streaking a left for my face, and I went under it and hit him with a barrage of blows that drove him back into the ropes. I nailed him there with a hard right and stabbed two lefts to his mouth.

He dished up a couple of wicked hooks into my middle that made me feel like I'd lost something, and then I clipped him with a right. He jerked his elbow into my face, so I gave his the treatment with my left and he rolled away along the ropes and got free.

I stepped back and lanced his lip with a left, hooked that same left to his ear, and took a wicked left to the body that jerked my mouth open, and then he lunged close and tried to butt.

"What's the matter?" I said. "Can't you win it fair?"

He jerked away from me and made me keep my mouth shut with a jolting left. I was counterpunching now. He started a hook and I beat him with an inside right that set him back on his heels. He tried to get his feet set, and rolled under a punch. I caught him with both hands and split one of his eyes.

Ludlow came in fast. It was a bitter, brutal, bloody fight and it was getting worse. His eyes were cut as badly as mine now, and both of us were doing plenty of bleeding. I was jolting him with body punches, and it was taking some of the snap out of him. Not that he didn't have plenty left. That guy would always have plenty left.

Sweat streamed into my eyes and the salt made me blink. I tried to wipe the blood away and caught a right hook for my pains. I went into a crouch and he put a hand on my head, trying to spin me. I was expecting that and hooked a left high and wide that caught him on the temple. It took him three steps to get his feet under him, and I was all over him like a cold shower.

He went back into the ropes, ripping

punches with both hands, but I went on into him. He tried to use the laces and hit me low once, but that wasn't stopping me. Not any. I was out to get this guy, and get him but good. I hung him on the ropes and then the bell sounded and I turned and trotted to my corner.

Tony Innes was there, and he leaned over. "Watch yourself, kid. Mark's got some muscle men here."

"Don't let it throw you," Buck said grimly, "so've we!"

I looked at him, and then glanced back at the crowd. Lanning was there, all right, and Gasparo was with him, but they both looked unhappy. Then I recognized some faces. Bulge Mahaney, the carnival strong man from Greater American, had a big hand resting on Lanning's shoulder. Beside him, with a heavy cane I knew to be loaded with lead, was Charley Dismo, who ran the Ferris wheel.

Behind them, around them, were a half-dozen tough carnival roughnecks. I grinned suddenly, and then, right behind my corner, I saw somebody else. It was Mantry, the big guy I fought several times. He lifted a hand and waved to me, grinning from ear to ear. Friends? Gosh, I had lots of friends.

Yet, in that minute, I looked for Marge. No, there was no love in me for her, but I felt sorry for the girl. I caught her eye, and she was looking at me. She started to look away, but I waved to her, and smiled. She looked startled, and when the bell rang I got a glimpse of her again, and there were tears in her eyes.

Van Ludlow wasn't looking at tears in anybody's eyes. He came out fast and clipped me with a right that rang all the bells in my head. I didn't have to look to see who these bells were tolling for. So I got off the canvas, accepted a steamy left hand to get close and began putting some oomph into some short arm punches into his middle.

He ripped into me but I rolled away, and he busted me again, and then I shoved him away and clipped him. His legs turned to rubber and I turned his head with a left and set Mary Ann for the payoff. He knew it was coming, but the guy was still trying, he jerked away and let one come down the main line.

That one got sidetracked about a flicker away from my chin, but the right that I let go, with all the payoff riding on it, didn't. It took him coming in and he let go everything and dropped on his face so hard you'd have thought they'd dropped him from the roof!

A cloud of resin dust floated up and I walked back to my corner. I leaned on the ropes feeling happy and good, and then the referee came over and lifted my right and the crowd went even crazier than they had been. The referee let go my hand, and when I started to take a bow, I bowed all the way to the canvas, just hit it on my face and passed out cold.

Only for a minute, though. They doused me with water and picked me up, and they were still working over Van Ludlow. I walked across toward his corner, writing shallow figure S's with my feet, and put my hand on his shoulder.

Duck Miller was standing there with his cigar in his face and he looked at me through the smoke.

"Hi, champ," he said.

I stopped and looked at him. "I won some dough on this fight," I said. "I'm going to open a poolroom, gym, and bowling alley in Zenith. I need a manager. Want the job?"

He looked at me, and something came

into his eyes that told me Duck Miller had all I'd ever believed he had.

"Sure," he said, "I'd never work for a better guy!"

I walked back to my corner then, and Buck Farley slipped my robe around my shoulders and I crawled through the ropes. I walked back to the dressing room. Pop was leaning on the table with a roll of bills you could carry in a wheelbarrow. "I bet some money," he said happily, "a lot of money!" He looked up. "And you," he said, "even if you never get a middleweight title fight, you are still going to be a wealthy young man!"

When I came out, Marge was sitting in the canary convertible.

"Everything all right?" I asked.

"Yes." She looked at me.

"If it isn't," I said, "let me know."

She sat there looking at me, and then she said, "I guess I made a mistake."

"No," I said, "you weren't brave enough to take a chance."

All the way back to the ranch I could hear Pop and Buck talking about how the G-men came in and picked Lanning up for some gyp deal on his income tax, an investigation stirred up by my stories from the West. But I wasn't thinking of that. I wasn't thinking of that at all.

I was thinking that in the morning I'd slip on some old brogans and a sweater to take a walk over the hills. I'd watch the grass shifting in the wind, see the brown specks of my cattle in the meadows, the blunt angles of my corrals and barns. I was thinking that after the frozen winters in Korea, the blood and sweat of the ring—choking down that smoky air . . . how I loved and hated it—I had a chance with something that was really mine. I had no one to fight anymore.

CRASH LANDING

Dyea was the first to speak. "Don't anyone move." His voice was quiet, and its very calm destroyed the moment of rising panic. "The plane seems to be resting insecurely, we must act carefully and with intelligence. I will investigate."

With infinite care, he straightened himself from his seat, glancing briefly at the wreckage of the nose. There was no possibility that pilot or co-pilot were alive. The stewardess was sitting in the aisle, where she had been thrown by the crash. She looked toward him uncertainly.

"Miss Taylor," he said, recalling her name from the tab above her breast pocket, "I was an officer in the Army, and I have some experience with this sort of thing. If all will cooperate, I'm sure we will be all right."

He could see the relief in her eyes, and

she nodded quickly. "Sit still," he said, before she could rise. "I'll only be a moment. The plane is resting, I believe, on a mountainside. Its position seems to be precarious."

The crashed commuter plane lay on the mountain, and could be no more than a dozen feet from the crest of the ridge. Balancing his weight, his body leaning against the slant, he eased down the incline to the door in the back of the cabin. Fortunately, it had not jammed. The wind, which had been blowing hard, seemed to have lulled, and he stepped carefully from the door.

Snow swirled around him as he took a few steps back, along the fuselage, and then he looked down into an awful void that dropped away beneath the very tail of the plane. For a long moment he stared, awed by what he could sense rather than see. The slightest gust of wind or concerted movement could start the ship sliding, and in an instant it would fall off into the black void.

Yet, where he stood, the rock was solid, covered only by a thin coating of ice and snow blown by the wind. Moving carefully, he checked the position of the cliff edge and the area nearest the crashed plane. Then he returned to the door.

Dyea stood outside and looked within. Five faces had turned to stare at him. "You must move one at a time, and at my direction. The ship is in an extremely dangerous position. If there is any confusion or hurry, it may start sliding. You, in the right front seat, rise carefully. If you're not sure you can move under your own power, please tell me now."

A voice came from that seat where no face showed. "I cannot move. You must all go first."

"Thank you." Dyea looked at a fat man who clutched a briefcase and was near the door. "You, sir, will begin. Rise carefully and cross to the door. Bring your blanket with you. Be sure the blanket will catch on nothing."

As if hypnotized, the man rose from his seat. Patiently, he gathered the blanket, and with extreme economy of movement, he folded it; then, with the blanket under his arm, he moved to the door. As he stepped to the snow, Dyea pointed. "Walk ten steps forward, then three to the left. There is a rock there that will protect us from the wind."

The man moved away, and Dyea turned to the next person. Only when the five who were capable of moving had been removed from the plane did Dyea look to the hostess. "Miss Taylor, get to your feet," he said, "move carefully and gather all the remaining blankets and pass them to me."

"What about this man?" She indicated the seat from which the voice had come.

"He must wait. All our lives are in danger. Free of the plane, they may still die of cold and exposure. We must think first of the greatest number. Furthermore," he added, "the gentleman's courage has already been demonstrated.

"When you've given me all the blankets and coats, get your first aid kit and as much food as you can. Move very carefully and slowly. The ship is resting upon the very lip of a cliff that looks to be more than six hundred feet high."

As the stewardess began her collecting of blankets, Dyea looked toward the seat back where the remaining occupant sat. "My friend, moving you is going to be extremely dangerous. Do not suggest that we shouldn't attempt it, for we shall.

However, I'll move you myself. Miss Taylor will be out of the ship at the time. We may both die. Therefore, think of any message you may want to send to anyone who survives you. Also, if there is any identification, pass it to the stewardess."

"And you?" The voice from the seat was calm, yet seemed tightly held against some pain, or fear. "What of you?"

"There is no one," Dyea said quietly, "I am a man alone."

Steadily, the stewardess made her trips; a dozen blankets, food, then medicine. One of the men appeared out of the darkness and accepted an armful of blankets. "One per person," Dyea said to him, "then a second as far as they go. The same for the coats. Then move this food and the medicine kit into the shelter."

"May I help?" the man asked, nodding toward the plane.

"Thank you, no. The added weight and movement would only increase the risk." He turned toward the stewardess. "Are any others alive?"

She looked into several of the seats, then stopped at one where he saw only a thin hand. "Yes, this girl is alive!"

"Good. We will proceed as planned. Come out."

Miss Taylor tiptoed carefully to the door and stepped out into the snow. Dyea turned to her, and she saw his strong, harshly cut face in the glow of the moon.

"If the plane carries us away," he advised, "you will keep these people huddled together until daylight." He glanced at the luminous dial of his wristwatch. "It is now three o'clock in the morning. It will begin to grow light shortly after six, possibly a little before. When it has become gray, make a stretcher of a couple of coats, load anyone who may not be able to walk, and move eastward along the ridge.

"When you've gone perhaps a quarter of a mile, away from this precipice, angle down the mountain toward the trees. Once there, build a fire and build a shelter. You have matches?"

"Yes." She hesitated. "Good luck."

"Thanks. I'll move the injured man first."

"I'll wait."

"No. Please don't." Dyea's voice was flat. "Now," he lifted his voice to the man in the plane, "your name and address, please? And any message for the stewardess?"

There was a moment of silence. "I am Victor Barclay, of Barclay and Paden, attorneys. My wife and children are living in Brentwood, California." He hesitated. "Only my love to them."

Miss Taylor turned her dark, serious eyes to the big man beside her. "And you, sir?"

"No message," Dyea said.

"Your name?"

"It does not matter."

"But isn't there someone?"

"No."

"I would like to know."

He smiled. She saw it clearly in the moonlight. The dark seriousness of his face changed. "My name is Dyea. Spelled D-Y-E-A. My family pronounced it dee-ah, the accent on the first syllable."

He hunched his shoulders against the cold. "Go now. Stay clear of the plane. I believe the wings are both gone, but some part might be under the snow and might drag you over. The rock will give you shelter."

When the woman was gone, Dyea stepped into the ship. With the decrease of weight, the situation was even more precarious. He walked carefully to the seated man. A blanket was over his legs, but obviously, both were broken. No other injuries were apparent. "All right, Barclay," Dyea said, "I'm going to pick you up. It may hurt like the devil. Despite that, you must hold yourself very still. If you move, you'll overbalance me on this incline and I'll fall. A fall would start the plane sliding."

"Very well. I'm ready."

Dyea's eyes flickered for the first time. He looked down the plane toward the tail, then at the door. He touched his lips with his tongue and, setting his feet carefully, stooped and picked up the injured man. As he straightened, he felt a sickening sensation of movement beneath him. He stood stock-still, holding the lawyer as if he were a child. The movement stopped with a faint grating sound; turning, Dyea took his first step. As he put down his foot with the combined weight of nearly four hundred pounds, he felt the ship shift beneath him. A queer sensation went up his spine, such a feeling as he had known but once before, when ice cracked beneath his feet out on a lake, a half mile from shore.

He took another step. There was no further movement, and he climbed down into the snow and walked over to the dark huddle of figures waiting in the lee of the rock.

Placing the lawyer on a coat spread out for him, Dyea straightened. "I think both thighs are fractured. I did not examine him. Possibly the lower part of the left leg, also. Keep him very warm and set the legs if you can."

Barclay looked up through the sifting flakes. His eyes were large with pain. "Don't go back," he said, "that little girl may not be alive by now."

"She was unconscious," Miss Taylor said.

"It's no matter. I'm going back."

"Don't be a fool, man!" Barclay burst out. "That plane almost went with us. It won't stand any more moving around. You know it and I know it. There's no use losing two lives when the one may go anyway."

Dyea did not reply. He turned, chafing his hands together. Then he walked quietly and stopped beside the plane. He looked around him, feeling the bitter cold for the first time. Then he glanced back to where the survivors were gathered, obscured by the swirling snow. The wind was rising. It would be a bitter night and a miserable tomorrow. Rescue parties might be days in coming but, with luck, the group could survive.

He balked at the door, and the thought that the girl must be dead by now flashed through his mind. Maybe, but probably not. He knew that was his fear of returning to the plane sneaking up on him. He shook his head and chuckled. The sound of it revived him, and he put a hand on each side of the plane door, a foot on the edge.

He stepped inside the plane and moved, gently as possible, to the girl's seat. As he bent to look at her, she opened her eyes and looked right into his.

"Don't move," he said, "there has been an accident."

She looked at him very carefully, at his eyes, his face, and his hair. In the plane, the moonlight shone through the windows, bright between scudding clouds. "I know," she said. "Who are you?"

"It does not matter. Think of this. Several of the passengers were killed, but six have been removed and are safe. If you and I can get out, we will be safe, too, and we're the last."

Her eyes were wide and gray. They bothered him, somehow. They reminded him of other eyes. "Where are we?"

"On a very high mountain. It is very cold and the wind is blowing hard. We're on the edge of a high cliff. When I pick you up, the plane may slip. It did with the last person I carried, but he was very heavy. So you must hold very still."

"Maybe I can walk. Let me try."

"No. If you stumbled or fell, the shock would start us moving. I must carry you."

"You're very brave."

"No, I'm not. Right now I'm scared. My stomach feels empty and my mouth is dry. I'll bet yours is, too, isn't it?"

"You're risking your life for me."

"You're a romantic child. And believe me, the risk is much less than you might suppose."

He had been on one knee, talking to her. Now he slid an arm beneath her legs and another around her body, under her arms. An arm slid trustfully around his neck and he got carefully to his feet. After Barclay's weight, she seemed very light. He stood still, looking toward the door. It was seven steps, every step an increasing danger.

She looked toward the door, too, then at him. "Isn't it strange? I'm not afraid anymore."

"I wish I could say I wasn't."

He took his first step, placing his foot down carefully, then, shifting his weight, he swung the other leg. Then the right and again the left. Nothing happened. He took a deep breath, looked at the black rectangle of the door, then took another step. As if moved by the added weight, the ship quivered slightly. The movement was only a tremor, but Dyea immediately stepped again, and then again.

Under his feet the plane started to move, and he knew that this time it was going all the way. He lunged at the door and shoved the girl out into the snow. He saw her land, sprawling. The nose of the plane was sliding down while the tail held almost still, the body rotating. Fortunately, it was swinging in an arc opposite from where the girl had fallen. Then the whole plane slid in one section over the edge of the cliff. As it fell free, Dyea, with one agonized, fear-driven snap of his muscles, sprang upward and outward into the blackness and swirling snow.

There was one awful instant when, hands spread high and wide, he seemed to be hanging in space. He hit a steep slope partially covered with snow. He slid, then felt his lower body going over . . . he clutched, grabbing a fingerhold just as he began to fall. His arms gave a frightful jerk but he held himself, swinging in black, swirling snow over a vast, cold emptiness.

The moon emerged from under a cloud, and he started upward. He was no more than four feet below the edge, the cliff before him not as sheer as he'd thought. The brow sloped steeply back, and on the very edge was the girl, peering over at him.

"I'll get help," she said.

"No." He knew his fingers would not retain their hold. "Can you brace yourself against something? Can your heels dig in?"

She glanced around, then nodded. "Then slip out of your coat and lower the end toward me. Hang on tight, but if you feel yourself going, just let go."

His fingers were slipping in their icy crack, already so numb he could scarcely feel them. Snow swirled in his face and the wind whipped at his mouth, stealing his breath away. He gasped, then the coat slapped him in the face. He let go with one hand and swung it around and up, grasping the suede coat. He felt the weight hit her, but she held it. Carefully, he drew himself up, hand over hand. When his feet were in the crack where his fingers had been, he climbed over and lay beside her in the snow.

"I never was an Army officer," he whispered. "I never was anything."

His arm was stretched out and his cuff pulled back. He could see the dial on his watch. It was just eleven minutes past three.

UNDER THE HANGING WALL

I

The bus bumped and jolted over the broken, heat-ribbed pavement, and I fought my way out of a sodden sleep and stared at the road ahead. My face felt sticky and my head ached from the gas fumes and heat. Twisting and turning in my sleep had wound my clothes around me, so I straightened up and tried to pull them back into place again.

We were climbing a steep, winding road that looked as if it had been graded exclusively for mountain goats. I ran my fingers through my hair and tried pulling my pants around to where they would be comfortable. In the process, my coat fell open and revealed the butt of my gun in its shoulder holster.

The fat man stared across the aisle at me.

"Better not let 'em catch you with that rod," he advised, "or you'll wind up in jail."

"Thanks," I said.

"Insurance is my line," he said, "Harbater's the name. Ernie Harbater. Do a lot of business up this way."

It was hot. The air in the bus was like the air over a furnace, and when I looked off across the desert that fell away to my left, the horizon was lost to dancing heat waves.

There were five people on the bus. Harbater, who wore a gray gabardine suit, the trousers stretched tight over fat thighs, his once white shirt bulging ominously over his belt, was the only one who sat near me. He looked as uncomfortable as I felt, and lying beside him on the seat was a crumpled and dog-eared copy of a detective magazine with a corner torn off the cover.

Three seats ahead a girl with stringy and streaked blond hair, and lipstick that didn't conform to the shape of her mouth, sweltered in her own little world. Across the aisle from her was another girl, who wore a gray tailored suit. The coat lay over the back of the seat beside her.

The fifth passenger was another man, with the rough physique and pale skin of a mining man. He squinted placidly out the window as the bus groaned unhappily and crept over the brow of the mountain. For a moment there was a breeze that was almost cool, and then we started down from the wide world in which we had existed, and into the oven of a tight little canyon.

We rounded a curve finally, and Winrock lay ahead of us, a mining town. Most of the buildings were strewn along the hillsides, empty and in ruins, the one graded street lying along the very bottom of the canyon. The business buildings were all frame or sheet metal but two. One was the brick bank, a squat and ugly thing on a corner, the other an ancient adobe that had once been a saloon. One of the reasons that I had gotten this job was because I'd worked in places like this, but that didn't mean I was wild about coming back.

Harbater had dozed off, so I shucked my gun from its holster and thrust it beneath my belt, under my shirt. Then I stowed the holster in my half-empty bag and slid gratefully out of my coat. My shirt was sweat-soaked.

The bus ground to a halt and dust sifted over it. Groggily, I crawled to my feet. Coat over one arm, and my bag in the other hand, I started for the door. The girl with the stringy hair was gathering up some odds and ends, and she looked up at me with that red blotch that passed for a mouth. Her lips, normally not unattractive, were lipsticked into what passed for a cupid's bow, and it looked terrible.

The other girl had awakened suddenly, and when I glanced down at her, I looked into a pair of wide, intelligent gray eyes. She sat up, pushing back a strand of hair. I swung down into the street, bag in hand.

Several loafers sat on a bench against the wall of the Winrock Hotel. I glanced at the sign, then walked up on the porch and shoved the door open with my shoulder.

A scrawny man in a green eyeshade got up from behind the desk and leaned on it. "Got a room?" I asked.

"Got fifty of 'em," the clerk said. He dug out a key and tossed it on the desktop. "End of the hall, second floor," he said. "Bath's next door."

I picked up my bag.

"That'll be ten dollars," he said.

I put the bag down again and fished for some bills. I pulled off two fives and handed them over, then went up the worn steps and down the creaky hall. If anybody ever dropped a match, the place would go up in one whopping blast of flame. It was old, and dry as tinder.

"You got yourself a lulu this time!" I said disgustedly. "What a guy will do for money!"

Tossing the bag on the old iron bed, I threw the coat over the back of a chair and peeled off my shirt. It was so wet it stuck to my back. Then I took off my shoes and socks and had started on my pants when I recalled the bath was next door. Still disgusted, I picked up a towel and, barefoot, stuck my head into the hall. There was nobody in sight, so I came out and went into the bathroom.

When I'd bathed and dressed, I put my gun back in my waistband and, taking my coat over my arm, walked downstairs.

The wide, almost empty room that did duty for a lobby had a bar along one side, two worn leather chairs and an old-fashioned settee down the middle, and four brass cuspidors.

Two men loafed at the bar. One of them was a big-shouldered, brown-faced man with a powerful chest. He was handsome in a heavy, somewhat brutal fashion and had the look of a man it would be bad to tangle with. The other was a shorter man, evidently one of the oldest inhabitants. I put a foot on the rail and ordered a bourbon and soda.

The brown-faced man looked at me. He had hard eyes, that guy. I turned to the bartender, who was an overstuffed party in a dirty shirt. He had a red fringe around a bald head, and red hair on his arms and the backs of his hands.

"Where do I find the law around here?"

He opened his heavy-lidded eyes, then jerked his head toward the brown-faced man. "He's it," he said.

"You the deputy sheriff?" I asked. "Are you Soderman?"

He looked at me and nodded.

I walked down the bar and flipped my badge at him. "Bruce Blake, I'm a private detective," I said. "I'm here to look over the Marshall case."

"It's closed." His hard eyes studied me like I was something dirty he'd found in his drink.

"His brother wanted it looked into. Just routine."

He hesitated, tipping his glass and study-ing his drink carefully. Then he shrugged. "All right. It's your time."

I shrugged my own shoulders and grinned. "Actually, it's Lew Marshall's time. I'm just going through the motions."

"You want to talk to Campbell? He's in jail, waitin' trial."

"Uh-huh. Might just as well."

On the way to the jail, Soderman told me about the case. "This Campbell owned the Dunhill mine. It had been rich once, then the vein petered out and they shut down. Campbell, he wouldn't believe the hole was finished. He'd helped locate the orig-inal claims, he an' Dunhill together. Ten years he worked around, tryin' to find what happened to that vein. Then he found a pocket and got enough ore out of it to hire an engineer. He hired Tom Marshall.

"Marshall came in here and worked for two months, and then quit, turning in a report that it was useless, the mine was played out. Campbell gave up then, and he took a regular job, mostly to pay his daughter's tuition at some school she was goin' to out in Los Angeles.

"Finally, he got an offer for the mine. It wasn't much, but it was something, and he sold. Sold it out for a few thousand dollars."

Soderman looked up, grinning wryly. His teeth were big, white and strong looking. "When the new outfit moved in, Marshall was the superintendent. They opened the mine up an' he had the vein uncovered in less than a week!"

"That's bad. He finds the vein, lies to Campbell, then gets backing. That was dirty."

"You said it!" Soderman's voice was hard with malice. I couldn't blame him. Probably most of the townspeople sympathized with Campbell.

"Anyway," he continued, "the day shift came out of the hole, and Marshall went down to look it over. They didn't have a night shift, but were plannin' one. Nobody ever saw Marshall again alive."

"How does Campbell tie in?"

"Weber, he was watchman at the mine, saw Campbell go into the mine. He ran to stop him, but Campbell was already inside. So Weber let him go."

"When did they find Marshall?"

"Day shift man found him when he came on the next morning."

"Nobody looked for him that night? What about his wife?"

Soderman shook his head. "Marshall usually worked at night, slept during the day. He'd been working night shifts a long time, and got used to it. Habit he had."

"Work at home?"

"He had an office at the mine."

I shifted my coat to the other arm and pulled the wet sleeve free of the flesh. Then I mopped my brow. The jail was at the far end of town. It was hotter than blazes, and as we plodded along in the dust, little whorls lifted toward our nostrils. Dust settled on my pant legs, and my shoes were gray with it.

This looked like they said, pretty open and shut. Why was Lew Marshall suspicious? He had told me nothing, just sent me along with a stiff retainer to look into the killing.

The jail was a low concrete building with three cells. It was no more than a holding tank for prisoners who would be sent on to the county building up north.

"You got him in there?"

The big man laughed. "The old fool cussed the prosecutor at the preliminary hearing. He wouldn't post a bond, so the judge sent him back here."

The air was like an oven inside. There was an office that stood with the door open, and we walked in. As we stepped into view of the three barred doors, I saw the gray-eyed girl from the bus standing in front of one of them. She started back as she saw us.

"Who are you?" Soderman wasn't the polite sort.

"I'm Marian Campbell. I've come to see my father."

"Oh?" He looked at her, then he smiled. I had to admit the guy was as good-looking as he was tough. I left him looking at her and stepped to the cell door.

Campbell was standing there. He was a short, broad man with heavy shoulders and a shock of white hair.

"I'm Bruce Blake, a private detective," I said. "They sent me down here to look into Marshall's death. You the guy who killed him?"

"I haven't killed anybody an' I told 'em so!" He looked right straight at me and his gray eyes reminded me of the girl's. "Tom Marshall was a double-crossing rat, an' maybe he needed a whippin', but not killin'. I'd not waste my time killin' him."

"What did you go to the mine for?" I mopped my brow. Soderman and the girl were both listening.

"To get some of that ore for evidence. I was going to start suit against him."

"You see him?"

He hesitated. "No," he said finally. "I never saw hide nor hair of him. The snake!"

If I was going to ask intelligent questions I was going to need more information. I ran my fingers through my hair. "Whew!" I said. "It's hot here. Let's go."

Soderman turned away and I followed him out into the white heat of the street. It was a climb back, and that didn't make me any happier. Certainly, Campbell had motive and opportunity. The guy looked straight at you, but a lot of crooks do that, too. And he was the type of western man who wouldn't take much pushing around. However, that type of western man rarely dodged issues on his killings.

"What do you think?" Soderman wanted to know. He stopped, sticking a cigarette between his lips. He cupped a match and lighted it.

"What can a guy think? Crotchety. Seems like he might have the temper to do it."

"Sure. Ain't even another suspect."

"Let's talk to the wife."

"Why talk to her?" Soderman said roughly. "She's been bothered enough."

"Yeah, but I can't go back and turn in a report when I haven't even talked to his wife."

Grudgingly, he admitted that. When he started up to the house, it was easy to see why he'd hesitated. It was a climb, and a steep one.

"What the devil did they live up here for?" I asked. "It would be a day's work to climb this hill, let alone anything else!"

"This ain't their home. She's just livin' here a few days. The Marshall house is even further up, but it's easier to get at." He pointed to a small white house with two trees standing on the open hillside in full view of the town. "That's it."

II

Donna Marshall was sitting in the living room when we rapped on the door. She looked up quickly when she heard Soderman's voice and started up from the divan.

"Private detective to see you," Soderman said sharply. "I tried to head him off."

She was something to look at, this Donna Marshall was. She made a man wonder why Tom Marshall worked nights. On second thought, if they had been married long, you could imagine why he might work nights.

She was a blonde, a tall, beautifully made woman who might have been a few pounds overweight, but not so that any man would complain. She was a lot of woman, and none of it was concealed.

"Come in, won't you?" she said.

We filed into the room and I sat on the lip of an overstuffed chair and fanned myself with my hat. "It's too hot," I said.

She smiled, and she had a pretty smile. Her eyes were a shade hard, I thought, but living in this country would make anything hard.

"What is it you wish to know?"

"I just thought I'd see you and ask a few questions. It looks like Soderman here has the right man in jail, so this is mostly routine. Anyway, it's too hot for a murder investigation."

She waited, a cigarette in her fingers. There was a bottle of beer on the stand beside the divan. I could have used one myself.

"Been married long?"

She nodded. "Six years."

"Happy?"

"Yes." Her answer was careless, and she didn't seem very positive or much interested. Her eyes strayed past me toward Soderman.

"Like living in these hick mining towns?"

For the first time she seemed to look at me, and she smiled. "I don't see how anybody could," she said. "There's simply nothing to do. I didn't care for it, but Tom had his work to consider."

Somehow I couldn't picture her fitting into such a town as Winrock. She was the sort of woman who likes nightclubs, likes dining and dancing. I didn't blame her for not liking Winrock, however, I didn't care for it myself.

"How much did Marshall have invested in this mine?"

"Not much," she said. "It was mostly a job."

Was that what she thought? I stared at the floor, faintly curious. Lew and Tom Marshall owned this mine, and from all the evidence it had turned into a whale of a rich hole. Well, maybe Tom Marshall was the cagey sort. Maybe he didn't tell his wife everything.

"Are you going to stay here?"

"Here?" She spoke so sharply that I glanced up. Her voice and her expression told me what she thought of the town a lot better than what she had to say. "I wouldn't stay here even a minute longer than I have to!"

She rubbed out her cigarette in the ashtray. Soderman got up. "Any more questions?" he asked. "We'd better move on."

"I guess that's right." We all got up, and Soderman turned toward the door. He sure was one big man. When he moved you could see the weight of muscle in his shoulders.

Donna Marshall started after him, and it gave me a chance to pick up a familiar-looking magazine that lay on the table near the ashtray. It wasn't exactly the thing to do, but I slid it into my coat pocket as casually as possible. They were going to the door together, so the move went unnoticed.

When we got outside in the sun, I mopped my brow again. "Good-lookin' woman," I said. "If I had a woman like that, I'd stay home nights."

He looked around at me, a question in his eyes. They weren't nice eyes when they looked at you like that, and I found myself being glad I wasn't a crook who had to come up against him. This Soderman could be a rough customer.

"Where to now?" he asked.

"Let's go up to their house," I said, "up where they lived."

"You got a craze for walkin'," he said with disgust. "Can't we let it ride until later? When it cools off a little?"

"You go on down if you want," I said. "I'll just look around a little more. I want to finish up and get out of here. I haven't lost anything in this town."

He led the way along the path that led to the Marshall house, and we swung back the gate and entered.

Once inside, I stopped and looked back. From the door you could see all the way down the winding path to the town and the Dunhill mine beyond. You could see everything that happened in town from this viewpoint, and likewise, anyone on the street in town could see anyone who came and went from this house.

There was little enough to see once we were inside. There were three rooms in the house, and a wide porch. The kitchen and living room offered nothing. There were dirty dishes on the table and in the sink, and one thing was plain enough: Donna Marshall was no housekeeper.

I wandered into the bedroom, not sure what I was looking for. More than anything, I was looking and hoping for a break, because I didn't even know why I was up here. Lew Marshall had given me little to nothing with which to work, merely telling me he wanted his brother's murderer punished and wanted to be very sure they got the right person.

Soderman had seated himself on the edge of the porch outside. He was plainly disgusted with me, and he wasn't alone. I was disgusted with myself, so when I'd taken a quick look around, I turned to go. Then I saw something under the head of the bed. I knelt quickly and picked up several fragments of dried red mud.

After studying them a few minutes, I put them into an envelope and slid them back into my pocket. Then I took the head of the bed and, with a lift, swung it clear of the wall. The dust under the bed was thick, but it had been disturbed recently, for something had been lying under that bed, something long and heavy, something that could have been a man, or the body of a man.

"What've you found?" Soderman appeared in the door behind me, the last person I wanted near right then. He must have moved swiftly and silently when he heard me moving the bed. He was staring at me now, and his lips were drawn over his white teeth. I shrugged and motioned vaguely at the room.

"Nothing," I said. "Just looking around."

"Haven't you had enough yet?" he demanded impatiently. "I'm gettin' fed up!"

"Then suppose you go on down to town?" I suggested. "I can find my way around now."

His eyes could be ugly. "No," he said, and

I didn't like the way he said it. "If you turn up anything, I want to be the first to know."

As we went out I palmed a map of the mine that I had noticed on the sideboard. It was creased where it had been folded to fit in someone's, probably Tom Marshall's, pocket. We started back down the steep path. I asked, "Rained around here lately?"

He hesitated before answering my question, and I could see he was weighing the question in his mind, trying to see what it might imply.

"Yes, it rained a few days ago," he said finally. "In fact, it rained the day before the killing."

The day before? I glanced off across the canyon. Whatever had been under that bed, it could scarcely have been Marshall's body, although it looked like something of the sort had been lying there. No man, not even so powerful a man as Soderman, could have carried a body from here, across town, and to the mine shaft.

Not even if he dared take a chance in leaving the house with an incriminating load when he had to cross the town from here. Certainly, crossing the town was not much of a task, but at any time, even in the dead of night, he might meet someone on that path or in the street itself. And if he, or anyone else, had done such a thing, he would have had to pass several houses.

There was no way a car could approach the house. It was on a steep canyon side, and there was no road or even a trail beyond the path on which we had come.

One thing remained for me to do. To have a look at the mine itself, to examine the scene of the crime. There was, in the back of my mind, a growing suspicion, but as yet it was no more than the vaguest shadow bolstered by a few stray bits of evidence, none of which would stand for a minute in court under the examination of a good lawyer. And none of them actually pointed to the guilty party or parties.

There was the magazine, a bit of red mud that might have come from a shoe, and some disturbed dust under a bed. There was also a very attractive young woman of a type who might have caused trouble in more selective circles than were to be found among the lusty males of Winrock . . . and she was tied in with a mining engineer who did not sleep at home.

. . .

We walked back to the jail. It sat close against the mountainside, and there had been some excavation there to fit the building into the niche chosen for it. There was a pump set off to one side of the entrance that leaked into the earth to one side of the path. Bright yellow bees hovered around the evaporating pool in a landing pattern like water bombers on their way to a forest fire. Soderman led the way inside. The jail office was scarcely more than the size of one of the cells.

"What did he have on him when he was found?" I asked.

Impatiently, Soderman opened his desk and dumped an envelope on the desktop. I loosened the string and emptied the contents. It was little enough. A box of matches, a tobacco pouch, some keys, a pocket knife, a couple of ore samples, and a gun.

The gun was a .38 Police Positive, an ugly and competent-looking gat, if you asked me. It was brand, spanking new. There were no marks in the bluing from the cylinder having been rotated, no dirt between the rear of the barrel and the top frame, and no lead in the rifling. It was fully loaded and had never been fired.

That gun was something to set a man thinking, and it needed no more than a glance to tell me how new the gun was. Why had Tom Marshall suddenly bought a gun, apparently just a few days before he was murdered?

"Wonder what he had that for?" I mused.

Soderman shrugged. "Snakes, maybe. Lots of us carry guns around here."

"He hasn't had it long."

"Listen." Soderman leaned his big heavy hands on the desk and glared at me. "What are you gettin' at? You've been nosin' around all day, diggin' into a closed case. We've got the guilty party right in this jail, an' we've got enough evidence for a conviction."

It was time to start something. If I was going to crack this one, I was going to have to get things rolling. If I could get them worried, perhaps I could do something. Anything I told him would get around. I hoped it would get to the right people.

"Then you can guess again," I told him. "I've a hunch Campbell didn't do it, and a better hunch who did!"

He leaned farther over the desk and his face swelled. "You tryin' to make a fool of me? You tryin' to come in here an' show me up? Well, I'm tellin' you now! *Get out!* Get out of town on the next bus!"

"Sorry," I said, "I'm not leaving. I'm here on a legitimate job, and I'll stay until it's wound up. You can cooperate or not as you please, but I tell you this: I'm going to hang this on the guilty parties, you can bet your last dollar on that!"

Turning on my heel, I left him like that, and walked back to the hotel. He didn't know how much of a case I had, and to be honest, I didn't have a thing. The mine remained to be looked at, and I was hoping there would be something there that would tell me what I wanted to know. Above all, something concrete in the way of evidence.

Yet why had Tom Marshall bought a gun before he was killed?

Why was the alarm clock in the Marshall home set for five A.M., when Tom Marshall remained at the mine all night?

And who, or what, had been under the bed on that last rainy day?

These things and a cheap magazine were what I had for working points, and none of them indicated a warrant for an arrest. And I had nothing to offer a jury.

Had he been afraid of Campbell, would he not have bought the gun before his return? Tom Marshall had been a rugged specimen, much more than a physical match for Campbell, and he did not seem to be a man who resorted to guns.

Hence, it stood to reason that he bought the gun for a man he could not handle with his fists. Flimsy reasoning, perhaps, but there it was.

Tom Marshall had spent his nights at the mine. Donna Marshall wasn't one to rise at five in the morning. Who had set the alarm I'd noticed beside the bed? It was set for five, and Soderman and I had been in the house from a quarter to five in the afternoon until at least quarter after. No alarm had gone off.

Daylight came shortly after five. Supposing someone wanted to be away from the house while it was still dark . . . An interesting speculation.

That afternoon I sent a wire, in code, to my home office. Soderman would find out that I had sent it, and that coded message was going to worry him.

My feet ached from walking. I went up the stairs to my room and lay down across the bed. There had to be an angle, somewhere. I sat up and took off my shoes, but when I had the left one in my hand, I froze with it there and stared at the rim of the sole and the space in front of the heel.

Both were marked with still-damp red mud!

It hit me like an ax. That red mud came from the wet place around the pump near the jail! Anybody getting water from that pump would get mud on their shoes. On a rainy day, it would be much worse.

Soderman.

Certainly it might not have been Soderman who killed Marshall. And yet it could have been.

III

It was full dark when I opened my eyes. Groggily, soaked with perspiration, I climbed off the bed and passed a shaky hand over my face. My head ached and I felt tired.

Fighting a desire to lie down again, I

stripped off my clothes and had another bath. I dressed in fresh clothing and slid my gun back into my waistband. Then I walked along the hall and down the stairs.

The usual gang was in the lobby. Four or five men loafed at the bar, and one of them was Soderman. He glanced up when I came down the steps, and he didn't look friendly. He looked as if he hated my innards. Several of the townspeople looked at me, but I didn't stop. Across the street was a small cafe, catering mostly to tourists. I walked over. I felt better, felt like eating.

A tall teenager waited on me, a girl who had not yet grown into her lanky body or her large, interested eyes.

When she put the glass of water on my table, she said, "There was a woman in here looking for you. Very pretty, too."

"Yeah?" I was surprised. "Not Mrs. Marshall?"

The waitress made a face. "No, much nicer!"

I said, "I take it that you don't care for Donna Marshall?"

"She's none of my business. I don't imagine she'll be here long, now that she has his money."

"This your home?"

"Me and my mother, she owns this place."

"Father?"

"Dead. He was killed in the mine."

"Cave-in?"

"Yes. It happened about ten years ago. They had to open a new drift into the mine, and sink a new shaft. The old one was down in the canyon, east of the new entrance."

The coffee was good. So was the steak.

"They never use that old entrance?" I asked her.

"Oh, no! It's very dangerous! No one has been in that way in years. It was tried, but there's a hanging wall of stone that is all cracked and it might collapse. Nothing has ever been done about it as they never go that way, but Jerry Wilson was in partway, and he said he never saw a worse-looking place. A shout or a sharp sound might bring the whole thing down. Anyway, the new part of the mine is west of there and so it doesn't matter."

That was interesting. Mines weren't new to me, especially hard rock mines. I'd run a stoper and a liner, those were drilling rigs, in more than one hole, and had done my share of timbering and mucking. I knew, too, that in a town of this size, in mining country, nearly everybody worked in the mines at one time or another.

A woman was looking for me. That would probably be the Campbell girl, but whatever she wanted would have to wait. I had plans. This was going to be my busy night, and with luck I could wind this case up tighter than a drum.

With luck.

It was going to take the devil's own luck to help me, for I was going to stick my neck out, way out.

Weber, the watchman at the mine, was the backbone of the case against Campbell. Weber had seen Tom Marshall go into the mine. He had seen Campbell go in, and nobody else had gone in at all. Campbell had motive and opportunity, and if others had motives, and none had been brought up, they hadn't had opportunity.

When I thought of what lay ahead, I had a notion to chuck it. A good night's sleep, the morning bus, and back to Los Angeles in a matter of hours. Lew Marshall hadn't told me how long I should stay on the job, only that I look into it. Well, I had looked into it. I had interviewed Donna Marshall, talked with the deputy sheriff and the accused, and I'd examined the situation. Out of that I could make a tight, accurate report that would earn me my money and look all right to anyone.

What it wouldn't do would be plenty. It would leave the murderer in the clear, for in my own mind I was morally certain that Campbell was not guilty. I've always thought there is no such thing as a perfect crime, there are just imperfect investigators. Contrary to what many believe, P.I.'s rarely get to solve crimes, but if I had a shot at it here, I didn't want myself listed with the imperfect.

Marshall went into the mine. Campbell went in. Campbell came out, and Marshall was found dead. That would make sense to any jury.

For me, it wasn't enough. I was always a contrary sort of a cuss, and when I looked at that sultry babe who had done duty as Marshall's wife, I began to wonder. She was sexy, she was lazy, she was untidy, but she had a body that would have stirred excitement in the veins of a crutch-using octogenarian.

Moreover, if I had ever looked into the eyes of a woman who was completely and entirely selfish, it was Donna Marshall.

Add to that one young, rugged, and handsome deputy sheriff and you've got trouble. They could have Campbell. For me, I'd hang my case on the skirts of Donna Marshall. She was the kind who bred murder and violence. And unless I had made a serious mistake, she had Soderman in the palm of her hand.

Or did she? Men like Soderman are not easy to handle. They live on a hair trigger and they backfire easily.

Sitting over my coffee, thinking of that, I heard the screen door slam and glanced up to see Marian Campbell coming toward me. She must have been hot and tired, but she looked as neat and lovely as she had when I first saw her getting on the bus in L.A.

She came right over to my table and sat down, and then the door opened again and the fat man I'd met on the bus came in. He glanced at me, then at Marian, and then he walked to another table and sat down. He ordered beer.

"What have you found out?" Marian's gray eyes were wide and beautiful.

"Not much, yet." It pays to be cautious. After all, why give her hope when there was no evidence?

"I know he didn't do it! You've got to believe me. Is there any way I can help?"

"Not yet," I said. Harbater was guzzling his beer. He looked at me, his sharp eyes probing.

The poor fool wonders if I'm still carrying that gun, I thought. Busybody if I ever saw one.

Marian Campbell sat there across the table from me, the picture of unhappiness. Me, I'm a sucker for an unhappy girl, and I looked up and stuck my neck out all the way.

"I don't want to raise any hopes," I said, "but I know in my own mind your father is innocent. And if I can, I'll prove it."

Her head came up sharply, and the look in her eyes was an excuse for anything. "Oh, if you could save him, I'd do anything for you!"

Why are women so free with promises like that?

The fat man was looking at me, then at the girl. I wondered what he was thinking, and if he had overheard. Suddenly, I was willing to bet a nickel he had.

The door slammed open and Soderman came in. He looked around, then saw me talking to Marian. He came across the room and sat down at the table, jerking a chair out with a quick movement and sitting down hard. He rested those big forearms on the table and stared at me, his eyes ugly.

"Didn't I tell you to leave town?" He spoke harshly, and it stirred something in me.

I've never hunted trouble, but in a lifetime of knocking around in rough places, I've had more than my share. Big guys always aroused something in me. They made the hair along the back of my neck stiffen like a strange bulldog would.

"You've been watching too many movies," I answered. "I told you I was staying, and I meant that. Until this case is busted wide open, I am staying."

Now I followed it up by saying too much, and I knew it, but I was mad. Mad clear through. "You've arrested an innocent man, and maybe you know he's innocent, but I'm going to free him, and brother, when I do, I'm going to hang a noose around the neck of the guilty parties!"

The veins in his forehead swelled and I thought he was coming right across the table at me. He glared for a moment or two, his big hands on the tabletop, and I sat there, tipped back a little in my chair, but my feet braced for quick movement.

Slowly, his face changed and it turned white around the eyes. He eased back into his chair, relaxing all his muscles. He was worried as well as mad. I knew then that I had him. If he had known nothing beyond what he was supposed to know, if he had been sure Campbell was guilty and not had some doubts of his own, he'd have slugged me.

"You're asking for trouble," he said, looking out from under his eyebrows at me, "and you're biting off more than you can chew."

"That's possible," I agreed, "but so has somebody else, and what they bit off is going to give them acute indigestion."

I shoved my hands down in my pockets. "Soderman," I said, "you've been a miner. You know enough about mines to get around in one. Well, I've worked in a few myself. And," I added, "I know something of the history of this one. Enough to know that Weber's evidence isn't worth a tinker's damn!"

His eyes flickered a little. "If you're thinking about the old shaft, you're wrong. It can't be used."

"Tried it?" I suggested.

He could see where that led, and he let something come into his eyes that told me he was going to like taking a poke at me.

"No," he said. "But it was abandoned because it was too dangerous. A man would be a fool to crawl into that hole. The hanging wall of that big stope needs only a jar and the whole blamed mountain would come down. It gives me the creeps even to look in there."

Knowing what unmaintained tunnels were like, I could agree with him. It made me sweat to think of it, and yet I knew then that I was going to sweat some more, because I was going to try it. If I could get from the old workings into the new, to the place where Marshall was killed, then I could establish a reasonable doubt as to Campbell's guilt.

Soderman shoved back from the table and got up. When he did, I happened to glance at Harbater sitting over his beer. His eyes were on Soderman, and in them was contempt . . . contempt and something more. The something more was hate.

Why should a stranger hate Soderman?

After a few more words I got up and left Marian, paid the check and went out.

It was cool and dark in the street, and I turned toward the hotel, taking my time. Across the way, and on the side of the ravine, the gallows frame over the shaft of the Dunhill loomed against the sky. It was too early for that. I went back to the hotel, up to my room.

Although I turned on the light, I didn't stay there. Stepping out into the hall, I took a quick gander each way, then moved down to the door of a room about twenty feet from my own. The lock was simple for my pick, and I went in, easing the door shut. The bag was locked, but a few moments with another pick and it opened. In the bag I found a pair of coveralls and a flashlight. Also, there was a small carbide miner's lamp, and a couple of letters that I glanced at, and some business cards.

"So?" I muttered. "It's like that, is it, my fat friend?"

There was no more time so I snapped the bag shut and slipped into the empty hall, locked the door, and returned to my own room. Ernie Harbater would have some things to explain, and it offered a new angle. I stretched out on the bed.

When my eyes opened, I was wide awake. A quick glance at my watch told me it was after midnight. Easing out of bed, I dressed, checked over my gun, and then picked up a carbide lamp, a more modern model than the one my neighbor down the hall had with him. For luck, I dropped a pencil flashlight in my pocket, then another clip for the rod.

The hall was like a tomb. I listened a moment, then slipped out and closed the door. At the end of the hall, I opened the back door and slipped out to the stairway. Cool air blew across my face. The door shut after me.

Only one light showed. It was the watchman's shack at the Dunhill. I turned and started away toward the ravine and the old workings that the girl in the cafe had told me about. The trail was overgrown with coarse grass, and at one point a small slide had blocked it. I crawled over and went along the trail to the collar of the old inclined shaft. There was a vague light, reflected off the nearby rocks from the shack above. It was just enough to see where I was walking and the shape of things nearby.

The abandoned hoist house was there, and beyond it I could see the shaft slanting steeply down. Rusted tracks were under my feet, and once I stubbed a toe on the end of a tie.

When I got there, to the collar of the shaft, I stopped. It had seemed cool, but I was sweating now.

IV

Here, where I stood, there was a level place where waste rock from the mine had been dumped and smoothed off. Across the narrow canyon the opposite side loomed up black against the night, and above it there was a scattering of bright desert stars. It was still, so still a person might almost have heard the movement of a bat's wing. Breeze touched my face gently, drying the perspiration on my cheeks.

To my left the mine opened, black as death. Nobody needed to tell me this might be my last look at the stars. Old mines were something I knew all too well. I knew the thick dust on the floor, gray and ancient, untouched by any breeze, undisturbed by any walking foot. I knew the pale gray dust that gathers on the side walls of the drifts and lays in a mantle over the chutes and the rusted ore cars.

I knew how the ancient timbers crack and groan with the weight of a mountain on their shoulders, and I knew how the strain on those timbers grew, how the hanging walls of the drifts and stopes began to buckle. Water would seep through, finding cracks and private ways, weakening the vast weight above. The guts of the mountain lay there suspended, a gigantic trap for the unwary.

I walked into the mine entrance. When I had felt my way along for thirty feet, and the opening was gray light in back and above me, I put my hand over the reflector of the carbide lamp and struck sharply to light it, brushing the tiny wheel against the flint. Flame spurted from the burner, a long, knifelike jet of flame standing out at least six inches and hissing comfortably. I turned it down to a mere two inches and, drawing a deep breath, started down the steep incline that led into the old workings of the mine.

When I had gone fifty yards or so, the floor became level and I passed the first ladder leading upward into a stope and, beside it, two chutes. Under one of them stood an ancient, rusted ore car.

A little farther on there were more chutes, and I continued walking. So far the timbering was in fair shape. From my few careful inquiries and a study of the map I'd obtained, I thought I could tell where the troublesome area began, but when I had gone beyond the last of the chutes, I realized I need not have worried about that. I stopped and flashed my light farther ahead; then I knew what hell was like.

When a vein of ore is discovered off of a mine tunnel, the miners follow it, hollowing out the richest rock to form what they call a stope. These man-made caverns are often too large to be supported by timbers and are the most dangerous areas in a mine . . . especially an older, unmaintained mine.

The tunnel before me fell away into blackness and vanished. It was not hard to see what had happened. Evidently, there had been a stope below the level on which I stood, and the unreinforced ceiling, or hanging wall, had caved in. Dead ahead of me the floor of the drift broke sharply off, and it was a good ten feet to the heaped-up, broken rock below. I raised my eyes and looked across at least a hundred feet of open space, lighted weirdly by the flame, turned up to its highest now.

The roof of the drift above me had been hollowed out, turning this section of tunnel into another stope, probably trying to follow the vein of ore from below. Flashing my light upward, I could vaguely see the hanging wall of the section ahead, and for the first time I could appreciate the term. The roof of upper stope was, literally, hanging.

Great cracks showed, and the rock on either side of the cracks sagged ominously. Water dripped through and the whole roof of the huge chamber bulged downward, waiting, it seemed, for no more than a gesture or a sudden sound to give way with all the crushing power of the mountain above it.

How long it had hung that way, I did not know. And I had to lower myself down to the rubble below and make my way across it to the tunnel beyond. I could not see that drift, nor did I know exactly where it was. I only knew it was there, and if I was to prove my theory, I had to cross this open stretch alive.

For a moment I stood, listening. There is no soundlessness such as the silence far under the earth. There is no dark such as that absolute blackness where there is complete absence of light. Yet here, it was not quite soundless, for there was something, vague, yet ominously present. A drip of water so quiet as not to be identified? A distant trickling of sand? Whatever it was, at times the mountain seemed to sigh, the earth to move, ever so slightly, like a restless sleeper.

Putting my lamp down on the lip of the cave-in at my feet, I lowered myself as far as I could, got my lamp in one hand, then let go. It was a short drop and I landed safely. Carefully, trying to forget the threatening bulges above my head, I began working my way over the heaped-up boulders and debris, mingled with a few timbers from smashed chutes, toward the opposite wall.

When I was almost halfway across, something made me turn and look back. On the lip of the old drift where a few minutes ago I had stood, there was a light!

Fear came up in my throat like a strangling

hand. Backing away, I watched the light like a bird watches a snake. I am not a coward, nor yet a brave man. A fight I always liked, but one thing I knew—I wanted no fighting here.

Then I saw the gun.

The man, or woman, who held the light had a gun. I could see the shine of the barrel in the glow from the flame. I was not afraid of being shot, for a bullet would mean nothing here. If that pistol was fired in this stope, neither of us would ever live to tell the story. It would mean complete and sudden extinction.

Moving back again, I saw the gun lift, and I spoke, trying to keep my voice low, for any sudden sound might be all that was needed.

"If you want to live, don't fire that gun. If you do, we'll both die. Look at the hanging wall."

The light held still.

"Look at the roof," I said. "The top of the stope."

The light lifted and pointed up, showing those ugly cracks and the great bulge of rocks.

"If you fire that gun, the whole roof will cave in. It will take that drift with it." I was still backing up with occasional swift glances around as the light allowed some vague outline of what lay behind me.

My mind was working swiftly as I backed away. I knew something now, something that had been disturbing me all day. It was a new idea and, while a puzzling one, it revealed much and made many things clear.

Whoever it was showed hesitation now. I could almost feel the mind working, could sense what he or she must be thinking. Trying to judge what was true and what not. The person over there wanted, desperately, to kill me, yet there was an element of danger.

Suddenly, the light went out. Then I heard a grating, a slide, and a sodden sound. Whoever it was had dropped to the floor of the stope!

Instantly, I put my own light out.

We were in complete darkness now. Gently, I shifted a foot. Backing as carefully as I could, I got to the wall. I wanted the killer, and I was sure in my own mind that the killer faced me in the stope, yet I wanted no trouble there. The slightest vibration might bring that hanging wall down, and I wanted no part of that.

My foot hit the wall behind me. If the drift was there, it would be above me, probably out of reach. The muck over which I had been crawling had been slanting down, carrying me even lower than the original ten feet.

I heard a rock fall, and knew the killer was coming up on me in the dark. He was closing in.

What did he expect to do? The chances were, he also had a knife. Sweat poured down my face and ran down my skin under my shirt. Dust came up in my nostrils. The air seemed very hot, and very close. I backed up. Then, suddenly, a cool movement of air touched my cheek.

Keeping it in my face, I edged toward it. I put my hand out and found emptiness. Feeling around, I found the arch of the top of a tunnel. The hole was no more than two feet wide, and chances were the drift was not over seven or eight feet high. Wedging myself in the hole, I dropped.

My feet hit first and there was a tiny splash of water. I got my balance and started rapidly along the drift. Once, I bumped hard into the wall at a turn, and once around it I got my light going, but turned it down to a very feeble glow. Then I ran swiftly along the drift, my lungs gasping for air.

Tom Marshall's body had been discovered at the bottom of a winze well back in the mine. Calculating my own descent through the stope, I believed myself to be on the level where the body had been found. He had been knocked on the head and dropped down the winze.

Hurrying on through the old workings of the mine, I came suddenly to some recent timbering. I had just crawled over a pile of waste that almost filled a crosscut running from the dead-end drift of the old workings into the new. In a matter of minutes I had found the winze.

Here it was. Dark stains on the rock were obvious enough. Once, I thought I heard a sound, and flashed the light down the drift that ran out the other side of the air shaft. There was nothing. Kneeling, I began to study the rocks. It was just a chance I could find something, some clue.

The tiny splash of water between the ties of the track jerked me out of a brown study. My lamp hung on the wall, and I came up fast. I was too slow.

A gigantic fist smashed out of somewhere, and I was knocked rolling. Lights exploded in my brain and I rolled over, getting to my knees. Soderman was calmly hooking his lamp to the wall. He turned then and started toward me, and I made it to my feet, weaving. He swung, low and hard, and I caught the punch on my forearm and swung my right. It caught him on the side of the face but he kept coming. Toe-to-toe we started to slug it out, weaving, smashing, swinging, forward and back, splashing in the water, our bodies looming black and awful in the glare of the two flickering lights.

There was blood in my mouth and my breath was coming hard. He closed with me, trying for a headlock, but I struck him behind the knee and it buckled, sending him down. I jerked my head free and kicked him in the ribs. He lunged to his feet and I hit him again, then he dived for me and I gave him my knee in the face.

Bloody and battered, he lunged in, taking my left and getting both hands on me. His fingers clamped hard on my throat and blackness swam up and engulfed me. Agonizing pains swept over me, and I swung my legs up high and got one of them across the top of his head, jerking him back. Then I crossed the other one over his face and, with all the power that was in them, crushed him back toward the floor. He was on his knees astride me, and I thought I'd break his back, but he was old at this game, too, and suddenly he hurled himself back, giving way to my pressure, and got his legs free.

Both of us came up, bloody and staggering. I swung one from my heels into his wind. He grunted like a stuck hog, and I let him have the other one. At that, it took three of them to bring him down, and I stood there in the flickering light, gasping to get my breath back.

Then the tunnel swam around me, the floor seemed to heave, and our lights went out. A moment later there came a dull boom.

V

Soderman, on the floor at my feet, came out of it with a grunt.

"What . . . was that?" The words were muffled through his swollen lips.

Feeling along the wall for my lamp, I let

him have it. "I think they've blown the entrance to this drift."

Holding the lamp in my left hand, I struck at the reflector with my palm. On the third strike I got a light. The flame leaped out, strong and bright.

Soderman was sitting up. His face looked terrible but his eyes were clear. "Blown up?" The idea got to him. "Bottled us in, huh!" That made me think, and I watched him closely.

He didn't throw a fit or start rushing around or exclaiming, and I liked that. He got up. Then he stared at me, frankly puzzled.

He said, "Who would do it? Why?"

"Soderman," I said, "you're a good fighter, but you've got nothing for brains. You and me, we're the only two people alive who know who killed Tom Marshall, and I'm the only one knows why!"

He stared at me, blinking. Then he got his light and set it going. He shook his head. "That ain't reasonable. It can't be!"

"It is," I said, "and it isn't going to do us much good. If I'm not mistaken, we're bottled up here. Anybody know you were coming here?"

"She did. Nobody else."

"Nobody knew I was coming, either. That means nobody is going to start wondering for a while where either of us are."

"She wouldn't do that! Why, she—" He was taking it hard.

"Buddy, Donna Marshall may have preferred you to her husband, enough to play around a little, anyway, but there was something she preferred to either of you."

"What was that?" He scowled at me, not liking it.

"Money."

"But how would she figure money?"

"This mine is worth dough. Also, Tom Marshall had a hundred thousand in insurance."

He studied that one over for a while, staring at his light. Then he started to move. "Let's have a look."

Soderman led the way and we slogged along through the mud and water toward where the main elevator station should be. Coming up from the old workings as I did, I had not been through here before, there was more to that hole than it looked like, and both of us were tired. Suddenly, after ten minutes or so of walking, our lights flashed on a slide of rock closing off the drift. He looked around a little, and his face got grim.

"Oh, they did it right!" he said. "They did it very right! This is a hundred yards inside the main drift. The chances are it caved all the way to the elevator station. We couldn't dig through that in a month!"

We didn't waste any time talking about it. We turned around and started back. "You must have come in through the big stope," he said over his shoulder. "How was it?"

"Nasty," I said, "and I'd bet a pretty penny there's no stope there now. That roof was the shakiest looking thing I've seen."

"Roof?" he said. "I thought you were a miner. You mean, hanging wall."

"Yes," I said, "that's what I mean." The reason I said it was because I was checking up on him, just to be sure, and things were clicking into place in my skull. "If I get out of this," I added, "I'm gonna see somebody swing!"

We only needed one look. The big stope through which I'd come a short time before was gone. Debris bulged into the drift from it, and part of the drift down which I'd come had caved in. We were shut off, entombed.

He stood there, staring at me, and he looked sick. I'd bet a plugged dime I looked sicker.

"Listen," I said, "you've worked in this hole. I haven't. Isn't there anyplace we could get out? An air shaft? An old prospect hole? Anything?"

"No." He shook his head. "Looks like we've bought it, bud."

I sat down on a boulder and got out my map.

"Let's look this over," I said. "If there's an angle, it's here."

Over my shoulder, he started to study it with me. Here, on paper, was a blueprint of the mine. And a cross section of all the workings, old and new.

We didn't have to study that blueprint long to know we were bottled up tighter than a Scotchman at a wake. There had been only two openings to this section of the mine, and they were plugged. On the other side of the elevator station there was a series of vent shafts, but they could just as well have been in China.

"We're sunk!" Soderman said. "She's fixed us plenty."

That blueprint lay there on my knee. "Hey!" I said. "Didn't I see a powder locker back down this drift?"

"Uh-huh, so what? Do we blow ourselves up?"

"Look at this two-twenty drift," I suggested. "It cuts mighty close to the edge of the hill. Supposing we set up a liner and see what we can do?"

He looked at me, then he bent over and turned a valve on the air pipe. It blasted a sharp, clear stream of air. "The compressor's still running." He looked at me and then chuckled. "What have we got to lose?"

The two-hundred-twenty-foot drift was higher than ours but it didn't connect to any of the shafts leading out of the mine. All the ore from that level was dropped down chutes to this level to be trammed out. We got a drill and carried it up into the two twenty and set it up facing the wall of the drift. Then we rustled some drill steel. None of it was very sharp, but there was still some part of an edge on it.

Neither of us was saying a thing. We both knew what the joker was. There were no figures on that blueprint to show how much distance there was between the wall of the drift and the outside. It might be eight feet, it might be ten, or twenty or fifty. The one figure we needed wasn't on that blueprint.

We didn't think about that because we didn't want to. Regardless of our fight, we went into this like a team. After all, we were miners, even though it had been a time since either of us had run a machine.

We connected the air hoses and started to work. The rattle and pound of the drill roared in the closed-in drift. He bored in with one length of steel, but when he'd drilled in as far as the steel would go, he didn't change to a longer bit, he shifted to another hole instead of completing this one. If need be, we could always load what we had and blast on chance.

Hour after hour passed. At times, despite the fact that we were afraid they would shut the main compressor down, we let the air blast freely into the drift, cooling us and making sure we had breathing air. Then we would connect the hose again and go back to work.

Nobody ever put in eight holes any faster than we did. Taking turns, we ran them in as deep as we could, having an ugly time fighting that dull steel. While he was working, I combed the mine for more of it, and while I was working, he brought up some powder and primers from the store on the level below.

We finally tore our machine down and lugged it out of there. Then we loaded the holes and split the fuses. Then we got as far away as we could, and waited with our mouths open for the blast. Maybe that wasn't necessary. Waiting with our mouths open, I mean, but neither of us knew what effect the blast would have when both openings of the mine were sealed.

We heard the *thump thump thump* of the blasts, and got up and started in after counting the shots. The air was still blue with powder smoke, but we moved over the muck to the face. A nice little crosscut was blasted, but there was solid rock at the end of it.

Without any talk, we mucked out a space and set up the liner again. This time he used several bits in the same hole, and I watched him. Suddenly, the drill leaped ahead. He just turned and looked at me, and neither of us needed to say a word. It had gone through!

We ran another hole and then, getting impatient, we loaded them and came out of the drift again. When the shots went, we started on the run, and before we had gone fifty feet we could feel the cool night air on our faces!

The hole wasn't big, but we got out. Soderman looked at me.

"We did it, pal! We did it!" he said. Then he added, "Mister, that's the last time I *ever* go underground until they bury me! I mean it!"

Me? I was already walking. I am not a guy who gets sore very often, but I was sore now, and I had my own ideas about what to do. My rod was still in my waistband, and that was where I wanted it.

There were swarms of people around the shaft collar when we came down the hill. Somebody saw us, and a yell went up. "Who set off that powder? Were you in there?"

Neither of us said anything; we saw Donna Marshall standing there in slacks and a sweater, and her face looked yellow as yeast. Behind her was a short, fat man with thick thighs and a round, pasty face. When I first saw him, I'd thought his eyes were cruel, and even now they looked it, frightened as he was.

Ten feet away from them, I stopped, and the crowd sort of fell back. I turned to Soderman. "Do it," I said.

"Donna Marshall!" he called out. "I'm arresting you for the murder of your husband, Tom Marshall!"

Harbater was edgy, and while I'd looked at her, I had an eye on him, too. When Soderman spoke her name and everyone's eyes shifted, Harbater's hand jabbed down in his pocket and he shot so fast it made me blink. The bullet went into the ground between my feet, and because he'd never pulled the gun clear of his pocket, he was having trouble raising it farther. He tried to jerk it out of his coat. I aimed and shot, my bullet breaking his kneecap and knocking him down. Then I stepped in, kicked his hand away, and pulled the gun from his pocket. He lay on the ground groaning.

We locked them up and called for the doctor. Mrs. Marshall cursed the deputy like a truck driver, then demanded a lawyer and went to sit in the corner of her cell. When we came out, Soderman was scowling at me. "Now fill me in. Who is this guy?" he wanted to know.

"He's the insurance salesman who sold Tom Marshall his policy. I spotted him on the bus coming up here. He had been reading a magazine on the bus, all crumpled and one corner torn off the cover. Later, I saw that magazine at Donna Marshall's, where he had evidently forgotten it. We probably only missed him by a few minutes.

"At first, I couldn't figure the guy. But I saw some of his business cards in his room and everything began to click into place. The only thing that messed me up was you."

"Me?" Soderman looked around, his neck getting red.

"Well," I said, "she's a good-looking babe, and you wouldn't be the first guy who got into trouble over one. I think Tom Marshall bought that gun for you. He was wise to you, but didn't want to tackle you bare-handed. I guess we'll never know. That alarm clock set for five was partly the tipoff. I knew *he* didn't need it." I chuckled. "It must have been tough that last time, under that bed. How long did you have to stay there?"

He scowled at me. "How did you know *that*?" Then he grinned sheepishly. "The alarm didn't go off that morning, and when I looked out of the window, he was coming up the hill. There I was in full sight of the whole town if I tried to leave, so I crawled under the bed, and that guy stayed there all day long!"

I laughed, and he scowled at me again. "It ain't funny!" he said. "And to think that babe made a sucker out of me! I thought you were tryin' to frame her to save the estate for Lew Marshall."

He rubbed his ear. "Who do you think actually did the killing?"

"I'm betting on the insurance man. Came in through that old working and killed Marshall, then got out. He followed me in there tonight, but I got away. Then he went back and blasted the mine entrance. But that'll be tough to prove."

"Oh, no. His pants will prove it. In that old working there's a streak of limestone, blue lime, and the ore evidently occurred as replacements of the limestone. In the new workings the ore mostly occurs with quartz monazite. There's no limestone at all in the new workings. If he crawled over those rocks in the big stope, some of that lime will be in his clothes."

"Now that's good!" I chuckled. "I've got more on Harbater. I frisked his room in the hotel and found some coveralls he used and a miner's lamp. He probably used the coveralls the first time he came into the mine. We could test those too. You know, it would have been easy," I added, "if you hadn't come into it from so many angles!"

"Coverin' up for a dame," he said. "Well, that cures me! They ain't any good for a man!"

"Some of them are, all right," I maintained, thinking of one in particular. "Some of them are very much all right."

I got up and started for the door. It was going to be nice to see Marian at breakfast and tell her that her father was cleared. It was one part of this job I was going to like. I was still planning the way I'd tell her when I fell asleep.

COAST PATROL

Dense fog blanketed the Siberian coast. It was cold, damp, and miserable. Turk Madden banked the Grumman steeply and strained his eyes toward the fogbound earth.

He could not see anything but the gray cottony thickness. Occasionally a jagged peak of the Sihote Alins loomed through the clouds, black and ugly where the wind had swept the snow away.

It was warm in the cabin of the plane, and glancing over his shoulder, Turk smiled to see Diakov asleep. The Ussuri Cossack gunner possessed an amazing ability to sleep at any time or place. And he never dozed. He was either instantly asleep or wide-awake. Well, a few more miles of patrol and they could return to Khabarovsk, to food and a warm bed.

Turk swung the ship lazily, detecting a rift

in the fog. Then, quite suddenly, he saw the freighter.

She was moored fore and aft, just inside the river mouth. A freighter of no less than four thousand tons tied up at a rocky shelf in the mouth of a lonely stream on a coast that rarely saw anything bigger than a fishing smack or occasional whaler. Since the war had begun, even the few Udehe fishermen had gone back up the coast to colder but safer waters.

Glancing back, he saw Diakov was awake. The big Cossack's black eyes were alert. "You see something? What is it?"

"A ship," Madden said. "A big freighter, tied up in the river."

"No Russian ship would be here," Diakov said. "I think not."

"I'm going down and have a look-see," Turk said. He rolled the plane around in a tight circle, heading upstream. His sense of direction had always been his greatest asset. He remembered that river, too. For two weeks he had been flying over it every day, and before that at odd times. Upstream there was a wide bend with a little backwater where he could land . . . with luck.

He landed.

Fog was around them like a shroud. Diakov straightened, his face pale under the tan. "Well," he shrugged, "I tell myself it is your life, too, so why should I be afraid? Nevertheless, I am afraid."

He leaped ashore and took a turn around a tree with a line, making the plane fast, then another tree, lashing it bow and stern. Then he got out skis and checked his rifle. "How far you think?" he asked.

"About three miles." Turk grinned at him, the smile making his lean brown face suddenly boyish. "You stay here, Muscovite. If I don't come back, you go over the mountains to Sidatun."

The Cossack lifted an eyebrow. "Even a ghost couldn't cross the Sihote Alins now," he said. "We fly out, or die."

It would have been simpler to have flown to Khabarovsk to report the ship, but finding a thread of river on that coast in a fog like this would be harder now than finding a Jap in Chungking. This way he could investigate first and have something definite to report.

A snow-covered forest trail followed the river. An expert on skis, Turk made good time and in only a matter of minutes stood on the edge of the forest, not a hundred yards from the ship.

The ladder was down, but the name of the ship was invisible in the fast-falling snow. Vladivostok, the nearest Siberian port, was miles away to the south, almost four hundred miles, in fact. Across the narrow Sea of Japan, however, were the Japanese islands.

Could it be a raiding party from Japan? An attempted invasion? It didn't seem likely. In any case, it was his job to find out. It was a chance he had to take.

Already, falling snow had covered him with a thin sifting of flakes. Moving carefully, taking every advantage of flurries of wind that veiled his movement, Turk crossed to the ship. He had abandoned his skis in the brush, so when he reached the ladder, he did not hesitate, but mounted swiftly.

There was no challenge, only the whisper of snow. The deck was white and still, unbroken by a footprint. Hesitating, flattened against the bulkhead, he studied the situation. Something here was radically wrong. It was almost an hour since he left the plane, and the snow had begun then, yet there had been no movement on the deck in that time. Every sense in his body was alert, and he hesitated, dreading to move, aware that his steps would be revealed in the snow.

Turk slid his hand inside his leather coat and loosened his Colt. Then he moved swiftly to the passage that led to the saloon and the officers' quarters.

The door opened easily under his hand, and he stepped into the warm passage. The door of the mate's cabin was on his left, but a glance showed it to be empty.

Before him was the door of the saloon. He opened the door, pushed it wide with his left hand as his right gripped the butt of his automatic.

A man lay with his cheek on the table, face toward the door, arms dangling. Between his shoulder blades was the protruding haft of a knife. His cap, bearing a second mate's insignia, lay on the table.

On most freighters the second mate had the twelve-to-four watch. The man had been murdered while eating, so apparently he had been killed just before taking over his watch. It was now nearly four.

Turk stepped back and closed the door gently, then mounted to the bridge. The wheelhouse was empty, except for a man lying sprawled on the deck. Even before he knelt over the body, Turk could see from the way the head lay that the man's neck was broken. There was a large welt on his head, and over him, a broken shelf.

Another cap lay nearby. Turk picked it up and glanced at it. *Third Mate.* He sized up the situation. "Nine bucks to a dime," he muttered thoughtfully, "somebody came in the port door. This guy rushed him, and the guy used judo on him. Threw him into that shelf."

Grimly, Turk stepped out on the bridge and closed the door. Visibility was low. He'd be unable to take off in this. He descended to the captain's deck and tried the starboard door. It was locked. Rounding the deckhouse, he tried the port door and it opened gently under his hand.

The very pretty brunette with the gun in her hand showed no surprise and no fear. "Come in," she said, "and close the door, or I'll kill you."

"Thanks," Turk said, "it's getting cold out there." If she had said she'd shoot him, he wouldn't have been surprised. But she said "kill," and he had a very good idea she meant it. "No need to hold that gun on me," he said pleasantly, "unless you're the one who murdered the mates."

She stiffened. "Who . . . murdered?"

"Yeah," he said. "Somebody played rough around here. Somebody who uses jujitsu and a knife. They got the second and third mates."

"Not Richards? Aaron isn't killed?" Her eyes were wide.

Turk frowned. "I don't know your pal Richards. I only know that you've got two less mates than you had, and I want to know why. I also want to know who you are, what this ship is doing here, and where the skipper is."

She stared at him suspiciously, making no move to put the gun down.

"It's all right," he said, exasperated. "I'm an American. I've been flying coast patrol for the Russians because of the war."

She hesitated, then decided to believe him. "This is the *Welleston*, out of Boston. My father, Mace Reardon, was in command. We were bound for Vladivostok with aviation fuel, machine oil, and M-3 tanks when Pearl Harbor was bombed. We had trouble with our radio, and the war had been going on for several days before we heard of it. Dad took the ship north around Sak-halin Island, hoping to slip down the Siberian coast to Vladivostok.

"When we got this far, Aaron—I mean Mr. Richards, the mate—suggested we tie up here and communicate with Vladivostok to get an escort through the most dangerous water."

Madden nodded. "Not a bad idea. Your Mr. Richards was smart. But how were you to communicate with them? Your radio would warn the Japs, and this is an American ship."

"We didn't use the radio. Aaron told Sparks to set out overland for Sidatun."

"For *where*?" Turk's eyes narrowed.

"Sidatun. It's several miles back from the coast. Sparks was good on skis, so he went."

"And Richards sent him?" Turk was beginning to understand . . . or suspect. "Where's Richards now?"

"I don't know." The girl was frankly puzzled. "Mutiny broke out, just after Sparks left. My father was . . ." She hesitated, and for the first time her poise wavered.

". . . killed. Then Aaron told me to stay inside and not to let anyone in but him."

A breath of cold air on the back of his neck warned Turk. He turned, letting his gun slide into his hand with that smooth efficiency that only comes from long familiarity and practice. He was just a little too fast for the tall, handsome man who stood in the doorway. "Hold it, buddy," Turk said softly. "I never like to kill people I haven't met socially."

"Aaron!" the girl cried out sharply. "I've been so worried. Where have you been?"

Richards ignored her question, his eyes intent, staring at Turk. He was a bigger man than Turk, which meant that he was well over six feet and weighed more than Madden's compact one eighty.

"Who is this man?" Richards asked coolly.

"The name is Madden," Turk replied, studying the man keenly. "I'm an American. I run a commercial airline in the East Indies. Made a long flight up to Siberia with a special passenger, and then went on patrol for the Soviet Army of the Far East. Come in and close that door."

Richards complied, moving warily and keeping his hands in sight. He didn't do anything suspicious, but something told Turk he was to be carefully watched.

Richards faced him again. "I'm afraid, Tony," he said to the girl, "that anything this man has told you is a lie. He cannot be on patrol. No plane could possibly land in this weather."

"I land planes in all kinds of weather," Turk said calmly, "and what you think or do not think does not happen to matter in the least. I am an officer of the Soviet government at the moment, and the cargo of this ship is the property of that government. The ship is flying the American flag, and I am a citizen of the United States. I want to know exactly what has happened on this boat."

"There was a mutiny," Richards said coldly, "a very minor one. I handled it. Everything is now under control. We need no help."

The man was listening for something. Turk remembered the door behind him was locked, the ports dogged down. Yet he felt an acute sense of impending danger.

"I wonder if the second and third mates thought it was minor?" Turk demanded. "Who murdered them? Did you?"

Richards stiffened, and his eyes widened

just a little, then turned cold and dangerous. "I think we might ask the crew about that, or *you*. You might be a Jap agent."

Turk laughed. "Yeah, I'd bet a lot of dough one of us is, and it isn't me. The second mate wasn't murdered by a stranger or by a crew in mutiny. He was murdered by someone he knew and trusted."

"How do you know that?" Tony asked sharply.

"Because he was stabbed in the back while eating by someone he knew was behind him. The third mate was killed by someone with a knowledge of jujitsu. But he was expecting trouble."

"Well, Mr. Sherlock Holmes," Richards sneered, his eyes hard, "you think you have it all figured out, don't you? Trying to pin it all on me? Well, I think you're a renegade, that you haven't any plane, and have no connection with any government whatsoever."

Tony Reardon was looking at Turk, her eyes cold. "Maybe you'd better put up that gun and leave," she said. "Whatever you came here for won't work. I know Mr. Richards, and now that my father is dead, he is in command. Your efforts to prejudice me against him won't do. I've known him for over a year, and he is not only the captain now, but my fiancé."

Turk grinned. "Which apparently makes him the head man around here. All right, darling, suppose you ask him why he sent Sparks out to die."

"What do you mean?" she demanded.

"You said he sent him to Sidatun to communicate with the Soviet officials. Sidatun, baby, is not several miles away, but several hundred, and across a range of mountains. In this weather even a man who knows the country couldn't make it."

"I don't believe it!" Tony said desperately.

Turk was watching Richards. The mate was half crouched, his eyes malevolent. Madden slipped his hand inside his coat and tossed a roll on the table. "Look at that map, honey."

There was a sudden step on the deck outside, and a sound of footsteps on the ladder. Triumphant light leaped into Richards's eyes at the sound, but Turk sprang for the door. Richards leaped to intercept him, swinging even as he sprang. Turk was lunging right into the path of the blow, and there was no way to avoid it. It struck him a smashing wallop on the chin and knocked him staggering into the wall. Even as he fell back, Richards steadied himself and lifted his gun.

Off balance and helpless, Turk was cold meat, when Tony caught Richards's arm, jerking it aside. The shot smashed a picture an inch over Turk's head.

Before the mate could free his gun hand, Turk sprang close and, grabbing him by the collar, literally jerked him from his feet, dragging him to the door. Throwing it open, Turk dumped Richards out at the feet of three startled Japanese sailors.

Madden drew back swiftly and slammed the door, turning the key in the lock. Tony Reardon's face was deathly pale. "What is it?" she asked. "What's happening? I don't understand!"

A shout of anger came from outside, and then a pounding on the door. It was a steel door, and Turk was unworried.

Her face was strained and Turk could see she was on the verge of hysteria. She had kept her father's death bottled up inside her, and now this.

"Hold it, kid," Turk said kindly. "You sit down and take it easy. We'll get out of this. The way I figure it, this Richards has sold out to someone. Now the Japs have arrived. Richards must have got in touch with them somehow."

He checked his gun. Without doubt they would move the ship at once. Every minute they stayed was dangerous. And that meant that unless he could do something promptly, they would be out on the Sea of Japan headed for a prison camp or death.

Turk crossed the room in a stride and peered out the port. A Jap seaman was opening the valves to get steam into the winch, another had put down his rifle and was clearing a line that had become fouled with some tackle. They would be casting off in a matter of minutes.

Tony came up to him. Her eyes were wide, her face tear-stained, but she was composed again. He looked down at her. "You've got nerve, kid," he said, "and that's what it's going to take."

"What are we to do now?" she asked simply.

"We've got to get out of here and away," he said, "an' there's a good chance we'll get killed trying. They can't release that line up there, an' don't dare cast off aft until they do, else they'll have the ship broadside to the current, an' probably run her aground.

"They will be getting up more steam now. When they do, the chances are someone will slip ashore an' cut the line. Then, like it or not, we'll be headed for Japan."

Turk hesitated. "I'm going to open that door and shoot the guard. It doesn't seem like there's many of them. Then we'll get down that ladder as fast as we can. The snow will help some. They can't see ten feet beyond the bow. It will be the last thing they expect, so we got a chance."

Tony picked up her gun, her chin firm. "Okay, honey," he said, "open the door an' follow me. We're blasting out of here."

Luck was with them. The guard stood by the rail, and even as he turned, Madden slashed him on the temple with the .45. They were halfway to the ladder before they were seen. A Japanese sailor patrolling the bridge let out a shout of alarm and threw up his rifle. Turk spun on his heel and snapped a quick shot at the man. It lifted the cap from the man's head, and he dropped out of sight behind the bulwark.

A shot glanced from the deck right ahead of them, and then Tony was running down the icy ladder. Turk turned coolly at the head of the ladder and laced the deck with a pattern of fire. Then he half ran, half slid, down the ladder. He stopped dead still and slid another clip into his automatic before he moved, then ran close alongside the hull.

Glancing back, he saw a sailor leaning out from the ship to level a rifle, and Turk fired. The man's face blossomed with crimson and he lost his hold, sliding through the rail to fall into the opening between the ship and the ledge.

Then, from the edge of the woods, a barrage of fire opened up, sweeping the ship's rail and bridge with a stream of bullets. Running, gasping for breath, the two plunged through the last of the snow and stumbled into the shelter of the forest.

Diakov met them on the edge of the woods, his face beaming, the CZ light machine gun cradled in his arms. "Skis here," he said. "We better leave quick."

"What about her?" Turk protested. "She—"

"Skis for her, too." The Cossack winked broadly. "I find a Jap out here on skis. I brought them along . . . a rifle too."

Turk glanced quickly at the trail to the

plane. Obviously, the Russian had been here some time, for his footprints were covered over with new snow. He turned at right angles to the river and started off through the timber. "Wrong way," Diakov protested.

"We'd get there just a few minutes ahead of their pursuit," Turk said, "and not time enough to warm up the plane and take off. No, we've got to lead them back in the hills."

Diakov's eyes lighted. "In the Sihote Alins? I hope they all follow us, comrade. We will show them something, no?"

In silence the three struck out through the timber. Behind them they knew pursuit would be organized. The Japanese dared not leave when there was a chance that other planes would catch them before they were far out at sea.

Turk said nothing as he followed Diakov through the timber. The big Cossack was a marvel on skis, and it took only a few minutes for Turk to see that Tony Reardon was able to muddle along.

"What kind of shape are you in?" he asked her.

She smiled for the first time. "I'll get the

hang of it. I used to do this when I was a kid in upstate New York. Don't worry about me."

After that it was grim business. There was no chance of eluding their pursuers, but they had a lead that they increased after a few miles. Diakov didn't look for easy going, and as often as possible he led them across bare, icy spots where the skis left no trail.

After a while Turk stopped. "You go ahead," he said to them. "I'm going to give these boys something to worry about."

The two headed away. He and Diakov in a murmured conversation had settled on a lonely peak for a rendezvous, deciding shortly after their start that would be their destination.

Turk took a limb from a tree and brushed the trail. The fast-falling snow would fill in the gaps. Then he walked back over a bare spot, carrying his skis. Down below, a half mile behind, he saw a knot of men, several others scattered out behind.

He rested the captured rifle on a branch and steadied it against his cheek. Allowing for the cold, he took careful aim, trying the rifle from several positions. He watched them come closer, then steadied the rifle and fired.

The group split like magic, and in an instant the trail was emptied of all but one man. He got up and, carrying one ski, hobbled into the brush. Taking his time, Turk fired three times, moving himself. Then slipping on his skis, he started out at a fast clip.

Shooting through an opening in the trees, he drove himself down a long slope in long, swift strides, took a quick turn around the bole of a huge tree, and started up a long slope through the brush, moving at an angle. Far below a shot rang out, and he knew he had been sighted, but he did not stop. Another shot, and then he stopped.

Taking a quick glance back, he threw up his rifle and fired. One of the men sprang aside.

"Stung him!" Turk muttered. "Well, that'll keep 'em worried."

He had gone no more than two miles before he stopped suddenly. Above him, on the steep side hill above the vague trail he was following, a huge boulder was poised. Behind it and on up the mountain were several tree trunks, more rock, and the makings of a small slide. He halted, studying the situation thoughtfully. There was a loose collection of rocks under the boulder, but apparently one stone held the bigger boulder in place. Using a broken limb, he cleared out some of the dirt and loose stuff from underneath and experimentally rocked the boulder back and forth.

Smiling, he continued on. Occasionally he glanced back, but kept to the trail, the boulder in sight. Twice he sighted his rifle over his back trail, and finally he halted.

Seating himself on a rock, he waited. From time to time he stood up and moved around to keep warm. Then he saw them coming. Slowly, the men began to wind along the trail below the boulder. Raising his rifle, he sighted carefully, took a long breath, and let a little out of his lungs. Then holding the rifle loosely, he squeezed the trigger.

He fired not at the men themselves, but at the spot where the rock was holding the slide suspended above the trail. Nothing happened. He shifted his position a little and fired again. Immediately there was a terrific roar, and he saw the slide wipe a black path across the mountainside.

When he moved on again, it was with the knowledge that two fewer men followed him.

It was dark when Turk reached the hollow

at the base of the peak. The spot was secluded, and the path he had taken brought him there only a few minutes after Diakov and Tony arrived. The Cossack was cutting dry wood from the underside of a fallen log to build a fire. When it was burning, they sat around talking in low tones. There was small chance of pursuit until daybreak, which was hours away. Traveling even in the day was not easy. At night, with boulders, ice slides, and heavy snow laced with fallen trunks, it would be infinitely more dangerous.

Diakov brewed tea over the fire, and after they had finished a bar of chocolate that Turk shared among them, Turk cleared a wider place in the snow and shifted the fire. Then he spread dry leaves from the bottom of a snow-covered pile over the warm ground where the fire had been. Tony could hardly keep her eyes open, and an instant after she touched the ground, she slept. Diakov and Turk shared watches.

It was just turning gray when Turk awakened. Diakov was putting fuel on the fire. "I went back to look," he said softly. "They are three miles back, but a mile and a half east of us. They have lost our trail and talk of returning."

Turk scowled. "That means we must make the plane today. The ship won't leave until these fellows return."

Turk awakened Tony and they hastily slipped on their skis and hit the trail. It was all downhill now. They had reached a high elevation and the trees had thinned out to a few fir, some Siberian larch, and spruce. The lower reaches along the valleys were covered with dense forest with few trails. Giant poplars reached toward the sky, some of them hundreds of years old. Sliding in among the trees, Turk led the way at a rapid pace. There was no time now for delay. Whatever was to be done must be done at once.

There was a chance that, casting about, the Japs would find their trail, but the risk had to be taken. The air was still and very cold, but the brisk movement kept them warm. Several times Turk stopped to study the back trail, but they moved so rapidly that almost before they realized it, they shot out of the woods beside the river.

The Grumman was lying quietly in the

backwater, her wings heavy with snow. Hastily, while Diakov and Tony brushed the snow away, Turk worked over the twin motors. After a few choking tries, they kicked off, roaring into life with a thunder that awakened the still cold of the taiga.

Tony got into the cabin, and then Diakov cast off. Instantly, gambling against the Japanese hearing his signals, Turk began to call the landing field at Khabarovsk. He glanced at his watch. Murzin would be on now. He sent his call out again.

"Madden, Ussuri coast patrol, calling Khabarovsk. Coast patrol calling Khabarovsk."

After a minute he heard Murzin. "Come in, Madden. Where you been, comrade?"

"S.S. *Welleston*, bound for Vladivostok, tied up in river mouth south of Nahtohu River. Mutiny aboard. Situation serious. Come loaded for bear."

"Stand by, Coast Patrol."

Turk Madden swung the Grumman around and headed for the shore. He was at home now. In the air, flying his specially built amphibian, he was always at home. For what she was, the ship was fast and maneuverable. He saw the gray line of the sea and then he was over it. Glancing down, he saw the freighter. There was no fog now, and he could see the line of men coming wearily through the trees from their fruitless chase.

Instantly, he banked, then pushed the stick forward and sent the ship down in a steep dive, opening up with the machine guns the Russians had installed. A blur of snow lifted near the men, and the line melted. He hauled back on the stick and the Grumman climbed steeply, then he swung back over the freighter and cleared her deck with a burst of fire.

Then Diakov was hammering on his back and pointing. He looked up to see a V of planes coming toward him about five hundred feet up. Turk's face turned grim and he climbed even more steeply. The Grumman went up and up and up, reaching for altitude. When he looked again, he could see the planes more closely. Three light bombers all painted with the rising sun. They were probably there in case the Russians had brought up a destroyer, or to sink the ship if it looked like it would get away. After all, it was an American ship.

Madden swung the Grumman around.

Stand by, they said. That meant to keep the situation in hand. One of the planes was climbing to meet him, and coming up fast. He had outflown the Japanese before, and could do it again, but in a ship like this, against a war plane, even the best of flying would have to be nine-tenths luck to come out alive. He streaked away from the climbing aircraft and went into a dive over the next lowest bomber.

The fellow swung away, and Turk's first burst of fire missed. Then he did an Immelmann and came in on the bomber's tail. His second burst painted a string of holes along the bomber's fuselage, and he saw the string reach the pilot. The bomber shot up, suddenly fell off, and going into a slow falling turn, burst into a bright rose of flame.

A streak of tracers shot by him, and Turk pulled the Grumman around, diving straight for the trees and the low-hanging fog with the other plane after him. The Japanese was a flier, and with his greater speed was coming up fast. Turk felt an icy blast of air as Diakov swung open the roof hatch behind the wing and deployed his gun mount. The Cossack slammed his machine gun onto the pivot and opened up as Turk banked the ship steeply, his wing tip almost grazing the treetops, and roared into the fog bank. The war plane pulled up slightly, and Madden's Grumman bucked and pitched through the mist with prayer the only force keeping him out of the invisible treetops.

Turk pulled up, into the clear, but the other plane had swung around and was coming at him from the side. The big Grumman was in a spot, and Turk banked around and headed straight for the nearest war plane, his twin motors wide open and all his guns hammering. The Japanese held on grimly, and the two planes shot at each other with terrific force, but in the split second before they would have come together, the Japanese lost his nerve and pulled back on his stick. The plane shot up, and Diakov raked his underside with a wild burst from his gun. Then he shot on by, and only had Diakov's shout of triumph to know that he had scored again.

Strangely, the last aircraft was streaking off over the Sea of Japan and climbing. Turk banked a little and glanced down to find himself coming in toward the freighter. A Jap on the shore was desperately trying to cast off. Turk shoved forward on the stick and opened up immediately with a burst of fire. The man crumpled, seeming to come all apart at the seams, and a second man, rushing for the woods, was caught on the edge of the raking burst and fell, his body tumbling in a complete somersault.

Turk came around and trimmed back for a hot landing on the river just before the freighter. The Cossack sprang ashore with a line, and Turk, leaving him to make the ship fast, grabbed his automatic and dashed for the ship.

Richards. The man was still aboard, and he needed to be apprehended.

Turk reached the top of the ladder just as Richards stepped out of the amidships house. The man's face turned livid and, without regard for Turk's gun, sprang at him. Madden hesitated only a second, then shoved the gun in his pocket and sprang forward, throwing punches with both fists.

Richards was not only big, he was tough and powerful. They grappled and he rolled over and scrambled free. Both men came up at the same time. Turk started to close in, but Richards kicked him away, and when Turk struck out, he caught his arm in a flying mare. Turk relaxed and went on over in an easy roll, landing on his feet. He spun around, slipped a fast left, and smashed a big fist into Richards's stomach. The mate backed up, his face dark with fury and pain. Turk followed, stabbing a left to the face, then crossing a jarring right to the chin. Richards's knees wilted and he almost fell. He lunged forward, and Turk broke his nose with a driving right hook. Richards went down, hitting the deck hard.

Aaron Richards scrambled to his feet. Wheeling, he rushed for the gangway that led to the bank of the river. He bent over and plucked the large pin that allowed the gang-way to swivel back and forth out of its hole. As Turk closed on him, Richards turned and swung the heavy piece of metal. It hit Turk a stunning blow on the back of his shoulder and knocked him flat on the deck, his pistol coming loose from its holster and rattling into the scuppers.

By the time Turk had picked himself up, Richards was stumbling down the ladder and out onto the muddy ground. When he saw Turk appear at the ship's rail, he turned and, taking hold of the gangway railing, gave a mighty heave. The entire assembly, now disconnected at the top, came loose.

Scraping down the side of the hull, it crashed into the gap between the ship and the riverbank. The mate took to his heels.

Diakov was returning from scouting the trees, and Richards straight-armed him like a football player. The big Russian went down, and Richards disappeared into the stand of fir along the water. Turk watched as he picked himself up, but instead of giving chase he limped toward the *Welleston*.

"There are still some left, comrade! They've a boat down the river!"

At that moment a heavy engine roared to life beyond the trees. Turk ran to the other rail in time to see a Japanese torpedo boat arc out into the river. She was going all out, bow high in the water and her stern sunk deep, a cloud of blue-gray exhaust trailing from her pipes. Within minutes Aaron Richards would make the inlet, and from there the open ocean.

Turk backed up, yanked off his low boots and coat and, vaulting the railing, took a running dive into the icy water. The height and the cold took his breath away, but within a dozen powerful strokes he was alongside the Grumman and scrambling onto the hull. His clasp knife made quick work of the mooring rope, and then he was pulling himself into the cockpit and firing the engines.

He flew down the river with the throttles wide open, leaving Diakov on the bank bellowing encouragement. As the plane clawed for altitude, Turk struggled out of his freezing shirt and turned up the mostly ineffective cabin heater.

As the water deepened, the patches of fog thinned, and then ahead of him he could see the torpedo boat. She was shooting across the swells like an arrow, kicking up blasts of spray and leaving a long wake. Turk put the plane into a shallow dive. Fast as the Japanese craft was, the Grumman came down on it at over a hundred fifty miles per hour. Turk triggered his forward guns, the burst cutting the water across the bow.

There were only two men visible on deck—a Japanese sailor at the helm, and Richards, who was struggling to pull the cover from the boat's antiaircraft machine gun. Turk wheeled around and came back, angling in on the fast gray boat carefully. The man at the wheel had begun evasive maneuvers, and Turk could tell it was throwing off Richards's aim; his gun flamed, but it was a moment before he hit the Grumman, and then the bullets found only the wing tip.

Turk held his fire as Richards swung his gun, and then he let go with a long burst just before the traitor could fire. The steel-jacketed slugs tore up the decking, forcing Richards to dive for cover, and continued ripping back and down into the engine compartment. Turk shot past, barely off the water, then pulled back on the stick, heading up toward the clouds.

Outside his left-hand window he saw his port engine stall and die. The drag pulled at the plane, and he leveled out, trying to compensate with his rudder. He turned the nose of the plane back toward land and was glancing at the motor for any signs of bullet damage or fire when the starboard engine died.

"This could be better!" he muttered to himself.

Grimly, Turk put the ship into a long glide and aimed for the calm water just inside the bar at the mouth of the river.

The amphibian set down upon the water smoothly, and when it came to a halt, Turk turned and flipped on the two-way radio switch.

"Calling Khabarovsk . . . calling Khabarovsk. Madden, Coast Patrol. Down at sea off Kumuhu River. Please send help. Out of petrol."

"Khabarovsk airdrome answering Madden, Coast Patrol. Stand by."

Another voice spoke through the radio. "Diakov calling from *S.S. Welleston*. I found the crew tied up. We're coming to fish you out. Are you all right, comrade?"

"Okay for now. Go pick up Richards first, no immediate danger . . . only I wanted to be shipwrecked with a beautiful dame."

"Well," a cool voice said in his ear, "you're not very complimentary!"

Turk turned and his jaw dropped. "Tony! What are you doing here!"

"I was in the plane, and you just jumped in and took off, so here I am!"

Turk must have left his mike switched on. "Comrade Madden . . . do you want to countermand that rescue order?"

Diakov waited for a reply, but there was no sound but the lapping of water against the hull. The Cossack had spent three years in the United States and had seen many movies. He sighed deeply.

THE GRAVEL PIT

Murder had been no part of his plan, yet a more speculative man would have realized that a crime is like a lie, and one inevitably begets another, for the commission of a first crime is like a girl's acceptance of a first lover—the second always comes easier.

To steal the payroll had seemed absurdly simple, and Cruzon willingly accepted the risk involved. Had he even dreamed that his crime would lead to violence, he would never have taken the first step, for he'd never struck a man in anger in his life, and only one woman.

But once he accepted the idea of murder, it was natural that he should think of the gravel pit. In no other place was a body so likely to lie undiscovered. The pit had been abandoned long ago, used as a playground by neighborhood children until the families moved from the vicinity and left it to the oil wells. Brush had now grown up around the pit, screening it, hiding it.

Now that the moment of murder approached, Cruzon waited by the window of his unlighted room, staring into the rain-wet street, his mouth dry, and a queer, formless sort of dread running through him.

He had been pleased with the detached way in which he planned the theft. The moment of greatest danger would be that instant in which he substituted the envelope he was carrying for the one containing the payroll. Once the substitution was made, the rest was simple, and the very casualness of it made the chance of detection slight. Hence, he had directed every thought to that one action. The thought that he might be seen and not exposed never occurred to him.

Yet that was exactly what had happened, and because of it, he was about to commit a murder.

Eddie Cruzon had been eating lunch at Barnaby's for over a year. On the day he overheard the conversation, nothing was further from his thoughts than crime.

"We've used the method for years," a man

beside him was saying. "The payroll will be in a manila envelope on George's desk. George will have the receipt for you to sign and the guard will be waiting."

"What about the route?"

"Your driver knows that. He was picked out and given the route not more than ten minutes ago. All you have to do is sit in the backseat and hold the fifteen thousand dollars in your lap."

Fifteen thousand was a lot of money. Cruzon considered the precautions, and the flaw was immediately apparent: the time when the payroll lay on George's desk in the busy office. For Eddie knew the office, having recognized the men talking. He worked for a parcel delivery service and had frequently visited the office on business. With that amount of money, a man could do . . . plenty. Yet, the idea of stealing it did not come until later.

Once his decision was made, the actual crime was as simple as he'd believed it would be. He merely walked into the office carrying a duplicate envelope, and seizing a moment when George was not at his desk, he put down his envelope and picked up the other. Walking out, his heart pounding, he mingled with people at the elevator, and then, in the foyer of the building, stamped and addressed the envelope to himself and dropped it in a large mailbox near the door.

It was Saturday morning and there was no delivery until Monday, so he went back to his work, pretending to be unconcerned as always. Yet when he finished his day and was once more in his room, he could scarcely restrain his exuberance.

Fifteen thousand, and all *his*! Standing before the mirror, he brushed his sleek blond hair and stared triumphantly at the vistas of wealth that opened before him. He would go about his work quietly for another month, and then make an excuse, and quit. After that, Rio, Havana, Buenos Aires! He was seeing himself immaculately clad on the terrace of a hotel in Rio when the phone rang.

"Cruzon?" The voice was low, unfamiliar. "That was pretty slick! Nobody saw it but me, and I'm not talking . . . as long as I can do business with you."

Shock held him speechless. His lips were numb and his stomach had gone hollow. He managed the words, "I don't know what you're talking about. Who is this?"

"You'll know soon enough. The only reason you're not in jail is because I've kept my mouth shut."

Eddie Cruzon had stared past the curtain at the drizzle of falling rain, his mind blank, his whole consciousness clambering at the walls of fear. "No reason why we should have trouble," the voice continued. "In ten minutes, I'll be sitting in the back booth of the coffee shop on your corner. All I want is my cut."

Cruzon's lips fumbled for words.

Into the silence the voice said, "They will pay five hundred for information. Think that over."

The man hung up suddenly, and Cruzon stared at the phone as if hypnotized. Then, slowly, he replaced the handset on its cradle.

For a long time he remained perfectly still, his mind a blank. One fact stood isolated in his mind. He must share the fifteen thousand dollars.

Yet almost at once his mind refused that solution. He had planned it, he had taken the risk, he would share it with no one.

The answer to that was stark and clear. The unknown, whoever he was, would inform on him if he didn't pay up.

He could share his loot, go to prison, or . . .

That was when he first thought of murder.

What right had the stranger to force his way into the affair? Theft was a rough game. If anything happened to him, it was just his bad luck.

Then he thought of the gravel pit. Only a few weeks ago he had visited the place, driving out the old road, now badly washed out and obviously unused. Curiosity impelled him to stop his car and walk up the grass-grown path along the fence.

The pit lay in the rough triangle formed by a wide field of pumping wells, the unused road, and the fence surrounding a golf course, but far from any of the fairways. It was screened by low trees and a tangle of thick brush. There was no evidence that anyone had been near it in a long time.

His car could be pulled into the brush, and it should take him no more than ten minutes to walk up to the pit and come back alone. There was small chance of being seen. It might be months before the body was found.

Even when the plan was detailed in his mind, something within him refused to accept it. He, Eddie Cruzon, was going to kill a man!

Later, looking across at the wide face of the man in the restaurant, he pretended to accept his entry into the affair with ease. "Why not?" he said. "I don't mind a split." He leaned over the table, anxious to convince the man of his sincerity. "Maybe we can work out something else. This job was a cinch."

"It was slick, all right!" The little man with the round face was frankly admiring. "Slick as anything I ever saw! It took me a minute or two to realize what had happened, and I saw it!"

Eddie had leaned forward. "The money's cached. We'll have to hire a car. . . ." He had decided not to use his own.

"I've got a car. Want to go now?" The little man was eager, his eyes bright and avid.

"Not now. I've got a date, and this girl might start asking questions. Neither of us should do anything out of the normal. We just act like we always have."

"That's right. I can see that," the fellow agreed, blinking. He was stupid, Cruzon thought, absolutely stupid! "When do we go after it?"

"Tomorrow night. You drive by and pick me up. We'll go out where I hid the money, split it two ways, have a good dinner to celebrate, and go our ways. Meanwhile, you be thinking. You're in a position to know about payrolls and can tip me to something else, later. With this parcel service job, I can go anywhere and never be noticed."

Nothing but talk, of course. Cruzon hated the milky blue eyes and the pasty face. He wanted only to be rid of him.

When he saw the car roll up before his apartment house, he felt in his waistband for the short iron bar he had picked off a junk pile. Then, pulling his hat brim lower, he walked out the door.

Weber opened the door for him, and Cruzon got in, striving for a nonchalance he did not feel. He gave directions and then sank back in the seat. His mouth was dry and he kept touching his lips with his tongue.

Out of the corners of his eyes, he studied the man beside him. Weber was shorter than he, and stocky. Once at the pit, he must kill and kill quickly, for the man would be suspicious.

They had seen no other car for miles

when he motioned Weber to pull off the road. Weber stared about suspiciously, uneasily. It was dark here, and gloomy, a place of slanting rain, wet pavement, and dripping brush. "You hid it clear out here? What for?"

"You think I want it on me? What if they came to search my place? And where could I hide it where I'd not be seen?" He opened the door and got out into the rain. "Right up this path," he invited, "it isn't far."

Weber was out of the car, but he looked up the path and shook his head. "Not me. I'll stay with the car."

Cruzon hesitated. He had not considered this, being sure the man would want to be with him. Weber stared at him, then up the path. Cruzon could almost see suspicion forming in the man's mind.

"Will you wait, then?" he asked irritably. "I don't want to be left out here."

"Don't worry!" Weber's voice was grim. "And don't try any tricks. I've got a gun."

"Who wants to try anything?" Cruzon demanded impatiently. Actually, he was in a panic. What could he do now?

Weber himself made it easy. "Go ahead," he said shortly, "and hurry. I'll wait in the car." He turned to get back into the car, and Cruzon hit him.

He struck hard with his fist, staggering Weber. The stocky man was fumbling for the gun with one hand when Cruzon jerked out the iron bar. He struck viciously. Once . . . twice . . . a third time.

And then there was only the softly falling rain, the dark body at his feet, and the night.

He was panting hoarsely. He must work fast now . . . fast. Careful to avoid any blood, he lifted the man in a fireman's carry and started up the path.

Once, when almost halfway, he slipped on the wet grass and grabbed wildly at a bush, hanging on grimly until he got his feet under him. When at last he reached the brink of the pit, he heaved Weber's body over and stood there, gasping for breath, listening to the slide of gravel.

Done!

It was all his now! Rain glistened on the stones, and the pit gaped beneath him, wide and dark. He turned from it, almost running. Luckily, there was nobody in sight. He climbed in and released the brake, starting the car by coasting. An hour later he deserted the car on a dark and lonely street, then straightened his clothes and hurried to the corner.

Walking four fast blocks, he boarded a bus and sank into a seat near the rear door. When he'd gone a dozen blocks, he got off and walked another block before catching a cab.

He was getting into the cab when the driver noticed his hand. "What's the matter? Cut yourself?"

In a panic, he looked down and saw that his hand was bloody. Weber's blood? It couldn't be. He'd worn gloves. He must have scratched his hand afterward, on the bushes.

"It's nothing," he said carelessly, "just a scratch."

The driver looked at him oddly. "Where to, mister?"

"Down Wilshire, then left."

Cruzon got out his handkerchief and wiped his hand. His trousers were wet and he felt dirty. It was a while before he got home. He stripped off his clothes and almost fell into bed.

Cruzon awakened with a start. It was broad daylight and time to dress for work.

His mind was startlingly clear, yet he was appalled at what he'd done. He had mur— He flinched at the word. He had killed a man.

He must be careful now. Any move might betray him. Reviewing his actions of the previous night, he tried to think of where he might have erred.

He had thrown the iron bar away. He had worn gloves in the car, and it had been left on a street in a bad neighborhood. He had taken precautions returning home. Above all, nobody knew he was acquainted with Weber.

There was nothing to worry about. He wanted to drive by the pit and see if any marks had been left, but knew it might be fatal. He must never go near the place again.

There was nothing to connect him with the payroll. When Weber turned up missing, there was a chance they would believe he had made the switch himself, then skipped out.

After dressing for work, he took time to carefully brush the suit he'd worn the previous night. He hurried out, drove to work, stopping only once, to buy a paper. There was nothing about the missing payroll. That puzzled and worried him, until he remembered it was Monday. That must have been in the Sunday paper, which he'd missed.

At his usual hour, he dropped around to Barnaby's. He took three papers with him, but waited until he had his coffee before opening them. A careful search netted him exactly nothing. There was no comment on the payroll robbery. Then, the two men whom he'd overheard came in and sat down near him. Another man came in a moment later, and Cruzon gasped audibly, turning cold and stiff.

The newcomer was short, stocky, and had a pale face. Cruzon almost gasped with relief when he saw the man was all of ten years older than Weber. The man carried a newspaper, and sat down one stool away from him.

Cruzon took off his uniform and cap and smoothed his blond hair with a shaky hand. No use getting jumpy whenever he saw a man even built like Weber; there were lots of them.

He had finished his lunch and was on his second cup of coffee, and trying so hard to hear what his neighbors were saying that he'd been prodded twice on the arm before he realized the stocky man on his other side was speaking to him. "How about the sugar?" he asked. Then the fellow grinned knowingly. "You must have had a bad night. I had to speak three times before you heard me."

Impatiently, Cruzon grabbed the sugar and shoved it at the man. The fellow took it, his eyes questioning and curious.

Cruzon got his attention back to the other men just in time to hear one say, ". . . good joke, I'd say. I wonder who got it?"

"Could have been anybody. You've got to hand it to the boss. He's smart. He puts so many twists in that payroll delivery, nobody could ever figure it out! I'll bet he lays awake nights working out angles!"

"Did Weber come in late? I haven't seen him."

"Not yet. Say, wouldn't it be funny if he took it? He's just dopey enough to try something like that!"

They paid their checks and walked out. Cruzon stared blindly at his coffee. Something was wrong! What did they mean by saying it was a good joke? He remembered all they had previously said, about not giving out the name of the driver or the route until the last minute, but had there been other precautions? Had . . . could he have been duped?

His spoon rattled on his cup and the man beside him grinned. "You'd better take on a lot of that, friend. You're in no shape to be driving."

"Mind your own business, will you?" His irritation, fear, and doubt broke out, his tone made ugly by it.

The fat man's eyes hardened. "It is my business, chum." The man got to his feet and flipped open a leather case, displaying a detective's badge. The name, Cruzon noted, was Gallagher. "We've enough trouble without you morning-after drivers."

"Oh . . . I'm sorry, officer." Get hold of yourself, get a grip, his subconscious was saying. "I'll be careful. Thanks for the warning."

Hastily, he paid his check and left. When he got into the truck, he saw the fat man standing by the building, watching him.

Watching *him*? But why should he? How could they be suspicious of him?

For the remainder of the day he drove so carefully he was almost an hour late in finishing deliveries. He checked in his truck, then hurried to his car and got in. Even more carefully, he drove home.

He saw it as soon as he entered the hall-way. Restraining an impulse to seize the envelope and run, he picked it up and walked to his room. The key rattled in the lock, and he was trembling when he put the envelope down on the table and ripped open the flap. He thrust in his hand, fumbling feverishly for the first packet. He jerked it out.

Newspapers . . . just newspapers cut in the size and shape of bills!

Desperately, his heart pounding, he dumped the envelope out on the table and pawed over the packets. More newspapers.

That was what they meant, then, and the joke was on him.

On him? Or on Weber?

Only Weber was out of it; Weber was beyond shame or punishment. Weber was dead, and he had been killed for a packet of trimmed paper.

But they did not know, they could not know. Weber could not talk, and that crime, at least, was covered. Covered completely.

Cruzon dropped into a chair, fighting for sanity and reason. He must get rid of the envelope and the paper. That was the first thing. It might be months before they found Weber's body, and he could be far away by then.

Frightened as he was, he gathered up the papers and, returning them to the envelope, slipped out to the incinerator and dumped them in.

Back in his room, he left the light off, then hastily stripped off his clothes and got into bed. He lay sleepless for a long, long time, staring out into the shadowed dark.

He was dressing the following morning when he first noticed his hands. They were red.

Red? *Blood on his hands!* The blood of . . . ! He came to his feet, gasping as if ducked in cold water. But no! That was impossible! There had been no blood on his hands but his own, that scratch.

The scratch? He opened his hand and stared at it feverishly; he pawed at it. There was no scratch.

The blood had been Weber's.

And this? But this was not the red of blood, it was brighter, a flatter red.

Leaving the house, he pulled on his gloves. A good deal of it had washed away, and there were parts of his hands it hadn't touched. Most of it was on the palms and fingers.

All morning he worked hard, moving swiftly, crisply, efficiently. Anything to keep his mind off Weber, off the newspapers, off the strange red tinge that stained his hands. Then, at last, it was lunchtime, and he escaped his work and went to Barnaby's almost with relief. Even removing his gloves did not disturb him, and nobody seemed aware of the red in between his fingers. A thought crept into his mind. *Was it visible only to him?*

Cruzon was over his coffee when the two men came in again. Eddie sipped his coffee and listened feverishly to the men beside him.

This time they discussed a movie they had seen, and he fought back his anxiety to leave, and waited, listening.

The red on his hands, he thought suddenly, might have come from a package he handled. Something must have broken inside, and in his preoccupied state, he had not noticed.

Then Gallagher walked in and dropped onto a stool beside him. He smiled at Cruzon. "Not so bad this morning," he said. "You must have slept well?"

"Sure," he agreed, trying to be affable. "Why not?"

"You're lucky. In my business, a man misses plenty of sleep. Like yesterday evening. We found a body."

"A body?" There was no way they could connect him with it, even if it was Weber.

"Yeah. Man found a gun alongside the road." Gallagher pulled a cheap, nickel-plated revolver from his pocket. "Not much account, these guns, but they could kill a man. Lots of 'em have. The fellow who found this gun, he brought it to us. We made a routine check, an' what d'you think? Belongs to a fellow named John Weber. He bought it a couple of days ago."

"John Weber?" So his name had been John? He had not known. "Has it been in the papers?"

"No, not yet. Well, anyway, that made us curious. A man buys a gun, then loses it right away, so we called this Weber, an' you know what? He'd disappeared! That's right! Landlady said his room hadn't been slept in, and he hadn't been to work. So we drove out to where this gun was lost and we scouted around.

"There was an old, washed-out dirt track up a hill away from the surfaced road. Nobody seemed to have been up there in a long time, but right up there on the track, we found the body."

"Where?" Even as the incredulous word escaped him, he realized his mistake. He took a slow, deep breath before speaking again. "But you said nobody had been there? How could he—"

"That's what we wondered. His head was battered, but he managed to crawl that far before he died. The killer had slugged him and dropped him over the rim of the pit."

Cruzon was frightened. Inside, he was deathly cold, and when he moved his tongue, it felt stiff and clumsy. He wanted to get away; he wanted to be anywhere but here, listening to that casual, easy voice and feeling those mild, friendly blue eyes. He glanced hastily at his watch. "Gosh! I've got to go! I'll be late with my deliveries!"

The detective dismissed his worry with a

wave of the hand. "No need to rush. I feel like talking, so I'll fix it with your boss. I'll tell him you were helping me."

Eddie had a feeling he was being smothered, stifled. Something . . . everything was wrong.

The gun, for instance. He had never given it a thought, having been anxious to get away without being seen. And Weber not dead, but crawling halfway to the road!

"I won't take much longer," Gallagher said, "it wasn't much of a case."

"But I should think it would be hard to solve a case like that. How could you find out who killed him? Or how he got there?"

"That isn't hard. Folks figure the cops are dumb, but nobody is smart all the time. I ball things up, occasionally, and sometimes other cops do, but we've got something that beats them all. We've got an organization, a system.

"Now take this Weber. It didn't take us long to get the dope on him. He'd only been in town a year, no outdoor fellow, he just bowled a little and went to movies. So what do we figure from that? That it must have been the killer who knew about the gravel pit. It was an abandoned pit, unused in years. Not likely Weber would know about it.

"Meanwhile, we find there's an attempted payroll robbery where this Weber works. We figure Weber either did it or knew who did and was killed because of it. That adds up. So while some of the boys checked on him, others checked on the gravel pit."

Gallagher flipped open a notebook. "It hadn't been used in eight years. The company found a better source for gravel, but one of the guys in the department knew about kids who used to play there. So we started a check on truck drivers who hauled from there, oil field workers who knew about it, and the kids.

"The guy who's in the department, he gave us a list. His name is Ernie Russell."

Skinny Russell!

"He remembered them all. One was killed on Okinawa. One's an intern in New York. A girl works down the street in a coffee shop, and you drive a parcel delivery truck. Funny, isn't it? How things work out? All of you scattered, an' now this brings it all back."

"You . . . you mean that was the same pit where we used to play?"

"Sure, Eddie. An' you know? You're the

only one who might have known Weber. You delivered to that office, sometimes."

"I deliver to a lot of offices." They had nothing on him. They were surmising, that was all. "I know few people in any of them."

"That's right, but suppose one of them called you?" The placid blue eyes were friendly. "Suppose one of them thought he saw you pick up the payroll envelope? Suppose he wanted a piece of it?"

The detective sipped coffee. "So it begins to add up. Suppose you were called by Weber? Weber was planning something because he bought that gun Saturday afternoon. He wanted to be on the safe side. And you knew about the gravel pit."

"So what? That isn't even a good circumstantial case. You can't prove I ever saw Weber."

"You've got something there. That's going to be tough unless you admit it."

He got to his feet. "I've got to go now. I've done nothing. I don't want to talk to you."

"Look, kid." Gallagher was patient. "You can tell me about it now or later. You muffed it, you know, from beginning to end. We know you met him somewhere, an' we can find it. Maybe it will take us a week, maybe two weeks or a month, but we'll find it. We've got you on the payroll job, an' we'll get you on the killing, too, kid."

"What do you mean, you've got me on the payroll job? I had nothing to do with it!"

Gallagher remained patient. "You've been trying to keep your hands out of sight. One of my boys was watching the house when you came out this morning. He was watching your hands, and he saw the red on them before you got your gloves on. He called me about it this morning. We checked your incinerator . . . closely packed papers have to be stirred around or they won't burn. Only the edges a little, and they'll brown over.

"That red on your hands? That guy in the payroll office, he's a funny one. He handles three payrolls a week for eight years, an' never lost one. He's always got an angle. The day you stole that envelope, he took the real payroll over in a taxi, all alone. But the papers you handled, they had red dye on them . . . hard to wash off."

Eddie Cruzon sat down on the stool again and stared blindly down at his coffee. He blinked his eyes, trying to think. Where was he now? What could he do?

"Another thing. Weber, he lives out in Westwood, an' he called you from home. It was a toll call, see? We got a record of it."

The fool! The miserable fool!

Gallagher got to his feet. "What do you say, kid? You haven't a chance. Want to tell us about it? My wife, she's havin' some friends over, an' I want to get home early."

Cruzon stared at his coffee and his jaw trembled. He was cold, so awfully cold, all the way through. And he was finished . . . finished because he'd thought . . .

"I'll talk." His voice was no more than a whisper. "I'll talk."

THE MONEY PUNCH

I

The girl in the trench coat and sand-colored beret was on the sidelines again. She was standing beside a white-haired man, and as Darby McGraw crawled through the ropes, she was watching him.

Darby grinned cockily at his second and trainer, Beano Brown. "That babe's here again," he said. "She must think I'm okay."

"She prob'ly comes to see somebody else," Beano said without interest. "Lots of fighters work out here."

"No, she always looks at me. And why is that, you ask me? It's because I'm the class of this crowd, that's why."

"You sure hate yourself," Beano said. "These people seen plenty of fighters." Beano leaned on the top rope and looked at

Darby with casual eyes. The boy was built. He had the shoulders, a slim waist and narrow hips, and he had good hands. A good-looking boy.

"Wait until I get in there with Mink Delano. I'll show 'em all something then. When I hit 'em with my right and they don't go down, they do some sure funny things standing up!"

"You come from an awful small town," Beano said. "I can tell that."

Darby moved in, feeling for the distance with his left. He felt good. Sammy Need, the boy he was working with, slipped inside of Darby's left and landed lightly to the ribs. Darby kept his right hand cocked. He would like to throw that right, just once, just to show this girl what he could do.

He liked Sammy, though, and didn't want to hurt him. Sammy was fast, and Darby wasn't hitting him very often, but that meant nothing. He rarely turned loose his right in workouts, and it was the right that was his money punch. That right had won his fights out in Jerome, and those fights had gotten him recommended to Fats Lakey in L.A.

Fats was his manager. Fats had been a pool hustler who dropped into Jerome one time and met some of the guys in the local fight scene. He'd been looking for new talent, and so the locals had talked McGraw into going to the coast and looking him up. With nine knockouts under his belt, Darby was willing.

He felt good today. He liked to train and was in rare shape. He moved in, and as he worked, he wondered what that girl would say if she knew he had knocked out nine men in a row. And no less than six of these in the first round. Neither Dempsey nor Louis had that many kayoes in their first nine fights.

When he had worked six rounds, he climbed down from the ring, scarcely breathing hard. He started for the table to take some body-bending exercise and deliberately passed close to the girl. He was within ten feet of her when he heard her say distinctly, "Delano will win. This one can't fight for sour apples."

Darby stopped, flat-footed, his face flushing red with sudden anger. Who did she think she was, anyway, talking him down like that! He started to turn, then noticed they were paying no attention to him, hadn't noticed him, in fact, so he wheeled angrily and went on to the table.

I'll show 'em! he told himself. He was seething inside. Why, just for that, he'd murder Delano; knock him out, like the others, in the very first round!

Darby McGraw's anger had settled to a grim, bitter determination by the night he climbed into the ring with Mink Delano. Fats Lakey was standing behind his corner, swelling with importance, a long cigar thrust in his fat, red cheek. He kept talking about "my boy McGraw" in a loud voice.

Beano Brown crawled into Darby's corner as second. He was not excited. Beano had seen too many of them come and go. He had been seconding fighters for twenty-two years, and it meant just another sawbuck to him, or whatever he could get. He was a short black man with one cauliflowered ear. Tonight he was bored and tired.

Darby glanced down at the ringside and saw the girl in the beret. She glanced at him, then looked away without interest.

"The special event was a better fight than this semifinal will be," he heard her say. "I can't see why they put this boy in that spot."

Darby stood up. He was mad clear through. I'll show her! he told himself viciously. I'll show her! He wouldn't have minded so much if she hadn't had wide gray eyes and lovely, soft brown hair. She was, he knew, almost beautiful.

They went to the center of the ring for their instructions. The crowd didn't bother him. He was impatient, anxious to get started and to feel his right fist smashing against Mink's chin. He'd show this crowd something, and quick! Why, it took them four hours to bring Al Baker back to his senses after Baker stopped that right with his chin!

The bell clanged and he wheeled and went out fast. Delano was a slim, white, muscled youngster who fought high on his toes. Darby moved in, feinted swiftly, and threw his right.

Something smashed him in the body, and then a light hook clipped him on the chin. He piled in, throwing the right again, but a fast left made him taste blood and another snapped home on his temple. Neither punch hurt, but he was confused. He steadied down and looked at Mink. The other boy was calm, unruffled.

Darby pawed with his left, but his left wasn't good for much, he knew. Then he threw his right. Again a gloved fist smashed him in the ribs. Darby bored in, landing a light left, but taking a fast one to the mouth. He threw his right and Mink beat him to it with a beautiful inside cross that jolted him to his heels. The bell sounded and he trotted back to his corner.

"Take your time, boy," Beano said. "Just take your time. No hurry."

Darby McGraw was on his feet before the bell sounded. He pulled up his trunks and pawed at the resin. This guy had lasted a whole round with him, and this after he'd sworn to get him in the first, too. The bell rang and he lunged from his corner and threw his right, high and hard.

A fist smashed into his middle, then another one. He was hit three times before he could get set after the missed punch. Darby drew back and circled Mink. Somehow he wasn't hitting Delano. He was suddenly vastly impatient. Talk about luck! This guy had it. Darby pawed with his left, then unleashed his right. Mink moved in and the right curled around his neck. He smiled at Darby, then smashed two wicked punches to the body.

Darby was shaken. His anger still burning within him, he pawed Delano's left out of the way and slammed a right to the body, but

Mink took it going away and the glove barely touched him.

Darby stepped around, set himself to throw his right, but Mink sidestepped neatly, taking himself out of line. Before Darby could change position, a left stabbed him in the mouth. Darby ducked his head and furrowed his brow. He'd have to watch this guy. He would have to be careful.

Delano moved in now, landing three fast left jabs. Darby fired his right suddenly, but it slid off a slashing left glove that smashed his lips back into his teeth and set him back on his heels. He took another step back and suddenly Delano was all over him. Before Darby could clinch, Mink hit him seven times.

Three times in the following round he tried with his right. Each time he missed. When the bell ended the round, he walked wearily back to his corner. He slumped on the stool. "Use your left," Beano told him. "This boy, he don't like no lefts. Use a left hook!"

Darby tried, but he had no confidence in that left of his. It had always been his right that won fights for him. All he had to do was land that right. One punch and he could win. Just one. He feinted with his right and threw his left. It was a poorly executed hook, more of a swing, but it caught Mink high on the head and knocked him sprawling on the canvas.

Darby was wild. He ran to a corner and waited, hands weaving. Delano scrambled to his feet at the count of nine and Darby went after him with a rush and threw a roundhouse right. Mink ducked inside of it and grabbed Darby with both hands.

Wildly, McGraw tore him loose and threw his right again. But Mink was crafty and slid inside and clinched once more. Darby could hear someone yelling to use his left. He tried. He pushed Delano away and cocked his left, but caught a left and right in the mouth before he could throw it.

In the last round of the fight he was outboxed completely. He was tired, but he kept pushing in, kept throwing his right. He didn't need to look at the referee. He kept his eyes away from the girl in the trench coat. He did not want to hear the decision. He knew he had lost every round.

Fats Lakey was waiting in the dressing room, his fat face flushed and ugly. "You bum!" he snarled. "You poor, country bum! I thought you were a fighter! Why, this Delano is only a preliminary boy, a punk, and he made a monkey out of you! Nine knockouts, but you can't fight! Not for sour apples, you can't fight!"

That did it. All the rage and frustration and disappointment boiled over. Darby swung his right. Fats, seeing his mistake too late, took a quick step back, enough to break the force of the blow but not enough to save him. The right smashed against his fat cheek and Lakey hit the floor on the seat of his pants, blood streaming from a cut below his eye.

"I'll have you pinched for this!" he screamed. He got up and backed toward the door. "I'll get you thrown in the cooler so fast!"

"No, you won't!" It was the white-haired man who had sat with the girl in the beret. They were both there. "I heard it all, Lakey, and if he hadn't clipped you, I would have. Now beat it!"

Fats Lakey backed away, his eyes ugly. The white-haired man had twisted a handkerchief around his fist and was watching him coolly.

II

When Fats was gone, the girl walked over to Darby. "Hurt much?"

"No," he said sullenly, keeping his eyes down. "I ain't hurt. That Delano couldn't break an egg!"

"Lucky for you he couldn't," she said coolly. "He hit you with everything but the stool."

Darby's eyes flashed angrily. He was bitter and ashamed. He wanted no girl such as this to see him beaten. He had wanted her to see him win.

"He was lucky," he muttered. "I had an off night."

"Oh?" Her voice was contemptuous. "So you're one of those?"

His head came up sharply. "One of what?" he demanded. "What do you mean?"

"One of those fighters who alibi themselves out of every beating," she said. "A fighter who is afraid to admit he was whipped. You were beaten tonight—you should be man enough to admit it."

He pulled his shoelace tighter and pressed his lips into a thin line. He glanced at her feet. She had nice feet and good legs.

Suddenly, memory of the fight flooded over him. He recalled those wild rights he had thrown into empty air, the stabbing lefts he had taken in the mouth, the rights that had battered his ribs. He got to his feet.

"All right," he said. "If you want me to admit it, he punched my head off. I couldn't hit him. But next time I'll hit him. Next time I'll knock him out!"

"Not if you fight the way you did tonight," she said matter-of-factly. "Fighting the way you do, you wouldn't hit him with that right in fifty fights. Whoever told you you were a fighter?"

He glared. "I won nine fights by knock-outs," he said defiantly. "Six in the first round!"

"Against country boys who knew even less about it than you did, probably. You might make a fighter," she admitted, "but you aren't one now. You can't win fights with nothing but a right hand."

"You know all about it," he sneered. "What does a girl know about fighting, any-way?"

"My father was Paddy McFadden," she replied quietly, "if you know who he was. My uncle was lightweight champion of the world. I grew up around better fighters than you've ever seen."

He picked up his coat. "So what?" He started for the door, but feeling a hand on his sleeve, he stopped. The white-haired man was holding out some money to him.

"I was afraid Lakey might forget to pay you, so I collected your part of this."

"Thanks," Darby snapped. He took the money and stuffed it into his pocket. He was out the door when he heard Beano.

"Mr. McGraw?"

"Yeah?" He was impatient, anxious to be gone.

"Fats, he forgot to give me my sawbuck."

The Negro's calm face quieted Darby. "Oh?" he said. "I'm sorry. Here." He reached for the money. It wasn't very much. He took a twenty from the thin packet of bills and handed it to Beano. "Here you are, and thanks. If I'd won, I'd have given you more."

He ducked out through the door and turned into the damp street, wet from a light drizzle of rain. Suddenly, he was ashamed of himself. He shouldn't have talked to the girl that way. It was only that he had wanted so much to make a good showing, to impress her, and then he had lost. It would have been better if he had been knocked out. It would have been less humiliating than to take the boxing lesson he'd taken.

With sudden clarity he saw the fight as it must have looked to others. A husky country boy, wading in and wasting punches on the air, while a faster, smarter fighter stepped around him and stuck left hands in his face.

What would they be saying back home now? He had told them all he would be back, welterweight champion of the world. His nine victories had made him sure that all he needed was a chance at the champion and he could win. And he'd been beaten by a comparatively unknown preliminary boxer!

Hours later he stopped at a cheap hotel and got a room for the night. What was it she had said?

"You can't win fights with nothing but a right hand."

She had been right, of course, and he'd been a fool. His few victories had swollen his head until he was too cocky, too sure of himself. Suddenly, he realized how long and hard the climb would be, how much he had to learn.

For a long time he lay awake that night, recalling those stabbing lefts and the girl's scorn. Yet she'd come to his dressing room. Why? She had bothered enough to talk to him. Darby McGraw shook his head. Girls had always puzzled him. But this one seemed particularly puzzling.

In the morning he recovered his few possessions at the hotel where he and Fats had stayed. Fats was gone, leaving the bill for him to pay. He paid it and had twelve dollars left.

He found Beano Brown leaning against the wall at Higherman's Gym. "Beano," he said hesitantly, "what was wrong with my fight last night?"

The Negro looked at him, then dug a pack of smokes from his pocket and shook one into his hand. "You ain't got no left," he said, "for one thing. Never was no great fighter without he had a good left hand. You got to learn to jab."

"Will you show me how?"

Beano lit his smoke. "You ain't goin' to

quit? Well, maybe I might show you, but why don't you go to Mary McFadden? She's got a trainin' farm. Inherited it from her daddy. She's got Dan Faherty out there. Ain't no better trainer than him."

"No." Darby shook his head, digging his hands into his coat pockets. "I don't want to go there. I want you to show me."

"Well," Beano said. "I guess so."

Darby McGraw was a lean six feet. His best weight was just over one hundred forty-five, but he was growing heavier. He had a shock of black, curly hair and a hard, brown face. The month before he had turned nineteen years old.

In the three weeks that followed his talk with Beano, he trained, hour after hour, and his training was mostly to stand properly, how to shift his feet, how to move forward and how to retreat.

He eked out a precarious existence with a few labor jobs and occasional workouts for which he was paid.

He saw nothing of Mary, but occasionally heard of her. He heard enough to know that she was considered to be a shrewd judge of fighters. Also, that she had arranged the training schedules of champions, that there was little she didn't know about the boxing game, and that she was only twenty-two.

"Seems like a funny business for a girl," he told Beano.

The Negro shrugged. "Maybe. Ain't no business funny for no girl now. She stuck with what she knowed. Her daddy and her uncle, she heard them talkin' fight for years, talkin' it with ever'body big in business. She couldn't help but know it. When her daddy was killed, she kept the trainin' farm. It was a good business, and Dan Faherty's like a father to her."

Beano looked at him suddenly. "Got you a fight. Over to Justiceville. You go four rounds with Billy Greb."

Justiceville was a tank town. There were about two thousand people in the crowd, however. Benny Seaman, crack middle, was fighting in the main go.

Darby went in at one hundred fifty. He was outweighed seven pounds. Beano leaned on the top rope and looked at him.

"You move around, see?" he instructed. "You jab him. No right hands, see?"

"All right," Darby said.

The bell sounded and he went out fast. Greb came into him swinging and Darby was tempted. He jabbed. His left impaled Greb, stopping his charge. Darby jabbed again. Then he feinted a right and jabbed again. Billy kept piling in and swinging.

Just before the bell, Greb missed a right and Darby caught him in the chin with a short left hook. Greb hit the canvas with his knees. He was still shaken when he came out for the second. Darby walked in slowly. He feinted a right and made Greb's knees wobble with another left. He jabbed twice, working cautiously. Then he feinted and hooked the left again. Greb's feet shot out from under him and he hit flat on his face. He never wiggled during the count.

"With my left!" Darby said, astonished. "I knocked him out with my left!"

"Uh-huh. You got two hands," Beano said. "But you got lots of work to do. Lots of work."

"All right," Darby said.

The next day he met Mary McFadden on the street. They recognized each other at the same moment and she stopped.

"Hello," he said. He felt himself blushing, and grinned sheepishly.

"Congratulations on your fight. I heard about you knocking out Bill Greb."

"It wasn't anything," he said, "just a four round preliminary."

"All fighters start at the bottom," she told him.

"I had to find that out," he admitted. "It wasn't easy."

"They want you back there, at Justiceville," Mary said. "Mike McDonald was over at the camp yesterday. He said they wanted you to fight Marshall Collins."

"Do you think I should?" He looked at her. "They tell me you know all about this boxing game."

"Oh, no!" she said quickly. "I don't at all." She looked up at him. "Tell Beano not to take Collins. Tell him to insist on Augie Gordon."

"But he's a better fighter than Collins!" Darby exclaimed.

"Yes, he is. Much better. But that isn't the question. Marshall Collins is very hard to fight. Augie Gordon is good, but he doesn't take a punch very well. He will outpoint you for a few rounds, but you'll hit him."

"All right," he said.

Mary smiled and held out her hand. "Why

don't you come out and work with us? We'd like to have you."

"Can't afford it," he said. "Your camp is too expensive."

"It wouldn't be if you were fighting for us," she said. "And Beano thinks you should be out there. He told me so. He's worried. You're causing him to work, and Beano likes to take his time about things."

He grinned. "Well, maybe. Just to make it easy on Beano." He started to turn away. "Say . . ." He hesitated and felt his face getting red. "Would you go to a show with me sometime?"

"You're an attractive man, Darby . . . but right now this is business. Maybe later, if you're still around."

"I will be," he stated.

"Then we both have something to look forward to."

Darby walked off feeling light-headed, although he realized that he didn't know what that "something" was.

Augie Gordon was fast. His left hand was faster than Mink Delano's. He was shifty, too. Darby pulled his chin in and began to weave and bob as Beano had been teaching him. He lost the first round, but there was a red spot on Gordon's side where Darby had landed four left hands.

Darby lost the second round, too, but the red spot on Augie's ribs was bigger and redder, and Gordon was watching that left. Augie didn't like them downstairs. Darby started working on Augie's ribs in the third, and noticed that the other fighter was slower getting away. The body punches were taking it out of him.

Darby kept it up. He kept it up with drumming punches through the fourth. In the fifth he walked out and threw a left at the body, pulled it, and hooked high and hard for the chin. Augie had jerked his stomach back and his chin came down to meet Darby's left. Augie Gordon turned halfway around before he hit the canvas.

He got up at nine, but he could barely continue. Remembering how Delano had stepped inside of his wild right-hand punches when he tried to finish him, Darby was cautious. He jabbed twice, then let Gordon see a chance to clinch. Augie moved in, and Darby met him halfway with a right uppercut that nearly tore his head off.

Mary was waiting for him when he climbed out of the ring. "Your left is getting better all the time," she said.

Dan Faherty smiled at him. "Mary says you may be coming out to the farm. We've got some good boys to work with out there."

"All right," he said, "I'll come." He grinned. "You two and Beano have made a believer out of me."

He started for his dressing room feeling better than he ever had in his life. He had stopped Augie Gordon. He had stopped Billy Greb. It looked like he was on his way. But next he wanted Mink Delano. That was a black mark on his record and he wanted it wiped clear. He pushed open the door of his dressing room and stepped inside.

Fats Lakey was sitting in a chair across the room. He was smiling, but his little eyes were mean. With him were two husky, hard-faced men.

"Hello, kid," Fats said softly. "Doin' all right, I see."

III

Beano's face was a shade paler and he kept his eyes down. "Yeah," Darby said, "I'm doing all right. What do you want?"

"Nothin'." Fats laughed. "Nothin' at all, right now. Of course, there's a little matter of some money you owe me, but we can take that up later."

"I owe you nothing!" Darby said angrily. He didn't even start to take off his bandages. "You never did a thing for me but try to steal my end of the gate and run away without paying Beano. The less I see of you, the better. Now beat it!"

Fats smiled, but his lips were thin. "I'm not in any hurry, Darby," he said. "When I get ready to go, I'll go. And don't get tough about it. I owe you a little something for that punch in the face you gave me, and if you don't talk mighty quiet, I'll let the boys here work you over."

Darby pulled his belt tight and slid into his sweater. He looked from one to the other of Fat's hard-faced companions, and suddenly he grinned.

"Those mugs?" he said, and laughed. "I could bounce 'em both without working up a sweat, and then stack you on top of them."

One of the men straightened up and his face hardened. "Punk," he said, "I don't think I like you."

"What do I do?" Darby snapped. "Shudder with sobs or something?"

"Take it easy, kid!" Fats said harshly. "Right now I want to talk business. I happen to know you're going in there next with Mink Delano."

"So what?"

"So you'll beat him. With that left you've worked up, you'll beat him. Then they'll have something else for you. When the right time comes, we can do business, and when you're ready, you'll do it my way. If you don't, bad things will happen to you and yours. . . . Get me?"

Fats got up, his face smug. "Wise punks don't get tough with me, see? You're just a country punk in a big town. If you want to play our way, you can make some dough. If you don't act nice, we'll see that you do."

He turned to go. "And that McFadden floozy won't help you none, either."

Darby dropped one hand on the rubbing table and vaulted it, starting for Fats. The gambler's face turned white and he jumped back.

"Take him, boys!" he yelled, his voice thin with fear. "Get him, *quick!*"

The bigger of the two men lunged to stop Darby, and McGraw uncorked a right hand that clipped him on the chin and knocked him against the wall with a thud. Then he leaped for Fats. But he had taken scarcely a step before something smashed down on his skull from behind. Great lights exploded in his brain and his knees turned to rubber.

He started to fall, but blind instinct forced stiffness into his legs, and he turned. Another blow hit him. He lashed out with his left, then his right, but suddenly Fats had sprung on his back, pinioning his arms. What happened after that, he never knew.

His face felt wet and he struggled to get up, but somebody was holding him. "Just relax, son. Everything will be all right." The voice was gentle, and he opened his eyes to see Dan Faherty on his knees beside him. "Lie still, kid. You've taken quite a beating," Faherty said. "Who was it?"

"Fats Lakey and two other guys. Big guys. They had blackjacks. I hit one of 'em, but then Fats jumped on me and held my arms. I'll kill him for that!"

"No you won't. Forget it," Faherty said quietly. "We'll take care of them later."

A week later he was in Mary McFadden's gym, taking light exercise. Fats had been right in one thing. McDonald the promoter wanted him against Mink Delano in a semi-final. A warrant had been sworn out against Fats, but he seemed to be nowhere around. Beano, with a knot on his skull from where he, too, had been sapped, was working with Darby.

The gym at the McFadden Training Farm was a vastly different place from the dingy interior of the gym in the city. Higherman's was old, the equipment worn, and fighters crowded the floors. This place was bright, the air was clean, and there were new bags, jump ropes, and strange exercise equipment that had come all the way from Germany.

In the week of light work before he moved on to heavier boxing, Dan Faherty worked with him every day, showing him new tricks and polishing his punching, his blocking, and his footwork.

"Balance is the main thing, Darby," the

older man advised. "Keep your weight balanced so you can move in any direction, and always be in position to punch. Footwork doesn't mean a lot of dancing around. A good fighter never makes an unnecessary movement. He saves himself. There's nothing fancy about scientific boxing. It's simply a hard, cold-blooded system, moving the fastest and easiest way, punching to get the maximum force with minimum effort.

"There's no such thing as a fighter born with know-how. He has to be a born fighter in that he has to have the heart and the innate love of the game. Then there is always a long process of schooling and training. Dempsey was just a big, husky kid with a right hand until Kearns got him and taught him how to use a left hook, and DeForest helped sharpen him up. Joe Louis would still be working in an automobile plant in Detroit if Jack Blackburn hadn't spent long months of work with him."

Darby McGraw skipped rope, shadowboxed, punched the light and heavy bags, and worked in the gym with big men and small men. He learned how to slip and ride punches, learned how to feint properly, how to make openings, and how to time his punches correctly.

"That Fats," Beano told him one night, "he's a bad one. A boy I know told me Fats is tied in with Art Renke."

"Renke?" Faherty had overheard the remark. "That's bad. Renke is one of the biggest and crookedest gamblers around, and he has a hand in several rackets."

The arena was full when Darby crawled through the ropes for his fight with Mink Delano. Since beating him, Mink had gone on to win five straight fights, two of them by knockouts. He had beaten Marshall Collins and Sandy Crocker, two tough middleweights who were ranked among the best in the area.

The bell sounded and Darby went out fast. He tried a wild right, and Mink stabbed with the left. But Darby had been ready for that and he rolled under the left and smashed a punch to the body. Then he worked in, jabbed a left and crossed a short right. Mink backed up and looked him over. The first round was fast, clean, and even.

The second was the same, except that

Mink Delano forged ahead. He won the round with a flurry of punches in the final fifteen seconds. The third found Mink moving fast, his left going all the time. He won that round and the fourth.

Dan Faherty and Beano were in Darby's corner. Dan smiled as McGraw sat down. He leaned into the fighter.

"Take him this round," he said quietly. "Go out there and get him. You've let him pile up a lead, get confident. Now the fun's over. Go get him!"

When the bell sounded, Delano came out briskly confident. He jabbed a left, but suddenly Darby exploded into action. He went under the left and slammed a savage right to the ribs that made the other fighter back up suddenly, but McGraw never let him get set. He hooked his left hard to the body, and then threw a one-two for the head, moving in all the time.

Delano staggered and attempted to clinch, then whipped out of it and smashed a wicked right to Darby's jaw. It hurt, and Darby moved in, started to clinch, then tore loose and smashed both fists to the body. He stabbed Delano with a left, and then they exchanged lefts. Fighting viciously, they drove back and forth across the ring.

Mink straightened up and started a jab. Anxious, Darby sprang in, smashing two ripping hooks to the body, then lifting the left to the chin. Delano staggered and fell back into the ropes, but Darby was set for him and stopped the spring with a stiff left that flattened Mink's nose into a blob of blood. Delano sidestepped and tried to get away, but Darby was after him. He stabbed a left, another left, then feinted and drilled his right all the way down the groove.

Mink tried to step inside of it, but took the steaming punch flush on the point of the chin. He hit the floor flat on his face.

Faherty was gathering up Darby's gear when he looked up. "Fats surrendered to the police," he said. "I don't get it. If the assault can be proved, he'll get a stiff sentence."

"There's me and Beano," Darby said. "We can prove it. Even if he has three witnesses. Nobody can deny I got beat up. I've got the doctor's report."

"Uh-huh." But Faherty was worried, and Darby could see it.

. . .

He was even more worried at workout time the next day. "You seen Beano?" he asked.

"No. Ain't he here?" Darby pulled on his light punching-bag mitts. "I saw him last night after the fights. He went down to Central Avenue, I think."

"He hasn't come back." Faherty shrugged. "He's probably got a girl down there. He'll be back.

"There's something else," he went on. "I've got you a fight, if you want it. Or rather, Mary got it. A main event with Benny Barros."

"Barros?" Darby was surprised. "He's pretty good, isn't he?"

"Uh-huh. He is good. But you've improved, Darby. You're getting to be almost as good as you thought you were in the beginning."

McGraw grinned, running his fingers through his thick hair. "Well," he said, "that big spar-boy, Tony Duretti, was hitting me with a left today, so I guess I can get better. When do I fight him?"

"Not for two months," Faherty advised. "In the meantime, we're taking a trip. You're fighting in Toledo, Detroit, Cleveland, and

Chicago. Once every ten days, then train for Barros."

"Gosh." Darby grinned. "Looks like I'm on my way, doesn't it?" He sobered suddenly. "I wish Beano would get back."

Two days later when the plane took off for Toledo, Beano Brown was still among the missing. In Toledo, Darby McGraw, brown as an Indian, his shoulders even bigger than they had been, and weighing one fifty-seven, knocked out Gunner Smith in one round. In Detroit he stopped Sammy White in three and flew on to Cleveland, where he beat Sam Ratner. Ratner was on the floor four times, but lasted the fight out by clinching and running. The tour ended in Chicago with a one-round kayo over Stob Williams.

The morning after their return to the coast, Darby rolled out of bed and dug his feet into his slippers. He shrugged into his robe and walked into the bathroom. There was a hint of a blue mouse over his right eye, and a red abrasion on his cheekbone. Other than that, he had never felt better in his life.

When he had bathed and shaved, he walked outside to the drive that ended at the main house. Mary's car was parked under a big tree, where she had left it the night before. She'd been strangely quiet all the way home from the airport. It was unusual for her to be quiet after one of his fights, but he had said nothing.

The sun was warm and it felt good. He walked across the yard, dappled with shadow and sunlight, toward the car. He dropped his hand on the wheel, the wheel Mary had been handling the night before, and stood there, thinking of her. Then he noticed the paper. He picked it up, idly curious if there was anything in the sport sheet about his fight with Williams.

He stiffened sharply.

FIGHTER DIES IN AUTO ACCIDENT

Beano Brown, former lightweight prize-fighter, was found dead this morning in the wreck of a car on the Ridge Route. Brown, apparently driving back to Los Angeles, evidently missed a turn and crashed into a canyon. He had been dead for several days when found.

"No," Darby whispered hoarsely. "No!"

The screen door slammed, but he did not notice, staring blindly at the paper. He had known Beano only a short time, but the Negro had been quiet, unconcerned, yet caring. In the past few weeks he had come to think of the man as his best friend. Now he was dead.

"Oh, you found it!" Mary exclaimed. She had come up behind him with Dan Faherty. "Oh, Darby, I'm so sorry! He was such a fine man!"

"Yeah," Darby replied dully, "he sure was. He didn't have a car, either. He didn't have any car at all. He wouldn't go driving out of town because he couldn't drive!"

"He couldn't?" Dan Faherty demanded. "Are you sure?"

"Of course I'm sure. You can ask Smoke Dobbins, his friend. Smoke offered him the use of his car one day, and Beano told him he couldn't drive."

Faherty looked worried. "Without him, it's only your unsupported word against Fats Lakey and his two pals that you were beat up. We'll never make it stick."

"But a killing?" Mary protested. "Surely they wouldn't kill a man just to keep him from giving evidence in a case like that!"

"I wouldn't think so," Dan agreed, "but after all, they could get five years for assault, or better. And Fats wouldn't have had any trouble getting someone to help him with the job, since he's Renke's brother-in-law."

"He is?" Darby scowled. He hadn't known that. He did know that Fats was vicious. He suddenly recalled things he had heard Fats brag about, thoughts he had considered just foolish talk at the time. Now he wasn't so sure.

"Renke manages Benny Barros," Dan said suddenly. "They'll be out to get you this time."

"It still doesn't seem right," McGraw persisted. "Not that they'd kill him. Beano was peculiar, though. He kept his mouth shut. Maybe there was something else he knew about Fats or Renke?"

IV

Smoke Dobbins was six-feet-four in his sock feet and weighed one hundred fifty pounds. He was lean and stooped, a sad-faced Negro who never looked so sad as when beating some luckless optimist who tried to play him at pool or craps. Darby McGraw, wearing a gray herringbone suit and a dark blue tie, found Smoke at the Elite Bar and Pool Room.

"You know me?" he asked.

Smoke eyed him thoughtfully, warily. "I reckon I do," he said at length. "You're Darby McGraw, the middleweight."

"That's right. Beano Brown was my trainer."

"He was?" Dobbins looked unhappier than ever. He shook out a cigarette and lit it thoughtfully.

"I liked Beano," Darby said. "He was my friend. I think he was murdered." He drew a long breath. "I think he knew something. To be more specific, I think he knew something about Renke or Fats Lakey."

"Could be." Smoke looked at his cigarette. "Ain't no good for you to be seen talkin' to me," he added. "Plenty of bad niggers around here, most of 'em workin' for Renke. They'll tell him."

"I don't care," Darby snapped. "Beano was my friend."

Smoke threw him a sidelong glance. "He was just a colored man, white boy. Just another nigger!" The man's voice took on a bitter tone.

"He was my friend," Darby persisted stubbornly. "If you know anything, tell me. If you're afraid, forget it."

"Afraid?" Smoke looked at his shoes. "I reckon that's just what I am. That Renke, he's a mighty bad man to trifle with. But," he added, "Beano was my friend, too."

Smoke looked up and met the fighter's eyes then. "Me, I don't rightly know from nothin', but I got an idea. You ever hear of Villa Lopez?"

"You mean the bantamweight? The one who died after his fight with Bobby Bland?"

"That's right. That's the one. Well . . ." Smoke took his hat off and scratched his head without looking at Darby. "Beano, he was in Villa's corner that night. Mugsy Stern was there, too. Mugsy was one of Renke's boys. At least, he has been ever since.

"Lots of people thought it mighty funny the way Villa died. He lost on a knockout, but he wouldn't take no dive. He got weak in the third round and Bobby knocked him out. Villa went back to his corner and died."

"You think Beano knew something?" Darby demanded. He was keeping an eye on a big Negro across the street. The Negro was talking to a white man who looked much like one of those with Fats that night when he got beat up.

"You fightin' Benny Barros, ain't you? What if somethin' happen to you? What if Beano was afraid somethin' goin' to happen to you? Somethin' like happened to Villa? Maybe if he thought that, he told Renke if anything funny happened, he would tell what he knew."

"The police? Go to the police, you mean?"

"No, not to the police." Smoke smiled. "Renke, he's got money with the police, but Villa, he had six brothers. A couple of them have been with the White Fence Gang. They good with knives. Good to stay away from. Even Renke is afraid of the Lopez brothers. If they thought, even a little thought, that something was smelling in that fight, there would be trouble for Renke."

"Where are they?" Darby demanded. "Where could I find them?"

"Don't you go talkin'," Smoke said seriously. "You talk an' you sure goin' to start a full-sized war. Those Lopez brothers, they are from East L.A. and down to San Pedro. Two of them are fishermen."

Darby McGraw walked down to the car stop when he left Smoke. When he glanced around, the tall colored man was gone. Then he saw two men walking toward him through the gathering dusk. The big Negro and the white man who had been with Fats. The man's name was Griggs. Darby stood very still, his thumbs hooked in his belt. He looked from one to the other. He was going to have to be careful of his hands, the fight was only three days off. There was no sign of the streetcar.

He waited and saw the space between the two men widening. They were going to take him. They were spreading out to get him from both sides.

"What you askin' that dinge?" Griggs demanded. "What you talkin' to that Dobbins for?"

"Takin' a collection for some flowers for Beano," Darby said. "You want to put some in?"

"I don't believe it," Griggs said. "I think you need a lesson. I thought you'd learned before, but I guess you didn't."

They were getting close now, and Darby could see the gleam of a knife in the Negro's hand, held low down at his side. He stepped away from them, stepping back off the curb. It put Griggs almost in front of him, the big Negro on his extreme left. Griggs took the bait and stepped off the high curb to follow Darby.

Instantly, Darby McGraw sprang, and involuntarily, Griggs tried to step back and tripped over the curb. He hit the walk in a sitting position, and Darby swung his right foot and kicked him full on the chin. Griggs's head went back like his neck was broken and he slumped over on the ground.

Quick as a cat, Darby wheeled. "Come on!" he said. "I'll make you eat that knife!"

"Uh-uh," Smoke Dobbins grunted, materializing from behind a signboard. He held the biggest pistol Darby had ever seen. "You don't take no chances with your hands. I'll tend to this boy. I'll handle him."

The big Negro's face paled as Smoke walked toward him. "You drop that frog sticker!" Smoke said. "Drop it or I'll bore a hole clear through you!"

The knife rattled on the walk. "You get goin', Darby," Smoke said. "I'm all right. I got two more boys comin'. We'll put these two in a freight car, and if they get out before they get to Pittsburgh, my name ain't Smoke Dobbins."

McGraw hesitated, and then as the street-car rolled up, he swung aboard. He did not look back. It was the first time in his life he had ever kicked a man. But Griggs had once slugged him with a blackjack from behind, and they had intended to cut him up this time.

Faherty held a watch on him next day. "You look good," he told Darby. "Just shorten that right a little more." He threw the towel around Darby's neck. "There's a lot of Barros money showing up. Mary's worried."

"She needn't be," Darby said quietly. "I want this boy and bad!"

"He's good," Dan told him, "he's three times the man Delano was. He knocked out Ratner. He stopped Augie Gordon, too. He's probably the best middleweight on the coast."

"All right, so he's good. Maybe I'm better."

Dan grinned. "Maybe you are," he said. "Maybe you are, at that!"

Beano Brown had lived in a cheap rooming house near Central Avenue. Darby knew where it was, and he had a hunch. Beano had always been secretive about his personal affairs, but he had told Darby one thing. He kept a diary.

The night before the fight, Darby borrowed Dan's car for a drive. He didn't say why, but he knew where he wanted to go.

It was a shabby frame addition built on the rear of an old red brick building. He had been there once many months ago. A man named Chigger Gamble had lived there with Beano. Chigger was a fry cook in a restaurant on Pico. He was a big, very fat Negro who was always perspiring profusely. If there was a diary, Chigger would know.

Darby parked the car two blocks away near an alley and walked along the dimly lighted street toward the side door of the building. If Beano had been murdered, Darby McGraw was going to see that somebody paid the price of that murder.

In his young life, Darby had learned the virtue of loyalty. Beano had given it to him, and if he was right, and if Smoke was right, Beano had died trying to protect him. In warning Renke away from him, Beano had possibly betrayed the fact that he knew the story behind the death of Villa Lopez. If that theory was correct, and Darby could think of no reason to doubt it, and if Renke had bet a lot of money and Villa had refused to go in the tank, Renke would not hesitate to dope him. Either the dope had killed him or left him so weakened that Bland's punches had finished him off.

Mugsy might have handled the dope in the corner, and somehow Beano had guessed it. Now Beano had died, and Darby meant to get the evidence if there was any.

The street was dark and the narrow sidewalk was rough and uneven. It ran along a high board fence for a ways. Behind the fence he could see the rooming house. There was a little dry grass growing between the sidewalk and the fence. Darby glanced right and left, then grabbed the top of the fence and pulled himself over. He was guessing that if Renke and Fats had not already found Beano's place, they would be hunting it. They might even be watching it.

The back door opened under his hand and he stepped into a dank, ill-smelling hallway. Beano and Chigger had lived on the second floor. He went up the back stairs and walked along the dimly lit hall to the door of number twelve.

He tapped lightly, but there was no response. He tapped again. After waiting for a moment, he dropped his hand to the knob and opened the door. He stepped quickly inside, then switched on a fountain-pen type flashlight.

The small circle of light fell on the dead, staring eyes of Chigger Gamble!

Quickly, Darby McGraw turned and felt for the light switch. The lights snapped on.

The room was a shambles of strewn clothing. Darby touched Chigger's shoulder. The man was still warm. Darby felt for his pulse. It was still, dead. He started to turn for the door to get help when he remembered the diary.

Yet, when he glanced around the room, he despaired of finding it here. Every conceivable place seemed to have been searched. A trunk marked with Beano's name stood open, and in the bottom of it was an open cigar box. Just such a place as the diary might have been kept. Darby switched off the light and went out the door.

A shadowy figure flitted from another doorway nearby and started down the hall on swift feet. "Hold it!" Darby called. "Wait a minute!"

But the man didn't wait, charging down the stairs as fast as he could run, with Darby right after him. They wheeled at the landing and the man went out the same door Darby had come in.

The fighter lunged after him and was just in time to see the man throwing himself over the fence. Darby took the fence with a lunge and went after him. He could see a car parked in the shadows near a trestle. He lunged toward the man as he fought to get the door unlocked.

It was Griggs, and the man grabbed wildly at his hip. Darby dropped one hand to Griggs's right wrist and slugged him in the stomach with the other. He slugged him three times, short, wicked blows, then twisted the right hand away and jerked out the gun, hurling it far out over the tracks. Then he smashed Griggs's nose with a left and clipped him with a chopping right to the head.

The big man went down, and Darby bent over him.

In his pocket was a flat, thick book. On the flyleaf it said, BEANO BROWN, 1949.

Darby turned and walked swiftly back to Dan's car. He was almost there when he saw the other car parked behind it. Suddenly he wished he had kept the gun.

But when the door of the second car opened, a girl stepped out and ran toward him. It was Mary.

"Oh, Darby!" she cried. "Are you all right?"

"Sure. Sure, I'm all right," he said. "How'd you get here?"

"I followed you," she said, "but I didn't see you leave the car and didn't see which house you went into. Then I saw the man come over the fence, but I couldn't tell who was after him. I waited."

"Let's go," he said, "we'd better get out of here fast."

They stopped in an all-night restaurant. "I got it," he said. "Beano Brown's diary. If he knew anything about the Lopez fight, it'll be in here."

The waiter stopped by their table, putting down two glasses of water. He was thin and dark. He looked at Darby, then at the book in his hand.

"What do you want, Mary?" McGraw asked.

"Coffee," she said. "Just coffee."

He opened the diary and started glancing down the pages while Mary looked over his shoulder. Suddenly, she squeezed his arm.

"Darby, that waiter's on the telephone!" she whispered excitedly. "I think he's talking about us!"

Darby looked up hastily. "Why should he? What does he know? Unless . . . unless Renke owns this joint. No, that's too much of a coincidence to figure we've hit one of Renke's places by accident."

"Not one of his places, Darby, but Renke's boss of the numbers racket here. All these places handle the slips. All of them have contact with Art Renke. And he pays off for favors."

"Finish your coffee," Darby said. "We'll save the diary."

They started to get up, and the thin, dark man came around the counter very fast. "Want some more coffee? Sure, have some . . . on the house."

"No," Mary said, "not now."

"Come on" the waiter said, smiling, "it's a cold night."

"The lady said no," Darby told him sharply, then turned to Mary. "Let's get out of here!"

They got into their cars and started them fast, but not fast enough. Just as Mary started to swing her car out from the curb, an old coupe with a bright metallic paint job wheeled around the corner and angled across in front of it. Two men got out and started toward her.

V

Darby left his car door hanging and started back, slipping on a pair of skintight gloves. Both men were small and swarthy, and both were dressed in flashy clothes. They looked at the girl and then at him. One of them had a gun.

"You gotta book, *señor*? You give it to me, yes?"

"No," Darby said.

"You better," the man replied harshly. "Hurry up quick now, or I'll shoot!"

The fighter hesitated, his jaw set stubbornly. This time there was Mary to think of. "If we give it to you, do we both go?"

"Si. Yes, of course. You give it up and you go."

Without a word, Darby handed over the

diary. The two men turned instantly and got in their own car.

"Well," Mary said, "that's that. We had it and now we don't have it. Art Renke is just as much in the clear as ever."

Darby was led through the crowd toward the ring. The place was packed and smoke hung in the air around the suspended lights. Coming through the stands, Darby and his second skirted a group of men and ran face-to-face with Fats Lakey. Fats grinned evilly; sweat ran down his neck. He wagged his finger. "Next fight, country boy . . . next time you fight you're gonna make me some money." He laughed and dodged back into the crowd. Darby knew what that meant. They would try to make him take a dive. His jaw tightened.

Darby tried to clear his mind. That was in the future, maybe. Tonight was what he had to worry about now.

Benny Barros was shorter than Darby McGraw by three inches. He was almost that much wider. He was certainly more than three inches thicker through the chest.

He was a puncher and built like one. Portuguese, and flat-faced, with a thick, heavy chest and powerful arms. He came into the ring wearing red silk trunks, and he didn't smile. He never smiled. When they came together in the center of the ring, he kept his eyes on the canvas, and then he walked back to his corner and they slipped off his robe, revealing the dark brown and powerful muscles of his torso. He looked then, with his flat, rattlesnake's eyes, at Darby McGraw. Just one look, and then the bell sounded.

Barros came out fast. He came out with his gloves cocked for hooking, and he moved right straight in. Darby's left was a streak that stabbed empty air over Benny's shoulder. Benny's right glove smashed into McGraw's midsection and Darby turned away, hooking a left to the head.

Both men were fast. Darby felt the sharpness of Barros's punches and knew he was in for a rough evening. He jabbed, then hooked a solid blow to the head, and Benny blinked. His face seemed to turn a shade darker and his lips flattened over his mouthpiece.

Between rounds Dan Faherty worked

over Darby. "Renke's here," he said. "So is Fats."

"I know. I wish I had that diary, though," Darby said. "We'd have them both in jail before the night is over."

The bell sounded for the second round and he walked out. Again Barros came in fast. He feinted and threw a high right that caught Darby on the chin. Darby took a quick step back and sat down. The crowd came to its feet with a roar and Darby shook his head, fighting his way to one knee. The suddenness of it startled him and he was badly shaken.

He got up at seven and saw Barros coming in fast, but Darby stabbed a left into Benny's mouth that started a trickle of blood. However, the punch failed to stop him. He got to Darby with both hands, blasting a right to the head and then digging a left into his midsection just above the belt band on his trunks. Darby jabbed a left and clipped Barros with a solid right to the head.

Darby stepped away and circled warily, then, as Barros moved in, he stabbed a left to the face and hooked sharply with the same left. Barros ducked under it and came in, slamming away at his body with both hands. Barros's body was glistening with sweat and his flat, hard face was taut and brutal under the bright glare of the light. A thin trickle of blood still came from the flat-lipped mouth, and Barros slipped another left and got home a right to Darby's stomach that jerked a gasp from him.

But Darby stepped in, punching with both hands, and suddenly Benny's eyes blazed with fury and triumph. Nobody had ever slugged with Benny Barros and walked away under his own power. The two lunged together and, toe-to-toe, began to slug it out. Darby spread his feet and walked in, throwing them with both hands, his heart burning with the fury of the battle, his mind firing on the smashing power of his fists.

He dropped a right to Benny's jaw that staggered the shorter man and made him blink, then he took a wicked left to the head that brought a hot, smoky taste into his mouth, and the sweat poured down over his body. The bell clanged, and clanged again and again before they got them apart.

Benny trotted back to his corner and stood there, refusing to sit down while he drew in great gulps of air. The crowd was still roaring when the bell for the third round sounded and both men rushed out, coming together in mid-ring with a crash of blows. Darby stabbed a wicked left to the head that started the blood from Benny's eye, and Barros ducked, weaved, and bobbed, hooking with both hands. Benny moved in with a right that jolted Darby to his heels. McGraw backed away, shaken, and Benny lunged after him, punching away with both hands.

Darby crumpled under the attack and hit the canvas, but then rolled over and came up without a count, and as Barros charged in for the kill, Darby straightened and drilled a right down the groove that put the Portuguese back on his heels. Lunging after him, Darby swung a wide left that connected and dropped Barros.

Barros took a count of four, then came up and bored in, landing a left to the body and stopping a left with his chin. The bell sounded and both men ran back to their corners. The crowd was a dull roar of sound, and Darby was so alive and burning with the fierce love of combat that he could scarcely sit down. He glanced out over the crowd once and saw two thin, dark men sitting behind Renke, and one of them was leaning over, speaking to him.

Then, as the bell rang, he realized one of the men was the man who had taken the diary. He knew he was lagging, and he lunged to his feet and sidestepped out of the corner to beat Barros's rush, but Benny was after him, hooking with both hands. Darby felt blood starting again from the cut over the eye that Faherty had repaired between rounds, and he backed up, putting up a hand as though to wipe it away. Instantly, Barros leaped in, and that left hand Darby had lifted dropped suddenly in a chopping blow that laid Benny's brow open just over the right eye. Barros staggered, then, with an almost animal-like growl of fury, he lunged in close and one of his hooks stabbed Darby in the vitals like a knife.

He stabbed with a left that missed, then hit Darby with a wicked right hook, and Darby felt as if he had been slugged behind the knees with a ball bat. He went down with lights exploding in his brain like the splitting of atoms somewhere over the crowd. And then he was coming up from the canvas, feeling the bite of resin in his nostrils.

The dull roar that was like the sound of a

far-off sea was the crowd, and he lunged to his feet and saw the brown, brutal shadow of Barros looming near. He struck out with a blind instinct and felt his fist hit something solid. Moving in, he hit by feel, and felt his left sink deep into Barros's tough, elastic body. He swung three times at the air before the referee grabbed him and shoved him toward a corner so that he could begin the count.

Darby got the fog out of his brain as Benny Barros struggled up at the count of nine. McGraw saw the brown man weaving before him and started down the ring toward him. The Portuguese lunged in, throwing both hands, and Darby lifted him to his tiptoes with a ripping right uppercut, then caught him with a sweeping left hook as his heels hit the canvas. Barros stumbled backward and Darby stepped in, set himself, and fired his right—the money punch—just like in the old days when he didn't know any better. Except now it was perfectly timed and he had the perfect opening. Barros went over backward, both feet straight out. He hit on his shoulder blades, rolled over on his face, and lay still.

The referee took a look, then touched him with a hand, and walking over, lifted Darby McGraw's right hand. Darby wobbled to the ropes and stood there hanging on and looking.

There was a wild turmoil at the ringside that suddenly thinned out, and he could see men in uniforms gathered around. Then Dan was leading him to his corner and Darby shook the fog out of his brain.

"What happened?" he demanded, staring at the knot of policemen. Over the noise of the crowd he could hear a siren whine to a stop out on the street.

Then one of the policemen stepped aside, and he saw Art Renke sitting with his head fallen back and the haft of a knife thrust upward from the hollow of his collarbone. Beside him, Fats Lakey was white and trembling, and there was blood all down his face from a slash across the cheek.

Mary was up in his corner. "Come on! Let's get you out of here!" Darby gathered his robe around him and she led him, his knees weak and uncooperative, back to the dressing room.

Darby was just getting his focus back when Dan came bursting through the door.

"It was the White Fence that got Renke," he said, "at least that's what the police think."

"The man in the cafe!" Mary gasped. "He must have been a friend of the Lopez brothers and called them!"

"Art Renke's dead," Dan said. "They just slashed Fats for luck. I'd heard they'd been suspicious, and when Beano was killed, it probably made them more so. Smoke may have told them something, too."

Darby McGraw let Dan unlace his gloves. "Who do I fight next?" he asked.

"You rest for a month now," Dan said. "Maybe more. Then we'll see."

"Okay," Darby said, smiling, "you're the boss." He looked at Mary. "Then we'll have time for a show, won't we? Or several of them?"

She squeezed his still-bandaged hand.

"We will," she promised. "I'll get the car."

He stopped her at the dressing-room door and took her chin in his right hand, tipping her head back.

"Thank you," he said seriously, "I'd thank Beano Brown too, if I could." He kissed her quickly then, and headed for the showers.

BEYOND THE GREAT SNOW MOUNTAINS

When the burial was complete, she rode with her son into the hills.

The Go-log tribesmen, sharing her sorrow for their lost leader, stood aside and allowed her to go. Lok-sha had been a great man and too young to die.

Only in the eyes of Norba and his followers did she detect the triumph born of realization that nothing now stood between him and tribal control. Nothing but a slender woman, alien to their land, and Kulan, her fourteen-year-old son.

There was no time to worry now, nor was there time for grief. If ever they were to escape, it must be at once, for it was unlikely such opportunity would again offer itself.

It had been fifteen years since the plane in which she was leaving China crashed in the mountains near Tosun Nor, killing all on board but herself. Now, as if decreed by fate, another had come, and this one landed intact.

Shambe had brought the news as Lok-sha lay dying, for long ago the far-ranging hunter had promised if ever another plane landed, he would first bring the news to her.

If the fierce Go-log tribesmen learned of the landing, they would kill the survivors and destroy the plane. To enter the land of the Go-log was to die.

It was a far land of high, grass plateaus, snowcapped mountains, and rushing streams. There among the peaks were born three of the greatest rivers of Asia—the Yellow, the Yangtze, and the Mekong—and there the Go-log lived as they had lived since the time of Genghis Khan.

Splendid horsemen and savage fighters, they lived upon their herds of yaks, fat-tailed sheep, horses, and the plunder reaped from caravans bound from China to Tibet.

Anna Doone, born on a ranch in Montana, had taken readily to the hard, nomadic life of the Go-log. She had come to China to join her father, a medical missionary, and her uncle, a noted anthropologist. Both were killed in Kansu by the renegade army that had once belonged to General Ma. Anna, with two friends, attempted an escape in an old plane.

Riding now toward this other aircraft, she recalled the morning when, standing beside her wrecked plane, she had first watched the Go-log approach. She was familiar with their reputation for killing interlopers, but she had a Winchester with a telescopic sight and a .45 caliber Colt revolver.

Despite her fear, she felt a burst of admiration for their superb horsemanship as they raced over the plain. Seeing the rifle ready in her hands, they drew up sharply, and her eyes for the first time looked upon Lok-sha.

Only a little older than her own twenty-one years, he was a tall man with a lean horseman's build, and he laughed with pure enjoyment when she lifted the rifle. She was to remember that laugh for a long time, for the Go-log were normally a somber people.

Lok-sha had the commanding presence of the born leader of men, and she realized at once that if she were to survive, it would be because he wished it.

He spoke sharply in his own tongue, and she replied in the dialect of Kansu, which fortunately he understood.

"It is a fine weapon," he said about the rifle.

"I do not wish to use it against the Go-log. I come as a friend."

"The Go-log have no friends."

A small herd of Tibetan antelope appeared on the crest of a low ridge some three hundred yards away, looking curiously toward the crashed plane.

She had used a rifle since she was a child, killing her first deer when only eleven. Indicating the antelope, she took careful aim and squeezed off her shot. The antelope bounded away, but one went to its knees, then rolled over on its side.

The Go-log shouted with amazement, for accurate shooting with their old rifles was impossible at that range. Two of the riders charged off to recover the game, and she looked into the eyes of the tall rider.

"I have another such rifle, and if we are friends, it is yours."

"I could kill you and take them both."

She returned his look. "*They*," she said, indicating the others, "might take it from me. You would not, for you are a man of honor, and I would kill you even as they killed me."

She had no doubt of her position, and her chance of ever leaving this place was remote. Whatever was done, she must do herself.

He gestured toward the wreck. "Get what you wish, and come with us."

Her shooting had impressed them, and now her riding did also, for these were men who lived by riding and shooting. Lok-sha, a *jyabo* or king of the Go-log people, did not kill her. Escape being impossible, she married him in a Buddhist ceremony, and then to satisfy some Puritan strain within her, she persuaded Tsan-Po, the lama, to read over them in Kansu dialect the Christian ceremony.

Fortunately, the plane had not burned, and from it she brought ammunition for the rifles, field glasses, clothing, medicines, and her father's instrument case. Best of all, she brought the books that had belonged to her father and uncle.

Having often assisted her father, she understood the emergency treatment of wounds and rough surgery. This knowledge became a valuable asset and solidified her position in the community.

As soon as Anna's son was born, she realized the time would come when, if they were not rescued, he would become *jyabo*, so she began a careful record of migration dates, grass conditions, and rainfall. If it was in her power, she was going to give him the knowledge to be the best leader possible.

Lok-sha was sharply interested in all she knew about the Chinese to the east, and he possessed the imagination to translate the lessons of history into the practical business of command and statecraft. The end had come when his horse, caught on a severe, rocky slope, had fallen, crushing Lok-sha's chest.

She had been happy in the years she'd spent as his wife, certainly she was better off than she would have been as a refugee in the civil war that gripped much of China or as a prisoner of the Japanese. But as happy as she had learned to be, as safe as she had finally found herself, Anna never forgot her home, nor ceased to long for the day when she might return.

Now, her thoughts were interrupted by

Shambe's appearance. "The plane is nearby," he said, "and there are two men."

Shambe was not only Lok-sha's best friend, but leader of the Ku-ts'a, the bodyguard of the *jyabo*, a carefully selected band of fighting men.

They rode now, side by side, Kulan, Shambe, and herself. "You will leave with the flying men?" Shambe asked. "And you will take the *jyabo* also?"

Startled, Anna Doone glanced at her son, riding quietly beside her. Of course . . . what had she been thinking of? Her son, Kulan, was *jyabo* now . . . king of six thousand tents, commander of approximately two thousand of the most dangerous fighting men in Asia!

But it was ridiculous. He was only fourteen. He should be in school, thinking about football or baseball. Yet fourteen among the Go-log was not fourteen among her own people. Lok-sha, against her bitter protests, had carried Kulan into battle when he was but six years old, and during long rides over the grasslands had taught him what he could of the arts of war and leadership.

Her son *jyabo*? She wished to see him a

doctor, a scientist, a teacher. It was prepos-
terous to think of him as king of a savage
people in a remote land. Yet deep within her
something asked a question: *How important
would baseball be to a boy accustomed to
riding a hundred miles from dawn to dusk,
or hunting bighorn sheep among the highest
peaks?*

"We shall regret your going," Shambe said
sincerely, "you have been long among us."

And she would regret losing him, too, for
he had been a true friend. She said as
much, said it quietly and with sincerity.

When she heard of the plane, her thoughts
had leaped ahead, anticipating their home-
coming. She had taken notes of her experiences and could write a book, and she
could lecture. Kulan was tall and strong and
could receive the education and opportuni-
ties that he had missed.

Yet she had sensed the reproof in
Shambe's tone; Shambe, who had been her
husband's supporter in his troubles with
Norba and chief of a minor division of the
Khang-sar Go-log.

Over their heads the sky was fiercely
blue, their horses' hooves drummed upon
the hard, close-cropped turf . . . there were

few clouds. Yes . . . these rides would be remembered. Nowhere were there mountains like these, nowhere such skies.

When they came within sight of the plane, the two men sprang to their feet, gripping their rifles.

She drew up. "I am Anna Doone, and this is Kulan, my son."

The older man strode toward her. "This is amazing! The State Department has been trying to locate you and your family for years! You are the niece of Dr. Ralph Doone, are you not?"

"I am."

"My name is Schwarzkopf. Your uncle and I were associated during his work at the Merv Oasis." He glanced at Shambe, and then at Kulan. "Your son, you said?"

She explained the crashed plane, her marriage to Lok-sha, his death, and her wish to escape. In turn, they told her of how they had seized the plane and escaped from the Communist soldiers. Their landing had been made with the last of their fuel.

"If there was fuel, would you take us with you?"

"Take you? But of course!" Schwarzkopf's eyes danced with excitement that belied his sixty-odd years. "What an opportunity! Married to a Go-log chieftain! So little is known of them, you understand! Their customs, their beliefs . . . we must arrange a grant. I know just the people who—"

"If it's all the same to you, Doc," his companion interrupted, "I'd like to get out of here." He looked up at Anna Doone. "I'm sorry, ma'am, but you mentioned fuel. Is there some gas around here somewhere?"

"Several months ago my husband took a convoy bound for an airfield in Tibet. He captured several trucks loaded with gasoline. They are hidden only a few miles away." She paused. "I can drive a truck."

Yet, first she must return to the Go-log encampment to meet with the elders and the fighting men of the Khang-sar. Kulan, as *jyabo*, must be present. It would be improper and even dangerous if she were not present also, for a decision was to be made on the move to new grazing grounds, and there might also be some question as to leadership.

The time had come for the Khang-sar to return to their home in the Yur-tse Mountains, and the thought brought a pang, for these were the loveliest of mountains, splendid forests and lakes in a limestone range near the head of the Yellow River.

"Whatever you do," she warned, "you must not leave the vicinity of the plane. Start no fires, and let no metal flash in the sun. When our meeting is over, Shambe will remain near you until Kulan and I can come."

She swung her horse around. "If you are found, neither Kulan nor I could protect you."

"Kulan?" The younger man looked at the boy in surprise.

Kulan sat straight in the saddle. "I am now *jyabo*," he replied sternly, "but our people think all outsiders are the enemy."

When they had gone some distance, Kulan sighed and said, "The machine is small. There will be no room for Deba."

She knew how much he loved the horse. "No, Kulan, there will be no room, but you would not wish to take him away. He was bred to this country, and loves it."

"I love it, too," Kulan replied simply.

She started to speak, but the horse herd was before them, and beyond were the felt yurts of the camp. Tsan-Po awaited them before their own tent. With Lok-sha gone, the Khang-sar Go-log would have need of the old man's shrewd advice.

Kulan waved a hand at the encampment. "How would we live in your country?"

"Life is very different there, Kulan, and much easier. You might become a fine scholar and lead a good life."

"If that is what you wish. I shall do my best, for both you and my father have taught me obedience. Only sometimes," his voice tightened, "sometimes I shall think of Deba and these grasslands, and of Amne Machin, the God Mountain."

For the first time she felt doubt, but quickly dismissed it. Of course she was doing the right thing. Once he was adjusted to life in civilization, he would be as happy there. True, he was mature for his years, as boys were apt to be among the Go-log. It was natural that he would miss Deba, and he would miss Shambe, as she would. Shambe had been a second father to him, even as Tsan-Po had been. The old lama had taught Kulan much that was beyond her.

Yet, how long she had dreamed of going home! Of luxuriating in a warm tub, conversing in English for hours on end, and the good, fireside talk of people who were doing things in the larger world of art, science, and scholarship. She longed for a life where she did not have to live with the fear that her son might die from something as silly as a tooth infection or as serious as the bullet from the rifle of a Communist soldier.

She was thirty-six, soon to be thirty-seven, and if she ever wanted a relationship with another man, it could not be here, where she had once been the wife of a king. Nor could she wait for too many years after the rough life on the steppes, a life that had been good to her so far, but was bound to leave her a wind-burned and arthritic old woman.

What Dr. Schwarzkopf had said was true. Her experience was unique. A book might sell . . . she could make a contribution to anthropology, and even to geographical knowledge. As for Kulan, he would do well in America. He was tall and wide-shouldered, and would be a handsome man with his olive skin, his dark, curly hair and truly magnificent dark eyes. There was a touch of the exotic about him that was romantic, and at fourteen he was already stronger than most men.

. . .

As she entered the yurt, she sensed trouble in the air. Shambe was beside her, but when had he not been present when she needed him?

All of the Khang-sar Go-log chieftains were there. Tsemba was the chief of two hundred tents and an important man whose opinion counted for much. Beside him were old Kunza, Gelak, and of course, Norba.

Norba was a towering big man with one muscular shoulder bare, as was the custom, his broad-bladed sword slung in its scabbard between his shoulder blades. His coterie of followers was close around him, confident now that Lok-sha was dead.

Norba had both hated and feared Lok-sha, but had no heart for a fight with the *jyabo*. Yet had Lok-sha left no heir, Norba would have become chief.

The impending shift to new grazing grounds promised trouble. A faction of the Khang-sar led by Norba wished to go to Tosun Nor, but Lok-sha had decided, under the present circumstances, it was better to graze far from the caravan trails and let a season go by without raids. The new sol-

diers from the east were not the undisci-
plined rabble of old. Something was afoot in
China proper, and Lok-sha had thought it
best to gather more information before test-
ing fate. Moreover, there had been rumors
of serious drought around Tosun Nor, and
drought meant losses from the herds.

She seated herself beside Kulan, with
Tsan-Po beside her, and Shambe seated on
the other side of her son. Norba had moved
to take the seat of *jyabo*, but Kulan was
before him. Norba's face flushed angrily
when he saw the boy take the seat where he
wished to sit.

"Move, boy. Go play with the children."

Kulan sat very straight. "Unless it is decided otherwise, I am *jyabo*," he replied.
"Until then, take your place."

For an instant there was utter stillness,
then a mutter from the followers of Norba,
but Kulan ignored them. Glancing at her
son, Anna Doone was astonished. Truly, he
looked every inch the young king. There
was strength in him, of that there would be
no doubt, strength and courage.

Norba hesitated, then reluctantly took a
seat. Anna could see his repressed fury and
knew there was trouble to come. It was well

that they were leaving. The thought of escape from all this sent a little tremor of excitement through her, excitement tinged with relief.

The yurt filled and the air was stifling. Anna studied the faces of the chieftains, but they were expressionless. Would they follow Kulan, or would they demand an older, more experienced leader?

Tsan-Po whispered to her that most of those within the tent were supporters of Norba, and Anna Doone felt inside her coat for the pistol she was never without.

Their very lives might depend on the selection of Kulan as *jyabo*, for if Norba were able to take power, he would at once seek to rid himself of his rival. It would not be without precedence if Norba attempted to kill Kulan here, now. Her hand on her pistol, Anna suddenly knew that if Norba even moved toward her son, she would kill him.

She accepted some tea, drinking from a bowl that had come to Tibet from India in the dower of a princess, more than a thousand years before. In those years, Tibet had controlled most of western China, as well as part of India and Kashmir.

Abruptly, without waiting for the others

to assemble, Norba declared himself. "Tomorrow," he said, "we will move to Tosun Nor to pasture upon the old lands."

There was silence as he looked around the yurt. That silence held for a slow minute, and then Kulan said one word.

"No."

The word was definite, the tone clear, the challenge accepted.

Norba's face flushed with anger, but Kulan spoke before Norba could frame a word.

"There is drought at Tosun Nor. The grass lies yellow and dead, the air is filled with dust. The beds of streams are cracked earth. We must go to the mountains, to the Yur-tse."

Again Norba prepared to speak, but Kulan interrupted. "My father is dead, but I am my father's son. We rode upon the high grass together and he taught me what I must do."

For the first time, he looked at Norba. "You are *deba* of two hundred tents. You may ride with us or go to Tosun Nor. I would advise you to come with us."

Norba looked around at his followers. "We are men, and not to be led by a boy. It is I who shall lead the Khang-sar. When you are of an age to lead," he added slyly, "you may lead."

Tsan-Po spoke. "The boy is his father's son. Leadership falls upon him."

Norba got to his feet. "Enough! I say that I shall lead. I say it, and my men say it."

Kulan arose, and Shambe and Anna arose with him. Anna held her gun in her hand. "The Ku-ts'a stand without," Shambe said, "and they follow Kulan . . . Unless all the chieftains say otherwise."

Norba's lips flattened against his big teeth, and for an instant Anna thought he would strike Kulan despite the fact that the body-guards surrounded the tent. The Ku-ts'a numbered fifty-eight chosen men, the hereditary guard of the *jyabo*. Norba had not expected the Ku-ts'a. With the *jyabo* dead, he had believed they would accept the situation.

He slammed his sword back into its scabbard. "We will go to Tosun Nor," he said. "You are fools."

"Go, if you will," Kulan replied, "and those who survive are welcome to return. Our herds will be fat upon the long grass of the limestone mountains."

With a pang, Anna realized that Kulan was no longer a boy. The discipline had been strict and the training harsh, but he was every inch a king. Yet she was impatient, for their time was short, and if the plane were discovered, the fliers would be killed and they would be condemned to more fruitless, wasted years.

Alone at last, she said to him, "What was all that about the drought at Tosun Nor?"

"It had been rumored, so while you talked to the old man of your people, I asked the other. He spoke of dense clouds of dust high in the heavens, and of sheep and horses lying dead from starvation and thirst."

He paused. "It is well that Norba goes, for when he returns, if he returns, his power will be broken."

He glanced at her slyly, his face warming with a smile. "My mother taught me to listen, to question when in doubt, and to keep my thoughts until the time for speaking."

After Kulan was asleep, she went outside the yurt and stood alone under the stars. There was moonlight upon the snows of the God Mountain, reflected moonlight that seemed born from some inner glory within the mountain itself.

She thought of home, of the quiet college town and the autumn leaves falling. It had been almost twenty years, but tomorrow they would fly over the mountains to India. To a fine hotel, a room of her own, a hot bath, and a real bed . . . it was impossible to imagine such things still existed.

For fifteen years she had been virtually a prisoner. True, Lok-sha had treated her well, and she had been respected among the Go-log, but their ways were strange, and her nights had been given up to dreaming of home.

The thought of Norba returned. If Kulan was gone, he would be in control, and would probably lead the Khang-sar Go-log to disaster. Lok-sha had always said he was a stubborn fool.

No matter. It was now or never. It was impossible that another opportunity would occur, for travel was restricted. No Europeans or Americans would be flying over this country. It was her last chance.

She looked around at the sleeping encampment. She would miss it. Lok-sha, despite their differences of background, had been a superior man. If he had been slow to appreciate her feelings, there had been no cruelty in him.

The icy peak was austere in its bath of moonlight; it was taller than Everest, some said, yet it gave an impression of bulk rather than height. It was no wonder the Go-log called it the God Mountain.

Tsan-Po was walking toward her. "Do you go tomorrow?"

She had ceased to be startled by his awareness of things. "Yes."

"You have been long away . . . does someone await you there?"

"No."

"We will miss you, and we will miss Kulan."

"He goes to a great land. He will do well, I think."

"Here he is a king. Ours is a small king, but even a small king is still a king."

She felt the reproof of his tone, and together they watched the moonlight on Amne Machin. "He will make a strong man," the lama said, "a stronger man and a better leader than Lok-sha."

She was surprised. "Do you really believe that?"

"You have taught him much, and he has character. We Go-log face a trying time, for as the world changes, even we must change.

"Kulan has a sense of the world. You taught him of your land and of Europe, and

I have told him of India, where I worked as a young man. He is schooled in the arts of war and statecraft, and I believe it is in him to be a great leader."

He was silent, then added, "Your country could use a friend here."

"Do you believe I am wrong to take him away?"

"We need him," Tsan-Po replied simply, "and he needs you. For several years yet, he will need you."

The lama turned away. "It is late." He took a step, then paused. "Beware of Norba. You have not finished with him."

When morning dawned, they rode swiftly to the hidden trucks. What Lok-sha planned to do with the trucks, she did not know, but presumably he intended to use them as a trap for Chinese soldiers.

She started the truck with difficulty for the motor was cold. There was no road, but the turf was solid, and she had driven on the prairie during her childhood in Montana. The old Army six-by-six was no problem.

Kulan followed, holding off to one side and leading her horse.

Keeping to low ground and circling to

avoid gullies or patches of rock, she needed all of an hour to reach the plane.

The pilot and Dr. Schwarzkopf rushed to the tailgate and started to unload the cans. As soon as the truck was empty, Anna drove back for a second truck, and by the time she had returned, the cans of the first had been emptied into the tanks of the plane.

Yet they had scarcely begun on the second load when Shambe came down off the ridge where he had been on watch. Kulan, also watching from a quarter of a mile away, wheeled his mount and raced back at a dead run, drawing his rifle from its scabbard.

"Norba comes," Shambe said, "with many men."

Schwarzkopf dropped his jerry can and started for his rifle, but Anna's gesture stopped him. "Finish refueling," she said, and when he hesitated, "Doctor, put that gun down and get busy!"

Kulan swung his pony alongside her as she mounted, and Shambe drew up on the other side. They sat together, awaiting the oncoming riders.

Norba's horse reared as he drew up, a

hard pleasure in his eyes. "So . . . you are traitors. I shall kill you."

Anna Doone's heart pounded heavily, yet she kept all emotion from her face. Her son's life, as well as her own, was at stake.

"These men are our friends. We help them on their way," she said.

"And I shall decide who is and is not a traitor," Kulan added.

From behind them the pilot said, "One more can does it."

Anna's heart lifted. Behind her was the plane that could take her home, the rescue of which she had dreamed for fifteen years. The time was here, the time was now.

The sky beckoned, and beyond the mountains lay India, the threshold to home.

"Go with them, Mother." Kulan's eyes did not turn from Norba. "I cannot, for these are my people."

Her protest found no words. How often had she taught him that kingship was an obligation rather than a glory?

Her eyes swung around the semicircle of savage faces, and then for one brief instant the dream remained, shimmering before her eyes: a warm quiet house, a hot bath, meals prepared from food from a market, life without fear of disease or crippling disfigurement, life without war.

"Dr. Schwarzkopf," she said, "you will leave your rifles and ammunition, they are in short supply here."

"If you are going," Kulan said, "you must go now."

"If these are your people, Kulan, then they are my people also."

The winding caravan of Norba's people appeared, heading north toward Tosun Nor. She should have remembered they would come this way.

Dr. Schwarzkopf brought the weapons and the ammunition. "You will not come with us, then?"

"I can't. This is my son."

"You will die," Norba said. His eyes flickered over the three he hated—the wife of Lok-sha, the leader of the Ku-ts'a, and the boy who stood between him and the kingship.

Norba's rifle started to lift, and Shambe's started up with it, but Kulan put out a hand to stop the movement, then stepped his horse toward Norba and looked into his eyes.

"I am *jyabo*," he said. "I am your king."

For an instant Norba's rifle held still, then slowly it lowered. With an oath, Norba whirled his horse and dashed away, followed by his men.

Behind them the motors broke into a roar, and throwing up a vast cloud of dust, the plane rolled off, gathered speed, then soared up and away, toward India, toward home.

"You should have let me kill him," Shambe said.

"No, Shambe," Kulan replied, "many go to die, but those who remain will remember that I spoke truth."

Three abreast, they rode to the crest of the ridge and halted. The caravan of Norba's followers moved north toward the great lake known as Tosun Nor, moved toward drought and death.

Anna Doone, born in Montana, looked beyond them to a bright fleck that hung in the sky. Sunlight gleamed for an instant on a wing tip . . . then it winked out and was gone, leaving only a distant mutter of engines that echoed against the mountains.

A NOTE ON THE DEDICATION

By Beau L'Amour

Since Louis's death in 1988 there have been no dedications on any of the new L'Amour books. This is as it should be. Louis's work was his to dedicate as he chose. In this one particular instance my family and I have felt it was appropriate to step in and change that policy. John Veitch was our family's great friend and his was one of the closest relationships that Louis, a man who had many acquaintances but few true friendships, ever had. John was the godfather to both my sister and me and was married to my mother's closest and oldest friend.

Just after he passed away, Mom told me that losing him was so hard that she felt it was like losing my father again. . . . I wasn't surprised since she had known him a decade before she met Louis, and John had lived a decade longer. In 1966 Louis dedicated "The Broken Gun" to the recently deceased Alan Ladd and Bill Bendix, Alan's partner in many movie adventures. Alan and Susie Ladd were John Veitch's good friends, almost like adopted parents. He was a member of their household for many years. He married their eldest daughter and in doing so became like a member of our family, too.

John was a production executive and ultimately *the* production executive at Columbia Studios. He was a movie producer and troubleshooter with no peer. To many of us whose lives have touched briefly on the film business (few more briefly than mine) he was a moral compass in a hall of smoke and mirrors.

John was the master of lengthy holiday toasts, a gentle Irish soul and a brave warrior who had left his war far behind him. We have dedicated this book to John and Louis in order to say: Godspeed old friends, we will not see your like again.

AFTERWORD

By Beau L'Amour

Beyond the Great Snow Mountains is the first in a series of four collections that will cover a broad spectrum of my father's work. "The Gravel Pit" and "The Money Punch" recall the late forties and early fifties when Louis had just moved to Los Angeles. Although written in the same period, "Sideshow Champion" and "Under the Hanging Wall" draw on his earlier experiences as a carnival boxer and miner. "Meeting at Falmouth" was an early experiment in the historical genre, when Dad was first attempting to break away from the label of being an author of westerns.

Both "By the Waters of San Tadeo" and "Beyond the Great Snow Mountains" are stories that either drew from Louis's mysterious travels in South America and China or sprang from his encyclopedialike knowledge of geography and obscure cultures. "Coast Patrol" may also be included in this last group and raises the added question of the character of Turk Madden. As represented in several of Louis L'Amour's early adventure stories, Turk is a fictional character. Some of the inspiration for Louis's writing about this tramp pilot was Jimmy Angel, the bush pilot for whom Venezuela's Angel Falls are named. But Dad claimed to have known an adventurer named Turk Madden in the Far East, and if this is true, then Turk is one of the few times when Dad gave a fictional character the name of one of his friends.

Work on the Louis L'Amour biography continues at its maddeningly slow pace. Information drifts in, sometimes proving, sometimes disproving, stories Louis told or ideas that I have had about what happened at certain times.

I want to extend my thanks to all the people who have written in with information for the book, and I want to apologize in advance because I will no longer be able to answer all of the wonderful fan mail that has come to me through the Biography Project's P.O. box. My staff and I are swamped with research and simply cannot keep up with all the nonbiography fan letters that keep coming in. We have decided that from now on *we can respond only to those of you who write in about a subject that directly pertains to the biography itself.* I regret this, I appreciate everyone's interest, but I'm not making enough progress on the story of my father's life and I must focus on only the things that help me get that into print.

The next book (which will be out in spring of 2000) will be *The Cross and the Candle.* It will contain the same eclectic mixture of stories as this collection. However, there will be a few that are like those stories in the *Yondering* collection, tales drawn from Louis's life or the lives of people that he knew. There will still be a few more westerns, more crime, and more sports stories to come.

Below are the names of the people whom I would like to contact. If you find your name on the list, I would be very grateful if you would write to me. Some of these people may have known Louis as "Duke" LaMoore or Michael "Micky" Moore, since Louis occasionally used those names. Many of the people on this list may have died. If you are a family member (or were a very good friend) of anyone on the list who has passed away, I would like to hear from you, too. Some of the names I have marked with an asterisk. If there is anyone out there who knows *anything at all* about these people, I would like to hear it. The address to write to is:

> Louis L'Amour Biography Project
> P.O. Box 41183
> Pasadena, CA 91114-9183

Because of the many demands on our time, we will no longer be responding to *fan* mail sent to this address . . . it is for correspondence regarding biography information only!

Marian Payne　Married a guy named Duane. Louis knew her in Oklahoma in the mid- to late 1930s. She moved to New York for a while; she may have lived in Wichita at some point.

Chaplain Phillips　Louis first met him at

Fort Sill, then again in Paris at the Place de Saint Augustine Officers' Mess. The first meeting was in 1942, the second in 1945.

Anne Mary Bentley   Friend of Louis's from Oklahoma in the 1930s. Possibly a musician of some sort. Lived in Denver for a time.

Pete Boering*   Born in the late 1890s. Came from Amsterdam, Holland. His father may have been a ship's captain.

Betty Brown   Woman Louis corresponded with extensively while in Choctaw, Oklahoma, in the late 1930s. Later she moved to New York.

Jacques Chambrun*   Louis's agent from the late 1930s through the late 1950s.

Des   His first name. Chambrun's assistant in the late 1940s or early 1950s.

Joe Friscia*   Joined Hagenbeck & Wallace circus in Phoenix in the mid-1920s. Rode freights across Texas and spent a couple of nights in the Star of Hope mission in Houston. May have been from Boston.

Harry "Shorty" Warren*   Shipmate of Louis's in the mid-1920s. Harry may have been an Australian.

Joe Hollinger* Louis met him while with Hagenbeck & Wallace circus, where he ran the "privilege car." A couple of months later he shipped out with Louis. This was in the mid-1920s.

Joe Hildebrand* Louis met him on the docks in New Orleans in the mid-1920s, then ran into him later in Indonesia. Joe may have been the first mate and Louis second mate on a schooner operated by Captain Douglas. This would have been in the East Indies in the later 1920s or early 1930s. Joe may have been an aircraft pilot and flown for Pan-Am in the early 1930s.

Turk Madden* Louis knew him in Indonesia in the late 1920s or early 1930s. They may have spent some time around the "old" Straits Hotel and the Maypole Bar in Singapore. Later on, in the States, Louis traveled around with him, putting on boxing exhibitions. Madden worked at an airfield near Denver as a mechanic in the early 1930s. Louis eventually used his name for a fictional character.

"Cockney" Joe Hagen* Louis knew him in Indonesia in the late 1920s or early 1930s.

Richard LaForte* A merchant seaman from the Bay area. Shipped out with Louis in the mid-1920s.

Mason or Milton* Don't know which was his real name. He was a munitions dealer in Shanghai in the late 1920s or 1930s. He was killed while Louis was there. His head was stuck on a pipe in front of his house as a warning not to double-cross a particular warlord.

Singapore Charlie* Louis knew him in Singapore and served with him on Captain Douglas's schooner in the East Indies. Louis was second mate and Charlie was bo'sun. He was a stocky man of indeterminate race, and, if I remember correctly, Dad told me he had quite a few tattoos. In the early 1930s Louis helped get him a job on a ship in San Pedro, California, that was owned by a movie studio.

Renée Semich She was born in Vienna, I think, and was going to a New York art school when Louis met her. This was just before WWII. Her father's family was from Yugoslavia or Italy, her mother from Austria. They lived in New York; her aunt had an apartment overlooking Central

Park. For a while she worked for a company in Waterbury, Connecticut.

Aola Seery Friend of Louis's from Oklahoma City in the late 1930s. She was a member of the "Writer's Club" and I think she had both a brother and a sister.

Enoch Lusk Owner of Lusk Publishing Company in 1939, original publisher of Louis's *Smoke from this Altar*. Also associated with the National Printing Company, Oklahoma City.

*Helen Turner** Louis knew her in late 1920s Los Angeles. Once a showgirl with Jack Fine's Follies.

*James "Jimmy" Eades** Louis knew him in San Pedro in the mid-1920s.

Frank Moran Louis met him in Ventura, California when Louis was a "club second" for fighters in the later 1920s. They also may have known each other in Los Angeles or Kingman, Arizona, in the mid-1920s. Louis ran into him again on Hollywood Boulevard late in 1946.

*Jud and Red Rasco** Brothers or cousins, cowboys, Louis met them in Tucumcari, New Mexico. Also saw them in Santa

Rosa, New Mexico. This was in the early to mid-1920s.

Olga Santiago Friend of Louis's from late 1940s Los Angeles. Last saw her at a book signing in Thousand Oaks, California.

Jose Craig Berry* A writer friend of Louis's from Oklahoma City in the late 1930s. She worked for a paper called the *Black Dispatch*.

Evelyn Smith Colt She knew him in Kingman at one point, probably the late 1920s. Louis saw her again much later at a Paso Robles book signing.

Kathlyn Beucler Hays Friend from Choctaw, taught school there in the 1930s. Louis saw her much later at a book signing in San Diego.

Floyd Bolton* A man from Hollywood who came out to Oklahoma to talk to Louis about a possible trip to Java to make a movie.

Lisa Cohn Reference librarian in Portland; family owned Cohn Bros. furniture store. Louis knew her in the late 1920s or early 1930s.

Mary Claire Collingsworth Friend and correspondent from Oklahoma in the 1930s.

C.A. Donnell   Guy in Oklahoma City in the early 1930s who rented Louis a typewriter.

Captain Douglas*   Captain of a ship in Indonesia that Louis served on, a three-masted auxiliary schooner.

Leonard Duks*   I think that this was probably a shortened version of the original family name. A first mate in the mid-1920s. I think that he was a U.S. citizen but he was originally a Russian.

Maudee Harris   My aunt Chynne's sister.

Parker LaMoore and *Chynne Harris LaMoore**   Louis's eldest brother and his wife. Parker was secretary to the governor of Oklahoma for a while, then he worked for the Scripps-Howard newspaper chain. He also worked with Ambassador Pat Hurley. He died in the early 1950s. Chynne outlived him, but I don't know where she lived after his death.

Mrs. Brown   Worked for Parker LaMoore in the 1930s to the 1950s.

Haig*   First name unknown. Louis described him as a Scotsman, once an officer in the British-India army. Louis said he was "an officer in one of the Scottish regiments." Louis knew him in Shanghai in the 1930s, and we don't know how old he would have been at the time. He may have been involved in some kind of intelligence work. He and Louis shared an apartment for a while, which seems to have been located just off Avenue King Edward VII.

Lola LaCorne   Along with her sister and mother, she was a friend of Louis's in Paris during World War II. She later taught literature at the Sorbonne and had (hopefully still has) a husband named Christopher.

Dean Kirby   A pal from Oklahoma City in the late 1930s who seems to have been a copywriter or something of the sort. Might have worked for Lusk Publishing.

Bunny Yeager   Girlfriend of Dean Kirby's from Oklahoma City. Not the famous photographer for *Playboy*.

Virginia McElroy   Girl with whom Louis went to school in Jamestown, North Dakota.

Guardsman Penwill   A British boxer in the period between the mid-1920s and the mid-1930s.

Arleen Weston Sherman   A friend of Louis's from Jamestown, when he was thirteen or fourteen. I think her family visited the LaMoores in Choctaw in the 1930s. Her older sister's name is Mary; parents' names are Ralph and Lil.

Harry Bigelow Louis knew him in Ventura. He had a picture taken with Louis's mother, Emily LaMoore, at a place named Berkeley Springs around 1929. Louis may have known him at the Katherine mine, near Kingman, Arizona, or in Oregon.

Tommy Pinto Boxer from Portland; got Louis a job at Portland Manufacturing.

Nancy Carroll An actress as of 1933. She may have been in the chorus of a show at the Winter Garden in New York and a cabaret in New Jersey where she and her sister danced occasionally, probably during the mid- to late 1920s.

Judith Wood Actress. Louis knew her in Hollywood in the late 1920s.

Stanley George The George family relocated from Kingman, Arizona, to Ventura, California, possibly in the late 1920s.

*Francis Lederer** Actor whom Louis knew in late 1920s Los Angeles. I'm looking for anyone who knew him in *Hollywood* between 1926 and 1931.

Lieutenant Rix Served in the 3622 Quartermaster Truck Co. in Europe in 1944-45.

*Pablo De Gantes** Ex-soldier of fortune who occasionally wrote magazine articles for *Lands of Romance* in the 1930s. This man used several names, and I believe he was actually a Belgian. He lived in Mexico at one time.

Lieutenant King Traveled to England with Louis when he was shipped overseas in early 1944.

K. C. Gibson or his two nephews In October 1924, they were crossing New Mexico and Arizona, bound for Brawley, California.

Wilma Anderson A friend of Louis's from Oklahoma who worked in the Key campaign headquarters in 1938.

Johnny Annette A boxer Louis fought a bout with in Woodward, Oklahoma (or Kansas) in the 1930s.

Harry Bell A boxing promoter Louis worked with in Oklahoma City in the 1930s.

*Joe Bickerstaff** An occasional boxing

promoter, in Klamath Falls, Oregon, in the late 1920s.

Pat Chaney Friend of Louis's from Choctaw, Oklahoma, in the late 1930s.

*Mr. Lettsinger** An older man whom Louis knew in Klamath Falls in the late 1920s. I think he was from the Midwest or the South.

*Tommy Danforth** A boxing promoter from Prescott, Arizona, in the mid-1920s. Was using the V.A. hospital at Fort Whipple.

*Ned DeWitt** Knew Louis in Oklahoma in the 1930s, also a friend of Jim Thompson.

Austin Fullerton Sold tickets for athletic events in Oklahoma City in the late 1930s.

Martha Nell Hitchcock A friend from Edmond, Oklahoma, in the 1930s.

*Tommy Tucker** Boss stoker on a British Blue Funnel ship in the mid-1920s to mid-1930s.

*Dynamite Jackson** An African-American fighter Louis helped promote in Oklahoma in the 1930s.

Orry Kelly Designer in Hollywood; Louis knew him in the late 1940s.

Dorothy Kilgallen A newspaper columnist who worked in L.A. in the 1950s.

Henry Li Louis knew him from 1943, when he was at Camp Robinson, Arkansas.

Savoie Lottinville* Of the University of Oklahoma.

Julio Lopez Louis worked for him very briefly in Phoenix in the mid-1920s.

Joe May A rancher Louis boxed with in Fort Sumner, New Mexico, in the 1920s.

Ann Mehaffey A friend of Louis's from the time he spent at Camp Robinson, Arkansas.

Sam Merwin or Sam Mines* Once worked with Leo Margulies at Standard Magazines/Better Publications.

Jack Natteford Screenwriter who worked with Louis in the 1950s.

Joe Paskvan Once of the Oklahoma Writers Project, who Louis knew in the late 1930s.

Billy Prince Went to sea in the late 1930s on the *Wallace E. Pratt*, a Standard tanker.

Countess Dulong de Rosney (Toni Morgan)* Louis knew her in France in the mid-1940s.

Dot and Truitt Ross   Brother and sister Louis knew in Oklahoma in the 1930s.

Mary Jane Stevenson   A friend of Louis's from L.A. in the late 1940s.

Orchid Tatu   Lived in Sparta, Wisconsin, in the mid-1940s.

Florence Wagner   Wife of Rob Wagner of Rob Wagner's Script.

Doris Weil   A roomer in the flat where Louis lived in the late 1940s.

Sandra Widener   Wrote an article on Louis called "The Untold Stories of Louis L'Amour."

Anyone who knew Louis in Los Angeles or New York between 1946 and 1956.

I would also like to hear about, or from, anyone who served on *S.S. Steel Worker* between 1925 and 1930. In particular: Captain *C.C. Boase*, 2nd Mate *Ralph Jones*, 3d Mate *Raymond Cousins*, Radio Operator *Stanley Turbervil*, Carpenter *George Mearly*, Bo'sun *H. Allendorf*, Chief Engineer *C. B. Dahlberg*, 1st Asst Eng. *O. E. Morgan*, 2nd Asst Eng. *W. Haynes*, 3d Asst Engineers *George G. Folberth* and *William Stewart*, Oilers *A. Chagnon* and *A. Kratochbil*,

Firemen *William Hohroien, J. Perez, Manfrido Gonzales, John Fennelly,* and *E. G. Burnay,* Wipers *A. Sanchez, J. J. Dalmasse* and *F. Clifford,* Steward *J. Shiel,* Messmen *Dean Bender, William Harvey,* and *J. H. Blomstedt,* Able-Bodied Seamen *Ernest Martin, Chris Moore, Karl Erickson, Steve Schmotzer, Michael Llorca, Louis Armand, Joseph Morris, Herbert Lieflander, William Reichart,* and *H. F. Waite.*

Also, anyone familiar with *Singapore in the late 1920s,* the old Straits Hotel, and the Maypole Bar. And anyone who is very knowledgeable in *military history and/or politics in western (Shansi, Kansu, and Sinkiang provinces) China* in 1928-36.

I am also looking for seamen who served on the following ships: the *Catherine G. Sudden,* between 1925 and 1936; the *Yellowstone,* between 1925 and 1936; the *S.S. Steadfast*, between 1924 and 1930; the *Annandale* (exact spelling uncertain), a four-masted bark, between 1920 and 1926; the *Randsberg*, a German freighter, between 1925 and 1937.

Also, anyone who knows anything about an old square-rigged sailing vessel called the *Indiana*, which was used in movies in the 1920s and 1930s. This ship was docked at San Pedro.

Anyone who knows anything about the following boxers: *Jonny "Kid" Stopper, Jack Horan, "Kid" Yates, Butch Vierthaler (Bill Thaler).* And *Ira O'Neil, Jimmy Roberts, Jimmy Russo, Jack McGraf,* or *Jackie Jones*—guys Louis met in Phoenix in October of 1924.

Anyone who knows anything about *a fight (I assume with small arms) between two trading schooners* that was stopped by a British warship near Pinaki in the South Pacific. This would have been between 1926 and 1932.

Anyone from *the family or group that Louis guided around Egypt* sometime between 1926 and 1937. Although he very much looked the part, Louis finally admitted that he wasn't a real guide and that he'd been using a tour book from a library to learn about where he was taking them. They may have been staying at Shepherds. Some or all of the party were Americans, and there may have been as many as twelve of them.

Anyone who might know about *a flight that Louis took across Africa* with a French officer, with stops at Taudeni and Timbuktu.

This would have been between the mid-1920s and late 1930s.

Anyone familiar with *an island in the Spratly group called Itu Aba.*

Anyone who knows anything about a very short-lived magazine published in Oklahoma City in 1936 called *Uptown Magazine.*

Anyone who knows if *Norman Foster* and *Rex Bell (George Francis Beldam)* ever went to sea during the 1920s or early 1930s.

Anyone who knows where the personal and business papers of *B. P. Schulberg (not Budd)* and *Sam Katz* are archived. Both of these men worked at Paramount Publix Pictures. The period that I am interested in is the late 1920s to the early 1930s.

Anyone familiar with the *Royal Government Experimental Hospital in Calcutta, India.*

I would also like to hear from men who served in the following military units: the *3622 Quartermaster Truck Company,* between June of 1944 and December of 1945; the *3595 Quartermaster Truck Company*, after October 1945 and before January 1946; the *670th Tank Destroyer Battalion,* at Camp Hood, Texas in 1943; the

808th Tank Destroyer Battalion, at Camp Phillips, Kansas, in 1943.

Also, soldiers or officers who took *basic training at Camp Robinson, Arkansas*, between September 1942 and January 1943; took *winter training at Camp McCoy, Wisconsin*, and near Land o' Lakes and Watersmeet in the northern Michigan peninsula between October 1943 and February 1944, or remember Louis in early 1944 when he was staying at the *St. Francis Hotel* and the *Belleview in San Francisco.* During this time he worked at the *Oakland Air Base* and *Fort Mason, California.* Later he was at *Camp Beale, California.*

Anyone who worked with the *Oklahoma WPA Writers Project.*

Any recordings that anyone knows about of any of Louis's speeches.

ABOUT LOUIS L'AMOUR

*"I think of myself in the oral tradition—
as a troubadour, a village tale-teller, the
man in the shadows of the campfire.
That's the way I'd like to be remembered—as a storyteller. A good storyteller."*

It is doubtful that any author could be as at
home in the world re-created in his novels
as Louis Dearborn L'Amour. Not only could
he physically fill the boots of the rugged
characters he wrote about, but he literally
"walked the land my characters walk." His
personal experiences as well as his lifelong
devotion to historical research combined to
give Mr. L'Amour the unique knowledge and
understanding of people, events, and the
challenge of the American frontier that
became the hallmarks of his popularity.

Of French-Irish descent, Mr. L'Amour could trace his own family in North America back to the early 1600s and follow their steady progression westward, "always on the frontier." As a boy growing up in Jamestown, North Dakota, he absorbed all he could about his family's frontier heritage, including the story of his great-grandfather who was scalped by Sioux warriors.

Spurred by an eager curiosity and desire to broaden his horizons, Mr. L'Amour left home at the age of fifteen and enjoyed a wide variety of jobs including seaman, lumberjack, elephant handler, skinner of dead cattle, miner, and was an officer in the transportation corps during World War II. During his "yondering" days he also circled the world on a freighter, sailed a dhow on the Red Sea, was shipwrecked in the West Indies and stranded in the Mojave Desert. He won fifty-one of fifty-nine fights as a professional boxer and worked as a journalist and lecturer. He was a voracious reader and collector of rare books. His personal library contained 17,000 volumes.

Mr. L'Amour "wanted to write almost from the time I could talk." After developing a widespread following for his many frontier and adventure stories written for fiction magazines, Mr. L'Amour published his first full-length novel, *Hondo*, in the United States in 1953. Every one of his more than 100 books is in print; there are nearly 260 million copies of his books in print worldwide, making him one of the bestselling authors in modern literary history. His books have been translated into twenty languages, and more than forty-five of his novels and stories have been made into feature films and television movies.

His hardcover bestsellers include *The Lonesome Gods, The Walking Drum* (his twelfth-century historical novel), *Jubal Sackett, Last of the Breed*, and *The Haunted Mesa*. His memoir, *Education of a Wandering Man*, was a leading bestseller in 1989. Audio dramatizations and adaptations of many L'Amour stories are available on cassette tapes from Bantam Audio Publishing.

The recipient of many great honors and awards, in 1983 Mr. L'Amour became the first novelist ever to be awarded the Congressional Gold Medal by the United States Congress in honor of his life's work.

In 1984 he was also awarded the Medal of Freedom by President Reagan.

Louis L'Amour died on June 10, 1988. His wife, Kathy, and their two children, Beau and Angelique, carry the L'Amour tradition forward with new books written by the author during his lifetime to be published by Bantam.

BANTAM BOOKS BY LOUIS L'AMOUR

Ask your bookseller for the books you have missed.

NOVELS
Bendigo Shafter
Borden Chantry
Brionne
The Broken Gun
The Burning Hills
The Californios
Callaghen
Catlow
Chancy
The Cherokee
  Trail
Comstock Lode
Conagher
Crossfire Trail
Dark Canyon
Down the Long
  Hills
The Empty Land
Fair Blows the
  Wind
Fallon
The Ferguson
  Rifle
The First Fast
  Draw
Flint
Guns of the
  Timberlands
Hanging Woman
  Creek
The Haunted
  Mesa
Heller with a Gun
The High Graders

High Lonesome
Hondo
How the West
  Was Won
The Iron Marshal
The Key-Lock
  Man
Kid Rodelo
Kilkenny
Killoe
Kilrone
Kiowa Trail
Last of the Breed
Last Stand at
  Papago Wells
The Lonesome
  Gods
The Man Called
  Noon
The Man from
  Skibbereen
The Man from the
  Broken Hills
Matagorda
Milo Talon
The Mountain
  Valley War
North to the Rails
Over on the Dry
  Side
Passin' Through
The Proving Trail
The Quick and
  the Dead
Radigan

Reilly's Luck
The Rider of Lost
  Creek
Rivers West
The Shadow
  Riders
Shalako
Showdown at
  Yellow Butte
Silver Canyon
Sitka
Son of a Wanted
  Man
Taggart
The Tall Stranger
To Tame a Land
Tucker
Under the
  Sweetwater
  Rim
Utah Blaine
The Walking
  Drum
Westward the
  Tide
Where the Long
  Grass Blows

*(continued on
next page)*